WICKED VAMPIRE
THE ROYALS: VAMPIRE COURT

MEGAN MONTERO

© MEGAN MONTERO

CHAPTER ONE

DICE

"You sure you're okay?" Andrew, the manager of the restaurant, stood on the other side of the bar. He handed me the case of beer that I'd asked for.

The noise around us nearly drowned out his words. The truth was, I wish they had. I was tired of everyone giving me the pitying looks and words of comfort, like what I needed right now was comfort. What I needed were answers. Until then, nothing would stop the tightness in my chest that came with grief. Or the knots in my stomach that came with worry. Sleep was a distant memory and food tasted like sand. I didn't know if my bestie was alive or dead, and yet they all assumed she was dead. But deep down, I knew she still walked this Earth. I just had to find her.

It was beyond me as to why people always asked me if I was okay. Like losing my bestie, my sister, would be anything near *okay*. The truth was . . . none of it was *okay*. Finding her in a hole in the ground was not *okay*. Watching her straight up attack someone a day later was not *okay*. And sitting in an interrogation room where they thought I had something to do with it was anything but *okay*. I wanted to scream that nothing was OKAY. Yet here I was keeping my head down and working. If I went back to the house I shared with Piper, I'd drive myself crazy. If I tried to find her, I'd just end up walking the streets with no direction and no answers.

The cops swore she was alive, but the picture of her dead would never leave my mind: her skin tinged with that pale blue hue, the stillness of her chest, and her lifeless body covered in dirt from where she'd been buried, or I should say dumped. The cops thought it was some kind of horrible prank and wouldn't help me find her. I had nowhere to turn and no one to ask for help. It was a constant battle in my mind because I'd seen her. I'd touched her cold, lifeless body. But the next day, I also watched a video of her rising off a slab in the morgue and attacking the coroner. She might not be dead, but I wasn't sure she was alive either. I'd lived in Salem for years, and that came with the belief in *other things*.

Things no one *could* see. Or *should* see.

"Yeah, I'm fine." *I'm not even close to fine.*

All I could do now was try to focus on work and making enough money to keep our place until Piper came home so that we at least had a place to come home to. I took the case of beer and dragged it across the top of the bar and placed it on the floor to shove the bottles into the bin of ice in front of me. Andrew gave me that boyish smile that made him look younger than he really was. He was the kind of guy who had nice and gentle written all over him. The kind of guy who a girl should settle down, marry, and have a couple kids with. The kind of guy Piper and I would've eaten for breakfast.

I couldn't put my finger on it, but deep down I knew it had something to do with Grayson, that smoot-talking British bastard who stole her heart. When I found him, I was going to kill him with my bare hands. Or something more gruesome, even if I had to fly my ass all the way to London and hunt him down. The word castration had crossed my mind a time or two. Everything was great before he arrived. We were great, living our best lives. Then it all went to shit. Anger boiled through my veins and my grip tightened on the bottle. As her bestie, I should've known better. I should've tried to stop her. But prince charming had both of our stupid man-pickers fooled.

Andrew eyed my white knuckles. "If you just want to talk . . . I'm around."

I stopped shoving beer into the cold bucket of ice and stood up straight. "What do you want me to say here, Andy?"

"Nothing." He ran his hand over his short blond hair and shook his head. "I'm just saying . . . if you need a friend, I'm here."

"I know what you're saying, but I'm good." I didn't

snap at him, but I also knew my tone gave off the — *this subject is closed—* vibe.

If I was being honest, it was closed to all my co-workers. They all lived pretty lives with their big families, friends, and significant others. But Piper and me, we'd grown up in the foster care system, aged out together, and made our own little family. Without each other, we were completely alone in this world. Whatever she was going through now, she needed me. I just knew it.

"I'm here for you, Dice." He melted back into the crowd of people and let me get back to work. Bartending wasn't the most glamorous job, but it paid the bills and put food on the table for us both.

"Yo, blondie." A guy at the end of the bar shook his empty beer bottle at me.

I did my best not to roll my eyes or start a fight. Before all this happened, Piper and I would've roasted this guy and probably made him cry into his next drink just for being an ass. But without her here, it just wasn't the same. I loathed when they called me things like blondie, sugar lips, baby, honey, blue eyes . . . the list went on and on. All unoriginal and all just as annoying.

I held up my finger. "Just a sec."

I took the order of the woman sitting in front of me who'd been patiently waiting. "Chardonnay? You got it."

The truth was, she looked about as run down as I felt, with her hair flying in all different directions and heavy bags under her eyes. When I handed her the glass, she took a big sip and sighed. "Thank you. Holidays and family. You know how it goes."

I really don't. "Yeah, I know." People were out to unwind and forget the madness of the impending holiday. Me? I was here to try and forget the questionable, unexplained chaos that was my bestie. The guy held up his bottle and shook it at me again. "Come on, blondie. Can I get a beer or what?"

I groaned and snatched one out of the ice. I ground my teeth together and popped the top off. Normally, I would've made him wait. I could out-stubborn anyone, but I just didn't have the venom it required when I was using so much of my energy trying to stay sane.

"Patience is a virtue, buddy."

I slid the bottle down the bar, and it was like watching it in slow-motion. It slid right off the corner of the bar and hit the ground where it shattered. Beer splashed all over the floor. "Let me guess, no hand-eye coordination?"

When I looked up, he hadn't moved. No one had moved. Bright, neon-green smoke filled the room. It drifted over the floor and up around everyone like creeping fog. I froze, just looking at the entire bar standing there like mannequins. They were all mid-motion, or mid-sentence, or smiling. Groups of people sat at tables, not moving. In the corner of the room in a dark booth, a couple froze moments before his lips touched hers. A slight smile played on her lips and her eyes were shut tight. At the pool tables, a man was bent

5

over his pool stick and had his eye on the cue about to take a shot while another watched from the high seat against the wall. Even the TV screens froze in time, their faint glow only illuminating the unmoving faces closest to them. A shiver went down my spine.

Eerie, heavy silence fell all around, and I could barely breathe. Even the kitchen fell silent. Had I finally lost my mind, or was there something more at play here? Panic filled my body, and I didn't know if I should run or call the cops. I glanced across the bar and a one-eyed black cat hopped up on one of the high tables. We locked eyes and he leaned down and snatched a fry from a basket of food, then he hopped to the next table, stealing a nacho, then to another where he took a chicken strip. Every one of its moves was as silent as a graveyard.

I shook my head and blinked my eyes hard. *I'm going insane.*

A blast of chilly air flew through the room and the green smoke rose even higher. I backed away from the bar and bumped into the liquor racks behind me. The bottles clanked together as the shelf shook. A tall, dark figure marched toward me from the back of the restaurant. He paused halfway to me and looked at the cat.

"Share."

The cat arched its back and hissed in his direction.

The man chuckled. "Odin, share or I'll tell Astrid you're cheating on your diet."

Another violent hiss and then it swiped its little claws toward the man, baring his claws. They seemed to have some kind of standoff. He stared at the cat, and the cat stared back. As if some unspoken decision had been made, the cat turned and grabbed another chicken tender from the plate and leapt across the room, landing on the man's shoulder. He dropped the tender into his waiting hand, then leapt away to steal food from more tables. The man took a bite and shrugged, then continued toward me.

His hair was inky black and fell to his chin. His eyes were milky white with a green glow behind them. Neon-green smoke swirled around him, and when he locked eyes with me, my body froze. I couldn't move, couldn't breathe. Beside him was a tiny woman with wild, wavy blonde hair that flowed past her shoulders. Her eyes flickered from the deepest brown to the brightest green. She wore a trench coat about three sizes too big, which billowed out around her. I instantly recognized them both.

"You . . . you're the ones . . ." My words halted for a moment. "Piper."

They were the ones who'd tempted me into their little tent and gave me an eerie tarot reading, then led me to where Piper was buried. They helped me dig her up. And they were the ones who'd left me in that graveyard alone with my best friend's body. I'd never forget their faces, except now magic swirled around them and they looked different. Harsher . . . scarier.

The girl held her finger over her cherry lips. "Shhhh."

I pressed my lips together. The guy opened the

pocket on his army pants and cards flew from them. They spiraled around the two of them in a swirling tornado. Wind blew my hair back from my face. I wanted to melt into the wall of booze behind me, but there was no place to go. I eyed the bar, wondering if I could make the leap over the counter and run for the door.

The guy took a step to the side, catching my wandering eyes. "Any move you make will get you nowhere."

I froze and swallowed. "Where is Piper?"

No answer.

"Did you kill her?" How else would they have known where to find her body? I looked from him to her and back again, waiting for some kind of hint or clue. All the while, that damn cat stared me down with that one vivid-green eye as he ate everything in sight.

The man tilted his head to the side, staring at me. "Did she deserve to die?"

"WHAT?" My heart leapt in my chest. "No!"

"Then we didn't kill her." His eyes left mine and drifted up toward the cards spinning around his head.

"What he means is we don't hurt people . . . unless they really deserve it." The girl gave me a smile that didn't comfort or convince me in the least.

I wound my hand around one of the bottles behind my back. If I hit a human with a bottle, it'd take a bitch out, but I didn't know what these two were or what they had planned for me. The truth was, they were my only connection to finding anything out about Piper. I needed them, for better or worse.

"Please help me find her. You did once before." What the hell was I thinking?

Desperate times, desperate measures.

The short blond stared up at the swirling cards. "Which ones to pick, Maze?"

Maze? Is that a name or location or game?

"Your power grows daily, Tilly. You can do it." He nodded up toward the spinning cards.

To me, they were all a blur, but somehow it looked like these two saw them perfectly. She beamed at him. "You first."

Maze, at least that's what I thought his name was, winked. "If you insist."

When he reached up and plucked a card from the whirling vortex, that green smoke lingered around his fingers and twisted down his arm. "The emperor."

"Defense. Protection. Starting off strong I see." She nodded with approval.

He shrugged. "We have things to accomplish."

Things to accomplish. Am I the thing? My breaths started to come in panicked puffs, and I had to force myself to breathe easy. I'd made it through some rough shit as a kid, and this wouldn't even come close to the worst of it . . . *I think*. So, I fought for the calm that I knew would come when I wanted it to.

He flicked the card at me, and it flew like a throwing star at my chest. When it smacked into me, my body jerked back and hit the liquor shelf. The bottles rattled so hard I thought they'd break. The neon smoke spread over my body, and when I lifted my arms, it settled on my pale skin, giving it a weird ghostly sheen. Suddenly, I felt stronger, ready for what was a head.

"I want to know about Piper. Now." My voice was firm, almost forceful.

They didn't respond.

"True. We do have things to do." Tilly ignored me and rested her hand on his arm. She went up on her tiptoes and bit her bottom lip. One of her little fangs popped out. "Four of Pentacles."

He smirked. "Interesting."

She threw it at me, and it too hit my chest and magic exploded all around me. Things started to feel hazy, like I needed to keep everything tight and controlled. Like I needed something but didn't know what. The green around me grew brighter, and I had to squint to see them through the powerful haze.

"We keep the things we need close to the vest." Tilly wagged her eyebrows. "Last one on the count of three?"

Was this a game to them? Pick a card and throw it at Dice and see what happens? The chemistry between the two of them was palpable. And yet I stood here full of panic, but ready to demand action. Except, they ignored my words, like I never spoke to them, like I didn't exist. I tried to snap my fingers, but my movements were slow, like I was trapped in sludge.

"One." She smiled.

"Two."

"Three."

"Eight of Wands." They reached for it at the same time.

He grabbed one side, and she grabbed the other. They shoved it toward me in unison. It didn't flip end over end. Instead, it floated perfectly flat. I tried to move my arm to swat it away, but the magic halted my movements. The card slammed into me, and the neon smoke grew so bright I wanted to close my eyes. But I couldn't. My feet lifted off the ground and I floated a few inches off the floor. Power and determination flowed through my body, and the gut-wrenching panic I felt earlier eased.

The smoke seeped into my skin, making it shine for a few long moments. I didn't move, didn't even try to. I let it all wash over me. It was warm and welcoming like a warm blanket next to a fire. I wanted to lie there and soak it in. The shining color began to fade, and my feet eased down onto the floor. Yet I still couldn't move.

"That'll see it through." Maze nodded toward me. "Kylian will never be able to find her. Nor any others they send for her."

Who the hell is Kylian?

"Fortitude. I think we did what we came to do," Tilly agreed. "She's well hidden."

They didn't say anything else. As if on cue, they turned away from me. He threw his arm over her shoulder, and she tucked in close to him. When he snapped his fingers, the cat grabbed a buffalo wing from a plate and leapt onto his shoulder. They strolled toward the door, and the cards flew around them before shuffling back into his pocket like obedient pets. The neon smoke drifted up from the floor and seeped around them, making them disappear before they even reached the door.

The moment they were gone, the hold on my body dropped and I placed my hands on the bar, sucking in a deep breath. I couldn't stay like that. I had to try to find them. They were my only answer to finding Piper. I darted from behind the bar just as the whole room unfroze. Everyone went back to moving, as if nothing happened. As if two people hadn't done some kind of spell on me. I ran toward the door.

"Oh, come on, blondie. I'm still waiting," The guy called after me.

"Lick it up," I snapped and pointed at the broken bottle on the floor.

I shoved my way through the door and out into the freezing night. The noise from the bar faded away, and I spun around. Essex Street was completely empty but for the lights coming from the bar. Snow crunched under my feet as I walked even farther onto the uneven gray cobblestone.

"Hello! Come on." I turned around once more. "You gotta help me ... please."

I wrapped my arms around myself, trying to fight off the cold. The door to the restaurant flew open, and

Andrew came running out with my jacket in hand. "Dice, you good?"

I didn't know what to say. I was losing my mind... or something crazy just happened to me... or I'd been cursed. Either way, my luck was shit. It always had been.

I shook my head and admitted the one thing I never admitted to anyone out loud. "No... No, I'm not."

And who the hell was Kylian? Why did I need to be hidden from him?

CHAPTER TWO

GRAYSON

Days Later

Warmth covered my chest and small puffs of breath tickled my skin, yet something wasn't right. Something was off in my room. My eyes flashed wide, and there stood Titus at the foot of my bed, looking down on me covered by a very naked Piper. She lay face down with only her back exposed to him. Her thick, dark hair was spread around us. It tickled over my skin. Her warm honey scent filled my nose. I knew what the bed looked like. It was completely torn apart. There were pillows on the floor and one on top of a beam overhead. Claw marks marred my mahogany headboard and every bit of clothing had been ripped to shreds at some point during our hours-long bout of lovemaking. Bite marks covered my neck, wrists, and arms.

I didn't know what time it was, but when I looked

outside, the sun had either set or still hadn't come up. My guess was the former. Titus stood there in all his kingly glory. His hair fell from his head in dirty blond waves past his shoulders, and he narrowed those honey-colored eyes at me. With that one look, I knew this was about to be a right pain in the bollocks.

The muscles in his jaw ticked and he balled his hands into fists, then released them repeatedly. "Outside. Now."

Without another word, he marched from my room. I ran my hand through my hair and pulled at the strands. *I've gone and done it now. Got myself into a right spot.* "Oh shittttt."

Piper lay fast asleep, sated from my blood . . . and other things. I reluctantly disentangled myself from her and slid out of the bed. I grabbed the first pair of trousers I saw and shoved my legs into them while making my way toward the door. I had the button done up just as I opened the door and stepped into the hallway. Titus barely let me get the door shut before he got in my face.

"Are you out of your bloody senses?" he hissed under his breath.

I scrubbed my hand down my face. "No."

"Have you forgotten all that we spoke about?" He turned away from me and took a few steps.

I knew he had a right to be angry. I was playing a game where the odds were not in my favor. "No."

He turned around and charged forward, getting so close to me that the velvet from his jacket brushed my arm. "Do you want to end up like your father?"

"No, I don't bloody well want to end up six feet under a headstone. Thank you very much." Why did they all keep asking me that? Like I was going to say, *yes, I want to end up dead?*

"You're toying with things you should not be." He shook his head and sucked in a deep breath. "Have you forgotten our deal? Because I will send her away from here for good. To a place where I can guarantee you will never find her."

It was a night of passion. One I did not regret in the slightest. "I haven't forgotten."

"I will do everything in my power to stop the curse from taking you, but it seems I am the only one."

When I said nothing, he glared at me and continued.

"Mark these words, avenge thy crime,
Bound by blood in space and time.
From kin to kin one wretched vine,
A wicked curse seals a shaded line.
What was denied shall now be taken,
For when thee love thee turn forsaken.
Deep in thee veins thy soul will burn,
Forever more thy thirst shall yearn.
Breath by breath thy mind unwound,
To madness now thy life is drowned.
And if fate shall deem thy love requited,
Don't speak the words or curse the blighted.
For if on the wrist thy souls entwined,
Death shall call and forever find."

Those words rang through my mind constantly. "I know the bloody curse."

Titus waved toward the door. "Well, someone had better remind you. The deal was one year with her to teach her how to become a vampire. Not to become besotted. That display in there is not part of the deal and can never happen again, or we will all lose you. Even her!"

"You don't think I know that?" The thought of one measly year with her just didn't seem like enough in the infinite line of years I had left to live. The mere thought of it pained me. It tore at my chest and pulled at my heart. Piper was everything. She was . . . life.

Titus leaned into me. "It is better to admire from afar than to lose everything. Now, you can have your one year if you agree to uphold your end of the bargain. I will overlook this one night. You may teach her . . . but you may never have her again. What say you, Prince Grayson, do we have a deal?"

The saying deal with the devil *always came from The House of Shade.*

The air left my lungs and I sagged against the wall. With everything that I was, I didn't want to give her up. It would pain me deeply to do so, but he wasn't wrong. I knew it.

He knew it.

I gave a single nod. "Deal. But if I could just explain to her about the curse . . ."

"You will do no such thing. It is forbidden for anyone

here to know, lest we lose our seats in the vampire world. And they need us. The Blood Borns would set us back, and the Night Spawn would revolt. No, she must not know. It is a weakness we cannot afford."

"But if I could just—"

"—NO!" His power washed over me like an all-consuming tide. I felt it seep into my body and hold me there. I fought the hold, and for a second, I pushed it aside. But his blood magic, the ability to control others that he had honed over his many years, came back stronger and hit me like a ton of bricks. He had never used it on me before.

"I forbid you to tell her anything about the curse. You will uphold your word. And if you go back on it in any way, she goes, and I will lock you up for your own good."

I straightened my stance and rolled my shoulders as his power faded from my body. "Was that necessary?"

"Until you grow out of this childish infatuation, I find it completely necessary." He glared at me.

"I hardly think at my age anything is childish." And now my lips were sealed when it came to the curse and telling Piper.

"Normally, I would agree, but your actions speak otherwise." He didn't speak another word to me. Instead, he just turned and left. His long velvet coat billowed out around him and trailed behind as he marched away.

I glanced back at the door where I knew I'd made a complete balls-up of the situation. Piper was so beautifully flawed in ways that only came from a world that made her too hard too fast. I wanted to show her there was a different way and that not every guy only fell on the broken picker scale. But in reality, all I'd done was smash the damn picker and hurt her more severely than I'd ever intended. If I wasn't held in place by royal obligations and curses, I'd commit to her with everything I was. I'd let myself fall into the abyss that was Piper and gladly never come out.

I knew what I had to do, but I just needed . . . a moment. I shoved away from the wall and marched down the long halls. Christmas decorations hung from the ceiling and down the walls. They glowed with warm light that gave the dark stone walls a light, welcoming sheen. Green Christmas trees lined the halls, complete with red and golden ribbons, sparkling ornaments, and twinkling light. The smell of pine lingered on the air and some courtiers stopped and gazed at me as I marched past, but I didn't pay them any mind. I turned down a couple more hallways before arriving at the one door I knew I could always walk through.

I didn't bother knocking. I simply turned the knob and shoved the door wide open. Atlas Savage, my eldest friend in the world and also the deadliest sod who ever lived. As far as loyalty went, there was no other who would serve The House of Shade so fully. He was the right hand of the crown, and everyone knew it. With a past as dark as he was in the present, very few ever messed with him. Yet here I was.

He sat in an oversized chair next to a fireplace. His

black shirt hung wide open from his collar down to the middle of his stomach. It showed the blood magic tattoos he could call upon at any moment in time. They'd peel from his body and do his bidding. Strands of his white hair mixed in with the black hair that fell from his temples all the way down to his shoulders. It was a tangled mess that covered some of his face as he read.

There were very few things in this world that he cared about. He cared even less about people. Poe, his raven, sat on a perch in the corner of the room. Black feathers littered the floor around the twisted wooden stand. His claws dug into the wood, leaving small scratches. When I entered, Poe gave a small *caw* and then went back to whatever meaty meal Atlas had given him. Atlas barely lifted his head when I walked in. Instead, he peeked up at me with those crazy intense eyes. They were dark brown near the iris and had a vivid blue outer ring. When the fire light reflected off of them, they looked like they belonged to a wild animal in a forest hunting its prey at night.

He flipped the page of his book. I let my frustrations get the better of me as I marched over and grabbed another book off the shelf, then threw it against the wall. It smacked into the dark wood and stuck there. A few pages hung loose from the binding.

Atlas didn't react. He barely gave the book a passing glance. "Something vexes you?"

"Vexes me . . . I'd say I'm bloody well vexed from the

look of it. Would you not agree?" I paced in front of the fireplace.

A heavy sigh slipped past his lips. "I tend to wonder, if one knows what isn't good for one, then why jump into the deep end of said horrible pool? It's like saying you're allergic to flowers and wandering through a field of daisies."

"Piper is like a field of daisies."

He rolled his eyes and turned the page. "More like a field of roses, with all the thorn marks you've got littering your neck and arms."

I ran my finger over the tiny bite marks Piper left. Even now they were healing, and in a few more moments, they'd be gone all together. "I've been offered a deal."

He scoffed.

"What?"

Snort.

"For a man of so many words, your lips are awfully tight." I shoved my hands into my hair and tugged at the strands.

"You look like you're in a strop. Not in the mood for deals." He flipped another page and the sound of it shuffling made me want to grab the bloody thing from his hands.

"It's quite obvious I'm in a strop." I stomped over to his closet and yanked the door open. I rifled through the hanging shirts and growled. "Haven't you got anything besides black linen shirts?"

"If only I'd known you'd be shopping in my wardrobe, I would've taken greater pains to shop where you deem fit." He rose from the chair and sauntered over to the closet, then bent down to the small chest of drawers. He yanked the drawer open, pulled out a sweater, and threw it at me. "To hide the love bites."

"The disapproval is evident on your face, *friend*." I shoved my arms into the sweater and pulled it over my head. It was slightly longer than I was used to, as Atlas was a touch bigger than me, but it'd work for now.

"Do tell me, when one watches their best friend walk right toward the hangman's noose, how would you proceed? Shall I tie the knot for you, or shall I try to stop you? It's quite the plight you've put me in." He moved to stand in front of the fire with his arms crossed over his chest and his back to the flames. It cast him in shadows and darkness. Atlas was rarely concerned with the well-being of others. But we'd been friends for ages. The fact was, I was sure that I was his only friend.

"No longer a plight for you." I sighed, thinking of the promise I'd just made to Titus. I could only hope Piper would understand. If I were her, I wouldn't. "As I said, I've been *offered* a deal."

His eyebrows shot up. "Do tell? Is it a deal worth making?"

"I'm to stop all dalliances with my progeny or she will be sent away . . . never to be seen or heard from again. You wouldn't know anything about that would you?"

Atlas shook his head. "No."

He stared at me, and I stared back at him. "Something vexes you now?"

"Did you take the deal or not?" Atlas stilled, visibly holding his breath. It made me realize there was more than just myself and Piper at risk here.

I should've drawn it out and made him wait for an answer. The way he drew out his words and actions . . . But I was too damn stressed to mess about with silly games. "I did."

"Good." He looked me up and down. "So, what's the problem?"

"The problem is . . ." I didn't know if I wanted to admit it. "The problem is it might be too late. And Titus has put the blood magic leash on me. I can't even explain the curse to Piper."

"As it should be."

I couldn't disagree. It was a centuries-old curse that my family held as the deepest of secrets. A new vampire who still couldn't control their urges wasn't the best place to trust that kind of knowledge. I didn't want her to be thrown further into this life I forced upon her until she was comfortable in her own skin. This was a right mess. All of it. There was no way around it. I'd created a chain of events that could damage us all. Deep down, it tore at my insides and twisted something deep in my chest.

"You might be right."

"So, stop thinking with your member below the belt and start thinking with the head above your shoulders."

He shook his head and moved back to the chair where he dropped down and rested his elbows on his knees. "Or..."

I didn't like the tone of his voice. It was the voice he used when he was shutting himself down and about to do what was good for the crown and no one else. I stilled, waiting for what he was going to suggest, but he didn't speak. My patience wore thin with him. I had a one-way ticket to hell, and he was just dallying about.

"Or?"

"Or I could kill her and end all of this. Clean and done."

He barely got the words out before I wrapped my hand around his throat and shoved him against the wall. My fangs dropped down, and I felt my lips roll back from them as I hissed only inches from his face. No one would harm a hair on Piper's head. Not now, not ever. She was like the air I breathed. Most people would've cowered in the face of my wrath, but Atlas wasn't most people. His face went cold and dead as he met my eye.

"Judging by your aggressive reaction, I will take that as a no."

I squeezed harder, watching the steady pulse in his neck. Would I kill my oldest friend over her? I wanted to say no. But the thought of anything hurting her drove me to a place I'd never been before, a dark place where nothing lived if she didn't.

He swallowed, then a slow smirk spread across his lips. "When it comes to matters of the heart, one must check to make sure one is sincere in their declarations of devoted love. If anything, to be sure it is worth it."

I took a deep breath and shoved away from him. "I may not be able to have her, but I will not live another day without her in this world. I may not possess her, but so long as I breathe, so will she. Piper has always and will always be more than worth it."

He straightened his shirt and cracked his neck. "Now who holds the flare for drama?"

"It's the truth." I turned from him and picked up the chair I knocked over when I slammed him into the wall. I motioned to the chair and his neck. "Apologies."

A light chuckle escaped his lips and he rubbed at his neck. "I would've questioned your sincerity had you done nothing."

"Violence does tend to convey the right message." I sat on the foot of his bed and hung my head. "I need to break the curse."

He rolled his eyes. "I've been saying this for ages, yet no one heeds my warnings."

"I never had a reason for it before." I met his eyes and sighed. "But now I do. Until then, everything needs to be in place for her. I suspect I won't be in her favor much longer. What about her best friend? Dice. Have you found her yet?"

Atlas shook his head. "Still no word."

Annoyance ran through my body. "Can nothing go according to bloody plan? We have Jester and the freaking black ops of the vampire world, and you can't find one human girl?"

"It's like she's disappeared off the map." He snapped his fingers. "She's gone, completely gone. What about your boy Kylian?"

Kylian was one of the best trackers in the world. If we needed something or someone to be found, he would find it. His elven skills gave him the edge he needed to hunt down whatever and whomever. They let him blend into any environment. He could also make a weapon out of any natural material, which made him about as dangerous as they came. Deep down, I didn't know if I trusted the elf or not. There was only one problem when it came to Kylian, he valued lining his pockets more than he did his own moral compass.

Anger and frustration warred within me. "I haven't heard back from him. He's a bit of a prat."

Atlas leaned back in the chair and Poe soared across the room to land on the arm of the wooden chair next to him. He stroked his fingers over the inky black feathers. The simple act visibly relaxed him. "It'll be a hell of a time sorting it."

I glanced at the door, knowing what I had to do next. Dread sat heavy in my stomach, and deep down, I wanted to melt into the floor. My stomach rolled. "I will do what must be done. But if it does not work out, then I will require one thing of you."

"Is this a favor as a friend or a command from a Prince of The House of Shade?" He didn't look up from

Poe or meet my eye. The air in the room seemed thicker somehow, like it was hard to breathe.

I'd never commanded Atlas to do anything. It wasn't in my nature to throw my weight around with The House of Shade. I got what I wanted in other ways. But I didn't have any other options here. "It is a binding oath to The House of Shade."

He paused from stroking Poe's feathers. His lips pressed into a thin line and a slight growl escaped his lips. Tension stole through his body, and he sat forward. "Name it."

"If I can't get it sorted, if the curse does take me, I want it to be you to put me down."

It was a lot to ask but there was no other I knew who could bear it and do what needed to be done. Any of the friends I'd gained over the last few months wouldn't be able to kill me. Not the Queens of the Witch Court, not my friends Tuck or Beckett. They all didn't have the stomach for it. Ophelia might be able to end me . . . but who would want to die in such a gruesome way? No, Atlas would be the one, and he would make it quick and virtually painless. It was odd planning one's own death, but here I was asking for the impossible. The truth was, I'd rather die than take on the curse or the consequences it'd have for Piper.

Atlas slouched back like the wind had been whipped from his sails. He groaned and rubbed his hand over his head. I'd known him long enough to know that this was asking a lot. Maybe it was too much. But there was no one else I'd trust with such a task.

A muscle in his jaw ticked as he ground his teeth together. "If I have to, I will kill you."

With that one guarantee, I knew he would keep his word. Atlas was loyal to a fault. I was his one and only friend, but he would do as he promised. "I'm counting on it, friend."

I rose to my feet and headed to the door. Atlas cleared his throat. "You get my promise of death and then leave me. Feels a bit like a one-night stand."

"I never took you for the needy sort." I wanted to make this moment lighter, to not let it linger on guarantees of death.

He gave a humorless chuckle, letting me breathe the moment of tension between us. If ever there was one thing I could count on, it was Atlas always knowing how to roll with the moment and let it go. There was no need to draw out the conversation any more than we had to.

"My needs are always met. Yet I find myself intrigued. Are we checking off boxes on a to-do-list? Like a final act?"

Tension riddled my body and my stomach twisted into knots. I opened the door, forcing myself to do what must be done. "No, only holding up my end of the deal."

"Good luck."

I didn't need luck. I needed a way to guard my heart from what I was about to do to the one creature I valued above all others.

CHAPTER THREE

GRAYSON

I crept into the room and let the door fall shut behind me. Darkness would've made it impossible for a human to see, but my vampire eyes adjusted in an instant. Piper lay in the bed peacefully sleeping. Her breaths were slow and even, her cheeks pink with color from my blood running through her body. Dark, tangled locks of her hair spread over my sheets. There was a deep satisfaction of having her in my bed, in my space, in my life. If I hadn't known better, I'd have thought she was the other half of me.

None of that mattered, not when all our lives hung in the balance, not when her future hung in the balance. I'd set out to help her learn that not every guy would be a letdown. Because after she'd gone through so much in life, she deserved hope and a happily ever after. I wanted to give her friendship, comfort, support. But my own weakness would forever ensure that her mindset when it came to men was right. In her book, we were all the same: unreliable, selfish liars, and out for our own ends. In the end, I'd done nothing to prove her wrong. That weight would forever sit on my chest and choke me all hours of the day. Regret wasn't a feeling I ever let linger, but I would regret her, my Piper, for the rest of my infinite days.

How would we move on from this? How could we? The connection was undeniable. We had fire. We had passion. We knew each other in and out. I found her to be the most fascinating creature I'd ever met. I didn't know if I could control my obsession for her, but I had to. Before all this started, I'd fancied her to be my companion. I never dreamt I'd feel the kind of emotions I'd so scarcely allowed myself to have. But she'd gotten under my skin like a missing piece of my soul, making me complete.

My skin crawled at the thought of hurting her, but what choice did I have? There was a mandate handed down through the generations of The House of Shade. We were not allowed to talk about it with anyone not brought into the royal inner circle, which didn't include Piper. This was one rule I agree with. I didn't need a — *we'll fight it together—* moment. It would only unleash a chain of events I wouldn't be able to stop. At least this way, there was a chance we'd all survive . . . slight as that may be.

If these were going to be my last minutes entangled

with her in a romance, I'd enjoy what little time we had left. I walked around the room lighting candles to let the soft light bathe her in warmth. It gave her tan skin a deep glow that reminded me of the sunrise of a new day. Her warm honey scent filled the room, and I sucked in a deep breath, letting it wash over me. I dropped down in the chair across from my bed and watched her blissful sleep. My nerves twisted into knots. I wanted to hit pause on this moment. But I couldn't. Nothing would stop this. I took another second to look at her and feel the peace between us.

Just one more moment.

But as she stirred and began to rouse, I found myself hoping she would sleep a touch longer. When her eyes fluttered open and she looked at me with those piercing bright-green eyes, a slow smile spread across her full red lips and she arched her back, stretching like a cat.

"Are you watching me sleep?" She sat up and pulled the sheet up, holding it pressed over her chest.

"You're like an angel." It was true. Her hair was wild around her, like an inky halo that shined in the candlelight. Her lips were a plump cherry red from the events of the night before.

She gave a light chuckle. "It's still creepy even if it's topped with compliments."

"Then I maintain my right to be creepy." I didn't move from the chair. I didn't try to get closer. If she laid one hand on me, my resolve would falter, and it couldn't.

She lifted the bed sheet and her little fang popped out

over her lip. She let the sheet fall away from her leg, exposing all of that soft, supple skin. "Care to join me?"

Just another moment.

"I would like nothing more." *Not a lie.* "But I can't."

She tucked her leg back under the sheet. She sighed and pulled more blankets around her. "Royal duties call again?"

I forced a smile I didn't feel. "Something like that."

The smile dropped from her face, and she narrowed her eyes at me. "What's going on?"

My heart sunk, and the breath left my chest. Piper had always been one to read a room, and I had no doubt I was giving off waves of turmoil that she'd sense right away.

Just one more moment of bliss.

"Hello? You're kind of freaking me out with all of this." She waved her hand at me.

I leaned back in my chair and crossed my ankle over my knee. "All of what?"

"All of that tension in your body and the way you're holding yourself back." She scooted back against the headboard.

Observant little creature. I was always amazed by her intelligence. Selfish as it was, I wanted, no, *needed* just one more moment with her before everything went balls-up. "You think you know me so well?"

She lifted her chin and strands of her hair fell into her eyes. "Better than anyone, actually."

"Cocky?"

"There's a difference between being cocky and being right." She crossed her arms.

And with that one move, I already felt her walls going up. "I just thought we'd talk."

"Talk?" She rolled her eyes. "Right."

I glanced around the room, trying to burn it into my memory. The state of the bed and how she looked in it. The lingering fragrance of the two of us that hung in the air. They way my skin felt after her little bites, and the way her cheeks flushed after I'd fed her so well. A thread of pride wound through my body at the thought of caring for her. It was something I knew she'd never let me do again after this conversation.

She waved me on. "You want to talk so talk."

I hesitated, unable to get the words out.

Piper, this has to end.

Piper, we can't continue like this.

Piper, I'm so sorry, but we can't.

Piper, my duties are such that we have to maintain a certain amount of distance.

No matter how I thought of the words, not a single one of them conveyed what I wanted to say with so few words at my disposal. I wanted her, needed her. I didn't want things to end. I wanted our affair to last ages.

"This cannot be."

She curled her legs up to her chest. "Oh."

"I have duties that require my full attention, and we can't be like this again. Last night was . . ."

". . . a mistake." Her words sounded so defeated, like every word I spoke was just another slap.

I didn't want to say it. I knew the moment I did I'd be the one who did the damage. "Yes."

"What kind of duties?"

I hesitated. "I'm sorry what?"

"What kind of duties do you have that would prevent us? Prevent this?" She wrapped herself even tighter like she was preparing for the hurt I knew I was about to inflict on her.

"I can't tell you." Even saying that burned against Titus' power. A prickling sensation ran over my whole body in warning.

"You can't tell me, or you don't want to?"

More burning. "Both."

"Talk to me, Grayson. Why last night and then this? I want to have faith in you but it's really hard when you're pulling me in and pushing me back like some kind of yo-yo."

"I know. But that was not my intention."

"Intention or not, that's what's happening." Her eyes were sad almost pleading when she looked at me. "This isn't you, and I don't want you to be that guy."

"What guy?"

"The guy who once again proves my broken picker is a real thing, the guy who I . . . trust but shouldn't. So just tell me why."

I ground my teeth together. "I will not."

"If I'm being honest, it sounds like a lame excuse to me. You want me, you don't. You need me but don't want to be with me. You're making it really hard to give you the benefit of the doubt right now, Gray. And trust me I want to."

I wanted to tell her it was the curse, to unload all my miseries on her. But I couldn't and she'd have to accept it, just as I would accept the sorrow and anger I inflicted on her. "I'm sorry but this, between us, is done. I'm your sire and you're my progeny. Nothing else."

She flinched back and squeezed her eyes shut for a long moment. "You're right."

"What?" My brows furrowed. That was not the reaction I expected.

"You and me, last night, was one big mistake." She let go of her breath, and when she opened her eyes, they blazed with rage. I felt it rolling off her like I could feel the magic coming off the witches.

"Piper . . . I . . ." I wanted to apologize. I'd lost my head with her. I shouldn't have bedded her and then ended things like this. Even from where I sat, I knew it was a hellish thing to do to her. But Titus had ruled, and I had no other choice. If I was to keep her it would always be at a distance and never where or when she needed me most. Piper was my drug of choice, and she was my addiction.

Her eyes widened for a moment before she ground her teeth together. She was the most observant person I'd ever met. She could read an entire novel from such subtle body language. "You son of a bitch . . . You're breaking up with me . . . again!"

Ah, my brilliant creature knew it all. And with that, my last moment with her was gone.

CHAPTER FOUR

PIPER

I cannot believe this!
What the hell was I thinking giving him a second chance after he messed around the first time? *I'm a fucking moron.* I wasn't a *fool me once, fool me twice* kind of girl. I was a *one fuck-up and done* kind of girl. He made me think we could be more, made me believe in us and all the pretty possibilities that I now knew were bullshit. In my mind, I saw it all. I saw . . . a future with him. Was it going to be perfect? No, but what future was? What world was? And yet I wanted it, wanted him.

"You know if you would just talk to me maybe I could help. We could figure this out . . . together."

"There is no together here. I have my duties, to you, to the crown, to a world of vampires. I can't have dalliances." He didn't move. He barely looked at me.

Here I was trying to understand why he'd cast me off

like this again and he couldn't even give me a reasonable explanation why. "Dalliances?"

"Indeed."

Rage and self-loathing warred within me. I had a feeling in the pit of my stomach that this would happen, like a sixth sense telling me in the back of my mind it would never work. But I talked myself out of backing away and putting up my walls. Because after years of shitty relationships, bad family experiences, and in general just being hurt repeatedly, I'd spent my time being a skeptic. I had held myself away from others. I told myself not to be like that with him. I told myself to be open to it. That maybe, just maybe, this time my happily ever after was on the horizon. When in reality, I was right about it all. I was right about him, even when I really didn't want to be. With my whole heart, I didn't want to be right. Yet I was . . . about everything.

How could I have been so careless? So stupid with my own heart?

Happily ever after didn't exist. At least not for me. It did for other people, but deep down, I knew it wasn't in my cards for me. I knew in life we played the cards we were dealt, but this was the shittiest hand of all because I was senseless enough to believe him. As he sat there with that blank look on his face, I wanted to throw something —to yell, to cry, to just make him feel or know what he'd done to me. But I knew it wouldn't matter. Because if I mattered to him, he wouldn't have hurt me in the first place. He knew my history, knew the ins and outs of my past, and yet he just went on his happy little way, which showed exactly how much I mattered to him . . . not at all.

I hopped out of the bed and yanked the sheets around me like a toga. Grayson sat forward. His eyes lingered on me and I hissed at him. "Do not look at me like that."

"Piper . . ."

"Don't. I'm trying here and you're just clearly not. I don't communicate like this with people, Gray. I leave when shit like this happens."

"I know."

"Then I feel like you need to tell me why."

"I already did."

"A magical duty that appeared out of thin air that you're only telling me about now." I scoffed. "I'm an idiot."

I suddenly felt too naked, too exposed to him. I didn't want or need him to see me like this. My clothes were ripped in tatters and spread over the floor. That didn't matter. Instead, I lifted my chin and marched to his closet. I threw the doors wide open and yanked out the first sweater I spotted. I dropped the sheet, giving him a full view of the figure he'd never see again.

"You're not an idiot." When I glanced over my shoulder, I watched as his eyes ran over my body and he scrubbed his hand down his face. A moment later, he adjusted his seat and sat forward.

Fucking suffer. I pulled the shirt over my head and let

it fall down to my knees. "So, what was last night? A goodbye fuck?"

Grayson shook his head, and for a second, I swear I might've seen a hint of regret. There was a shadow in his eyes and a tightness to his lips I could only chalk up to that. Or maybe it was my own stupid hope that he would know what he was about to lose and might actually care. But no, that was me searching for feelings that didn't exist in a man willing to cast me aside so easily.

He sighed. "Don't be like that."

"Like what?" I pulled my hair from the collar of the shirt and tossed it over my shoulder, letting it fall in wild waves down my back.

"Angry with me." He shoved his hands into his hair. "This is just . . . how it has to be."

"Angry? Me? Nooo. And why would I be angry? For all the . . ." I did my best impression of his sly British accent, ". . . I'm so reliable, you can count on me, not everyone is the same. I'm so different."

He groaned. "I am different than those wankers."

I glared at him. "Funny how they all look the same from where I'm standing. More excuses."

"I just can't handle anything like this right now." He motioned between the two of us. "Any of this. I have duties to my people, to the crown."

"And you won't even tell me what they are, or how I can help, or work with you on it. Your solution is just to get rid of me."

"For now, this is how it must be."

"For now? You can't just pull me and push me like this, Gray. If you want this done and me gone then I will be. But not for you to come back and pick up later when you feel like it."

He let go of a heavy sigh. "I'm not pulling or pushing you. I can't do this and handle the other things that need doing. I'm just... not ready."

Not ready? Is he for real? Not ready would've been good to know before we actually slept together.

"Awww, poor you. I'm so sorry YOU aren't ready for US. Then let me ask you this: why did you give me that bullshit you spewed to gain my trust when I shouldn't have given it in the first place?" I wanted to be reasonable but the desire to throat punch him was overwhelming. "You've proven to be EXACTLY what I thought you would be. Just tied up in pretty words and no action to back it up."

He rose to his feet. "Don't compare me to your past exes."

I crossed my arms over my chest. "Then don't act like them. I thought we were more. I thought we were different."

"I am not them. I am more, and we are different. You know it, and I know it. There are just things that need to be dealt with. Things I can't explain right now. But you are the most amazing—"

"—Let me just stop you right there." I held my hand up, cutting him off. "Pretty words are like pity flowers, and no one wants those."

I wanted him to give me a reason not to be hurt or angry with him. I wanted there to be something important enough that I could believe in, something that made this all make sense. In my heart I thought we were meant to be, and I wanted him to give me a reason to still think that. But he was giving me nothing and now... now I felt like a fool.

His brow furrowed. "What the devil are pity flowers?"

I gave him a smirk to try to hide my hurt. "They're flowers given as a gift just because someone feels bad for you. So, excuse me if I don't need your pity flowers. Or, in your case, pity compliments."

"I've never said a word to you out of pity," he snapped. "I've meant it all."

I couldn't stop the humorless chuckle that burst from my chest. "Fine then. Pity *lies*."

He stilled. "Lies?"

"What else would you have called this fake relationship?" If he couldn't give me a logical reason why we were done, then that's all this was... fake. Even though I didn't want it to be.

"Nothing between us was fake or a lie." He spoke through gritted teeth.

"And yet you tell me nothing." I held my fingers up only an inch apart. "This is about how much I believe you right now."

He turned from me and began to pace. "I had no intention of hurting you."

Anger rolled inside me. I tried to stay calm to talk

things out, but he was giving me nothing. "You know, I would believe that if you hadn't just spent the whole night rolling in bed with me and then dumping me before the sun came up. Makes you a bit of a dick, don't you think?"

He nodded. "Yes, yes it does."

"First truth I've heard you speak since we met." I threw my hands up. I wouldn't be able to stay here and argue for much longer. My tattered insides were crushing on one another. It was hard to breathe, hard to think. If my anger hadn't started to take over, there was no telling what kind of depressed puddle I'd be.

Do not cry in front of him. Do . . . not . . . cry.

"That's not fair." He stilled. "It's just too much for me right now. I hoped you would understand."

"I don't understand at all. Because you won't actually tell me what it is about. So, you turned me into a vampire to keep me . . . but also not. Close but at a comfortable distance. Honestly, why'd you do it? Why make me believe you'd be there? Why earn my trust just to turn around and say you aren't ready? I wish you'd left me alone and taken your —*not ready*— somewhere else because I was happy on my own until you had me thinking more was on the horizon." I groaned and shook my head. I felt so stupid.

Pain lanced through my chest, but I'd be damned if he saw one ounce of it. A tight ball gathered in my throat, but my tears weren't for him. If there was one thing I'd learned in all my life, it was to never let them see you cry.

I really thought this was it. I thought all the games and all the dates and all the random guys were done. I thought my picker finally pointed me in the right direction. It hurt less when I expected betrayal. If I saw something like this coming, it was easy to guard my heart. But I never saw him coming. He'd climbed over my walls as if he were stepping over a curb . . . and butchered me from the inside out.

Screw him and screw this. It might've hurt, it might've secured my belief that love was not for me, but I'd be damned if it would break me. A life hard lived taught me that. It was okay to get knocked down, hurt for a while, but I learned a long time ago to bury the hurt deep down until it was killed. I would suffocate it until there was nothing left of him or *us* in my mind, then I'd get back up, only I'd be smarter and there wouldn't be a next time. I tried to understand, I wanted to help. All he did was shut me out, so I would do the same. There were only so many times I could put myself out there before it looked and felt pathetic. He would be nothing but a distant memory of the guy who almost got close enough to having me. I would forever be his regret and he would forever be a memory. I'd set fire to this sham of a relationship and let it burn with the rest of the bullshit this truly unfair world had to offer.

"I wish you'd just let me die instead of being trapped here like a caged bird you want to look at."

A pained groan escaped his lips. "Letting you die

would be the greatest kind of tragedy the world could suffer."

More words that meant nothing. I was done. Done with this, done with him. I gave him a second chance, there damn sure wouldn't be a third. "I won't wait for you to get your shit straight."

Grayson held his hands up in surrender "I'm not asking you to."

I needed to leave. I felt the crash of my broken heart weighing down on me. It was like I wouldn't be able to breathe or smile again. I had a picture in my head of what life could be with us and now I had to let that go. We could've been great. We could've been something. It was true what they said, this would be like mourning the death of someone who was still alive but would never be a part of my life—no matter how much I needed him to be. "Good, because I deserve so much more than this."

I yanked the door open and stormed out. If I hurried fast enough, I'd make it back to my room before the first tear fell. I pumped my arms, moving at a speed I wasn't used to. I was only a few feet from my door when a hand reached out and grabbed my arm. I was moving so fast I dragged him a few feet, then stopped. When I glanced up, Atlas had a hold on my upper arm.

When I looked down at his fingers, his gaze followed mine. One by one, he pried his fingers loose. "Apologies, my hand acted of its own accord."

"I'll remember to use that excuse the next time you touch me and my hand rips your nut sack right off."

"Noted." He tilted his head and looked at me in that freaky, overly observant way I hated. It felt like being a bug under a microscope. "I sense things are not going well."

What was it with naive men feeling the need to state the obvious when it came to women? "As you Brits would say, piss off. Or is it fuck off?"

"Take a moment to contemplate the things you perceive. He's not what you think." He pressed his lips together.

"I can't tell you how much I wish right now." I had only moments before I broke down and I was wasting them standing here with him. I didn't say another word. I turned from him and walked down the hall, trying to ignore the Christmas decorations. I would be alone again for the holidays, and this time it was even worse because I wouldn't even be with my best friend, Dice. We got each other through things like this. We were a family and always there for each other. Just when I needed her the most, I couldn't go near her.

"Piper," a smooth voice called. "Is all well?"

I turned to see Martin standing in the hall with his iPad in hand. He was always so perfectly dressed. With his neat blond hair, burgundy suit, and crisp white shirt. "Not really, Martin."

"Anything I can do?" His light eyes were round with genuine concern.

I didn't know why but I just walked up to him and hugged him. His arms wrapped around me for a brief moment. I wasn't a hugger, but the events of the last few days just made me need one. "Not unless you've got a boat load of chocolate I can actually eat."

"I think that can be arranged." He winked and hit a bunch of buttons on the screen. "I'll have it sent to your room. Anything else?"

I shook my head. I needed to get to my room before the tears began to fall. "No, you're too kind."

Before I could turn away he cleared his throat. "I'm always here if you need anything... even if it is just a friend."

I hugged him again. "Thank you, Martin. I might take you up on that."

I turned from him and ran the rest of the way until I got to my room. I hurried inside and let the door click shut. That single click of the latch was like a gun going off at the start of a race. My legs went weak and they gave out. They hit the ground, and I placed my hands out in front of me. The first tear was silent as it trickled down my nose and hit the floor. Another, then another. I couldn't do this, couldn't be here. I was surrounded by opulence in this room he'd picked out and furnished for me. It was my gilded cage. I was even wrapped in his shirt that smelled like the deep-red wine I was addicted to.

I jumped up and ran for the bathroom and ripped the shirt over my head. I needed him gone, needed him off my skin and out of my head. I hurried to the shower and cranked the water to as hot as I could get it. Steam billowed, nearly erasing the white marble walls and floor in a cloud of warmth. Each of my breaths came in panicked puffs, and I tried to hold each of them in. All I wanted was to feel the warmth on my skin and let the scalding water burn him away. I stepped under the water and let my body drop to the floor. I scurried back against the wall and pulled my knees to my chest, letting the water run over the top of my head and down my body. A sob broke past my lips and the tears fell freely. The water washed over me and blended in with my tears, and yet I felt each one like a slap in the face.

How could I have been so stupid?

There was one thing I knew for sure. I would never be again . . .

CHAPTER FIVE

GRAYSON

Three Days Later

I rapped my knuckles on the door to Piper's room. It'd been three days since our disastrous end—three days since she emerged from her room, three days since she spoke a word to me, and three days since I made the biggest fuck up of my life. Yet I was bound by Titus to a secret I didn't wish to keep. It weighed heavily on my mind and soul. The lack of her presence in my life pressed on me, and it'd only been three bloody days. There were stipulations to her staying as my progeny and I as her sire. I had to train her to survive in this world with her new vampire abilities and weaknesses. It had to be me. I couldn't trust anyone else but myself with her. My conscience wouldn't allow for it. I brought her into this world of blood and mayhem. I would assure that she thrived within it.

I knocked again. "Piper, I realize I'm the last person you want to see, but I must insist we begin training so you can control your vampire powers."

"Have you peered in a mirror lately? It's a sad state of affairs when a prince appears at the door of a lady looking in such horrible disarray." Atlas pulled up a big ornate chair and shoved it against the wall. He dropped down in it and let his arms fall on the arm rest.

"Aren't you supposed to be doing something?" I growled.

He gave his head a slow shake. "I tend to wander around and find the best form of entertainment until I'm called into action."

"Piss. Off." My hands balled into fists at my sides.

"Ohh, are we sour today? I'm here for dinner and a show. You seem intent on putting one on. I can't say I've ever seen you quite such a mess. Look at your rumpled clothing and let us not discuss the state of the rest of you. Horrid sight." He shook his head and wrinkled his nose.

I looked down at myself and knew he wasn't wrong. My shirt was wrinkled, as were my trousers. I hadn't bothered with my hair or anything else. Sleep was a distant memory I didn't care for at this point. Each time I let my lids close, there she was with her devastated eyes. "I'm in a spot of trouble, and here you are lounging about like there isn't a care in the world. You could be out searching for a way to help me with my plight, not sitting here taking the piss."

Atlas shrugged. "Don't be dramatic."

I did a double take. "There is this theory about a pot and a kettle. Remind me to educate you some time."

Atlas scoffed and shook his head. "And yet my dramatics are called for. For the plights of the simple-minded are simple, but the plights of the depths deserve the time to ponder and wallow. There is a difference."

"Did you just call *me* stupid and *you* the deep thinking one?" My fist shot out and connected with his shoulder. The chair tipped back and smacked into the wall. Atlas forced it forward until all four legs smacked into the floor. He deserved it. "If you're going to be a bloody wanker, go and do it somewhere else."

He rubbed at his shoulder and hissed. "Let us not think of it in such simple terms, but more like easy truths."

I pressed my hand to the door. "You're a right prat, you know that?"

"See? There's the simple analysis." He rose to his feet and stretched his arms over his head and yawned.

Must be nice to not have a care in the world.

I flipped him a very American finger. "Fuck you."

A loud clatter came from behind the door and we both froze. A scream echoed so loud it sounded like she was right next to us. My eyes darted to his, and we both knew that sound. Atlas rolled his sleeves up and ran his fingers over the dagger tattoos he had on his forearms. Red mist seeped from him and swirled around his arms. The daggers emerged from his skin, dark and terrible looking. They were so sharp the soft candlelight glinted off them.

"Watch where you're pointing those things." Another scream ripped through the air followed by the shattering collapse of a wooden bed frame.

"My aim is always true. Is yours?"

I didn't have time to find out. My heart thrummed in my chest as I gazed at the door and heard more things breaking. She was in there trashing the room to pieces. I took a step back.

"On three?"

Atlas nodded in agreement. "Three."

"Three!" I grabbed the doorknob and forced it wide open. Atlas was at my side as we hurried through the opening and into the chaos that was Piper's room.

Piper stood on the bed with a crazed look in her eyes. Blood marred her face and dripped down her legs. Deep scratches ran down her arms and legs. Her hair was a tangled mess that hung loose down the sides of her face. Her eyes were wild and glowing. She crouched down and hissed in our direction.

"What the hell is happening?" Atlas began to move to the side while keeping her in his sights.

"I don't know." If I hadn't known any better, I'd say she was a feral . . . again. But why?

I let my eyes quickly roam around the room. Empty blood bags littered the floor along with ripped clothing, broken furniture, and shards of shattered mirror from the bathroom. It looked like an 80s heavy metal rock band set up shop and destroyed the place. Claw marks riddled the walls, floor, ceiling, and furniture. Pieces of the wall were missing, like they'd been chewed by a dog. Chunks of the floor had been ripped up and cast aside. Holes were punched sporadically in the walls. If it wasn't so terrifying, it'd be almost impressive.

Piper clawed at the air and growled at the two of us. This was worse than cornering an animal. I took a step toward her, and she leapt to the end of the bed. Her sweatpants were torn and hanging from her body, as was her black tank top.

"She's gone feral, mate." The muscles in Atlas' arm tightened like he was going to throw a dagger at her.

I held my hand out toward him. "Stop."

"I'll not let her kill us both."

"So leave."

"Are you out of your senses?" He glanced from me to her and back again. "I've faced her before. She's the strongest I've ever seen."

Of course she was the strongest. Her nature demanded greatness. But I also knew she could control this. I had to bring her back from the edge of insanity. I had to. Piper deserved a life, and damn it I would ensure she'd have it. She would come back from this. She had to. Determination flowed through my veins. It was the first emotion I'd felt other than being a sad sod. As if on cue, Piper leapt from the bed and went right to the ceiling. She dug her nails through the rafters and hung there for a moment just watching the two of us. The lights from the candles reflected off her eyes like an animal in the night.

"I can handle this." I didn't know what made me think I could handle her or this situation. But deep down, I knew I had to be the one. I made her, and if she was going to kill me, then so be it. The curse would be no more, and this constant state of misery would die along with me.

"Are you daft? That makes about as much sense as me knitting a bloody sweater. I was born in this world at night, but I can assure you it wasn't last night."

I motioned for him to move away, and we both stepped back in unison. Piper's eyes tracked our movements, and she dropped back down onto the bed. She crouched down low, every muscle in her body tensed like she was going to attack. My blood magic wasn't something I liked to tap into, but if she attacked, there was no telling what Atlas would do, or what he'd be forced to do. I let it flow through my body and outward. A fine red sparkling mist seeped from me. To anyone else, it'd be invisible. Only a vampire would see it. I'd used it so few times I'd nearly forgotten what it looked and felt like. To use it on Piper almost seemed like blasphemy.

"Stop!"

She halted. I felt the strength in the way she fought my power. What the hell happened to make her revert back to this? Then it hit me—the state of her, the way the room smelled of blood and sickness. She was thin, paler than any vampire I'd ever seen, and she looked like she was on the verge of death. Her eyes were bloodshot, jaundice had set in, and dark circles surrounded her eyes. The blood was doing this to her, but why? How?

"Leave now. And make sure no one else comes in," I snapped to Atlas.

I knew what Piper needed, and I knew I had to give it to her. There was only one way this was going to end, and it would be me sacrificing myself for a moment. I knew I would enjoy it as much as she needed it. Did that make me a piece of shit? Maybe. But I was already there when it came to how I treated her before all this. I needed Piper to survive, and right now I would do anything to assure it.

A growl ripped from his mouth. "Fine, but if she kills you . . . then she dies."

"Touch a hair on her head and you die." I never threatened my most trusted friend, but for Piper, I would.

He straightened his stance and turned for the door. "Fine."

"Keep all of them away, Sav."

"Like they'd dare come close to me," he muttered as he marched to the door and yanked it open. "Love is a plague on The House of Shade and makes fools of kings."

Once he slammed the door behind him, my full attention was on Piper. She hadn't made a move yet, but I felt the tension and hunger within her. My power could barely contain her. If this wasn't such a dire situation, I ripped my shirt over my head and threw it to the ground.

Her eyes landed on the pulse point in my neck, and my body filled with tension knowing what those little fangs would feel like piercing my skin. *Heavenly.* She leaned her head back and sniffed the air.

"That's it. You know you're thirsty. Come on and get it." I dropped my hold on her. I slid my nail down the side of my throat and felt my blood well and trickle down my skin.

Her eyes dilated a split-second before she leapt at me. Our bodies smashed together, and she wrapped her legs around my hips. The force sent me spinning, and we slammed into the wall. Her teeth sank into my skin. Bliss shot through my body. Her warm honey scent surrounded me, and I held her there close to me as she took her first pull of my blood. I groaned at the feel of her skin against mine. Strands of her hair fell over my bare chest and shoulders. I held myself back from what I wanted to do, what I needed to do. My fangs extended in my mouth with the throbbing need to sink them into her, but this wasn't about me, it was about her.

Another deep pull from my neck and my eyes rolled into the back of my head. I felt my fingers press into her thighs as I held her against me. A warm flush crept over my skin, and the world faded away until I felt like I was completely on fire. I was only with Piper. I was only in this second. Here it was, the one more moment that I'd been praying for. I fought the desire to do more. That's what she'd always been for me . . . pure desire and more . . . always more. Everything about her appealed to me.

Her legs slid down my hips and still she pressed into me. When she pulled her little fangs from my skin and began to lick at the tiny punctures, I let my head fall back and a moan escaped my lips.

With her this close to me, nothing else mattered but her hands pressed into my chest and the feel of her against me, each of those little fingernails making a dent in my skin. I was lost to her, lost in a stolen moment I didn't deserve. Piper was the world, like the air I needed to breathe. How could I stay away? How would I resist?

My body was jerked back and suddenly the warmth of her was gone. She shoved me back so hard I dented the wall. Piper leapt across the room and stood there staring at me. She wrapped her arms around herself and looked around the room with wide eyes. "What the hell happened?"

I curled my hands at my sides, forcing myself not to go comfort her in her confusion. "You got . . . thirsty."

"So you figured you'd strip down and volunteer as tribute to the cause?" She rubbed her arms as she huddled into herself. She might've been pissed at me, but she'd regained her senses in no time. The madness of her thirst didn't take her away from me like it could with so many other vampires. Even physically she seemed to steadily recover. Her curves filled out, and there was a healthy pink hue to her cheeks. The dark circles under her eyes were gone and the jaundiced color of her skin disappeared in an instant.

Annoyance rolled off her in waves as she glared at me

with accusation in her eyes. But I had no other choice in the matter. She'd been starving and mad with thirst. Had I let her go in the castle she would've attacked someone else and pretty much signed her death warrant. It was illegal to keep feral vampires alive. It was for the good of all if they were put out of their own misery. It kept the rest of society safe. For her sake and mine, we had to figure this out, and I had to be the sire I was meant to be. If I could train her to understand her thirst and control it, perhaps this wouldn't happen again . . . maybe. Either way, she was a liability I had to fix.

"Get dressed. We have to train . . . now."

I staggered toward the door before I was lost to the temptation to grab her and kiss those plump lips of hers, to pull her close and tell her everything would be okay. I wanted desperately to be that person for her, but I knew I couldn't. Lines had been drawn and I would live my lot. I'd bear it because there was no other choice. I pulled the door shut behind me and leaned against the wall. Atlas took one look at me and unbuttoned his own shirt and threw it at me. "Put it on."

The dark-burgundy shirt wasn't exactly my style, but it would do. I slid my arms into the sleeves and quickly buttoned it up. Scratches ran over my chest and two little puncture wounds throbbed in my neck.

I tucked the shirt in. "Better?"

I held my arms out to my sides. He shook his head and sighed. "No."

Atlas motioned to the mirror across the hall. I looked

at myself and pulled the collar up higher. Even though the shirt was dark, two little dots of blood seeped into the material. There wasn't a thing I could do about it, but I didn't give a shit. I'd wear the bloody fang marks with pride.

"You think that'll help? Like putting lipstick on a pig."

"Come off it." I gave him a half-grin. "We both know I'm the better looking of the two of us."

"Oh, that's yet to be seen, my darling," a light familiar voice drifted to me from a few feet away.

"Mother!" My mother was the epitome of delicate grace.

She had long chestnut hair that flowed down her back in loose waves. Her eyes were a warm rich chocolate with only the barest hint of mahogany. Where Piper was wild and robust, my mother had a gentle way of getting exactly what she wanted, and yet both of them were amazing in their own right. My mother was all the good of a traditional vampire and none of the bad. Her features were elven with her tiny nose, little pink lips, and big doe eyes. She wore a navy-blue dress that was cinched in tight around her torso and puffed out from her waist in flowing sheer layers. The plumed sleeves were loose around her arms and tight at the wrist.

She looked Atlas up and down with his bare chest on full display. "New look for you, darling."

Atlas rarely put his tattoos on display. They were his own secret kind of deadly weapon. Each tattoo could be summoned from his skin and used however he wished.

Poe, his raven, was stretched across his chest, the knives were on his forearms, and a hooded figure on his back could change him into the night hunter that he was. New ones I'd never seen wrapped around his ribs and flowed down into the top of his pants.

He shrugged in that nonchalant way he had, like nothing in the world mattered to him. "Thought the ladies might like it, Moira."

My mother pressed her lips together, ignoring Sav's comment like she was trying to hold in a chuckle. She turned to me, giving me the side-eye. "Everything all right, dear?"

She placed her hand over the side of my neck where Piper had bitten me. Her warm blood magic forced my cells to heal even faster. I felt them buzzing under my skin and through my neck. I cleared my throat. *Nothing like your mother discovering your love bites.* "Never better."

She moved her hand from my neck to gently cup my cheek. "Careful with that one, darling. If you're after pleasure and pain, I'm sure she'll be the one to give it to you."

A snicker broke past my lips. She was too close to being right for my own comfort. "I have no doubt of that."

"For when thee love thee turn forsaken." She didn't say another word. She just patted my shoulder and silently glided away. It was a line from the curse and enough to send a chill right down my spine and into my bollocks.

CHAPTER SIX

PIPER

I tightened my arms around myself and stood across from Grayson. I didn't know how many days it'd been since we'd broken things off. Things got a bit hazy between the time I gorged myself on chocolate-flavored blood and the time when I upchucked it all. After that, there were only flashes. Whatever happened, it'd resulted in my room being trashed and my fangs in Grayson's neck . . . again. It was so freaking exasperating that my vampire side couldn't resist him when my brain wanted to so badly. My heart was an entirely different story I could barely figure out. I wanted him so badly but the sting of his rejection hurt even worse.

I didn't want to go to *training*, as he called it, but there was no one else to turn to and I had to get the blackouts under control. I'd always been in complete control of my life and my actions. To not have that now was beyond frustrating . . . and slightly terrifying. I knew I was stronger and more powerful than ever. My ability to hurt others had increased exponentially, and with that, I had to learn control, even if it was from Grayson. I had no choice. Perhaps the training would be a welcome distraction from the messes we both seemed to be.

So here I was in leggings, a sporty tank top, and a baggy off-the-shoulder sweater. I put sneakers on, but I didn't even know if I needed them anymore. Was I strong enough to run through the forest barefoot? Twilight style? If so, the smooth stones of the castle might've even felt good under my bare feet.

"Piper!" he snapped.

I jumped to face him. "What?"

"I've been saying your name for three sodding minutes." He had the audacity to stand there looking that good with that much attitude . . . *bastard*.

"Lost in thought."

The truth was, I was getting flashes of memory from my little losses of time: throwing things in my room, a dark-haired girl sitting in the lab with me . . . My eyes locked on the rocky ceiling and thick cement walls of the training room as I fought to find the pieces of my lost mind. I shook myself, pushing away the broken thoughts.

I focused on my surroundings, trying to find a moment of clarity in the last few days. It was hard to discern the contrast of the opulent castle, the high technology lab, and now a training room that looked like it belonged in the pits of hell. There was a damp basement smell to the room along with a chill that hung in the air from the dank England weather. The floor was made of a dark rubbery surface that would cushion any impact. Across the way in a small corner of the room, streams of daylight came in. Each one was a tiny dot of light that made the wall look like Swiss cheese. Was this room for training or torture? Made vampires couldn't stand the sunlight, only the born ones like Grayson, yet I found myself drawn to the dazzling rays. I knew I couldn't touch it, but the desire to test how much pain it might cause was there. I didn't know what he planned to do with me down here, but I wanted to learn and leave.

Grayson smoothed his hand over his perfectly imperfect hair. He had the nerve to look delicious in that burgundy shirt and black trousers. Two little dots of blood marred the collar of the shirt, and he wore it like some kind of badge of honor. Or a taunt. I couldn't decide which. There was a thin line between love and hate, and sometimes when it came to Grayson, I danced between the two. He was beautiful and charismatic in a way that drew me to him, and yet he'd broken my heart, and for that I couldn't just forgive and forget. People said forgiveness was divine, but if I wanted to be nominated for sainthood, that ship had sailed long before I'd met him.

He sighed. "We haven't got time for lost in thought, Little Creature."

"Don't call me that." Anything *creature* from him was an endearment I didn't want to listen to in that sexy as fuck British accent.

When he looked at me with those hypnotic mahogany eyes, I froze. He stared at me for what felt like long moments. Tension sizzled between us and every muscle in his body tensed like he was going to spring toward me. I took a step back, not wanting any part of that. Love was a fickle thing, and if I was being honest with myself, I'd fallen for Grayson the second he strolled into the bar. The fall had been steep. The crash was even harder.

"Apologies, Sassy Creature, but words roll off the tongue when it comes to you." His lip pulled up at the corner in that half-smirk.

I rolled my eyes. "Shut up."

He chuckled. "Has anyone ever told you an angry Piper is a sexy Piper?"

"Are you . . . are you flirting with me?" This man made no sense at all. *I can't be with you, but I love to flirt with you.*

"One does inspire the need to . . . play." He rested his hand on a stack of cinder blocks standing next to him.

"Listen up, bub, you made the decision to fuck all this up with no explanation other than some duty that came from thin air, so you get to live with it. There's nothing between us." If I said it out loud enough perhaps my heart would start to believe it. I didn't know why he had to be so damn confusing. *I want you, I don't. I need you, but I can't.* Playing yo-yo with my heart was not an option.

"Understood." His smile fell and he grabbed up a block. He tossed it up, then caught it again with one hand like it weighed no more than a coin.

He glanced at me a moment before he used his vampire speed to hurl the thing at me. I stepped to the side, and it sailed an inch from my face and embedded into the cement wall behind me. I looked at the block, then looked at him.

"Are you insane?" My voice rose.

"You can move faster." He grabbed another and threw it, then another, and another.

I ran halfway around the training room dodging each one of them. When he paused, I narrowed my eyes at him. "Is this your idea of a lesson?"

"Got you running, did it not?" He moved to a table a few feet away. "You need to be able to tap into that side of yourself at any moment and get used to the way your body moves."

"I'm fairly certain my body moves exactly how I want it to." What were we doing here? Having a little work out? I was a vampire now. Speed felt natural.

"I've always been a fan of cockiness."

He pulled a black cloth off the table, revealing a line of knives. He lifted one and held it out, letting the light reflect off the sharp edge. He turned it in all different directions, and my eyes locked on the distinctive facets of the silver blades. As a human, I remembered being afraid of the sharp pointies, but now I could see every piece of them and my fear all but disappeared. Like if I knew exactly where the cutting parts were, then I could avoid them easily enough.

Grayson flicked his wrist, and the knife flew end over end right toward my chest. It wasn't as fast as I'd thought it'd be. It moved in slow-motion as it came closer. I leaned back and let it soar by me. It thunked into the wall, the blade so deep in the cement there was only an inch showing past the hilt. I turned and arched my eyebrow at him. He smiled to himself and grabbed three more knives. He tossed one after the other at me. I spun, twisted, and dodged them easily. When he grabbed a fourth knife and threw it at me, I watched it head right toward my face. I didn't move, and at the last second, I snatched it from the air and held it there, only an inch from my nose.

"You're twisted, you know that, right?" I dropped my arm to my side. "Who throws knives at people?"

"You're a vampire now." He groaned and rubbed his hand over the back of his neck. "This world is a dangerous place, Piper. Beautiful but dangerous, and I've seen enough of it to know a knife is the least of your worries if you cross the wrong people."

I tossed it up and down easily, catching it by the hilt and never touching the sharp blade. It was something I'd never do as a human. "I don't plan on crossing anyone. I want to learn what I need to learn and go."

"Go?" His head snapped up as he turned toward me. "Where will you go?"

"Who knows?" I shrugged.

"No, I forbid it." He shook his head.

I pulled my arm back and let the knife fly end over end toward him. His eyes widened as he caught it a millimeter from his temple. "Now is not the time for cheek."

"I mean, I was aiming for your neck." Not a lie. Just a tiny scratch, just so he'd know I could. I winked.

He chuckled and dropped the knife, and it clanged on the ground as he moved over to a medicine ball the size of a small car. He leaned against it and crossed his arms over his chest. "Part of being a vampire is knowing how to control your strength."

"I think I'm good."

"The few broken ribs you gave me says you don't."

"... I didn't break your—"

"—didn't you?" He raised his eyebrows.

"When?" I crossed my arms.

"Do you really want me to answer that right now?" He shook his head. "I don't think you do."

My eyes widened at the thought that'd I'd hurt him during our extracurricular nighttime activities. I didn't know if I was impressed or disgusted with myself. The truth was, he always made me feel conflicted, and I didn't like it. I opened my mouth to apologize—

He waved his hand, cutting me off. "Don't you dare apologize . . . I enjoyed it."

"Such an ass." I groaned and started heading toward the door.

"Ah, but an ass with a point." He lifted the medicine ball over his head and threw it at me. "Catch!"

"Catch?" I backed up a few steps as this thing soared across the room right at me. My old instincts died hard. I wanted to run out of the way, but if I was supposed to train with my strength, then this was the moment. I put my arms out and caught the damn thing. My feet skidded across the floor as I flew backwards.

My back slammed into the wall and the cement dented, causing little pieces to roll down from the crack in the wall. Dust rained down into my hair and across my shoulders. I took a step forward and held the ball above my head with one hand. I tossed it up and caught it, then threw it right back at him. "Catch."

He stood in front of it and caught the ball, but when it hit him, he too skidded back a few feet. I smiled to myself. I was strong . . . Really strong. He lifted the ball over his head with one hand. "It's not a bloody game."

"Incorrect. I do believe catch is, in fact, a game."

"Right, wise ass. Now hold on to it." He threw it back, and I marveled at how easily I was able to hold and move something the size and weight of a car. It made me curious to see what else I could do.

Grayson pulled another black cloth off the table,

revealing a dozen eggs laying there beautifully. He grabbed one. "Now, hold the ball and catch this."

He hurled it at me so fast it was a blur, even for my vampire eyes. I reached out and caught it. It cracked in my hand, sending slimy yoke down my fingers and onto the floor. I shook my hand out. "Gross."

"And that'll teach you. The secret to being the best of the best is finesse." He was at my side in an instant. His fingers trailed down my arm to my hand like the whisper of a butterfly. "Gentle, Little Creature."

Before I could shove him away, he was back on the other side of the room, like he knew he'd only have a second to touch me before I threw him and used it to his advantage. "Right, you think you could try that?"

"You mean not to throat punch you the next time you touch me? Yeah, I could try . . . but I doubt I would succeed."

His lips twitched like he fought not to smile. "Noted."

It wasn't that I hated Grayson, but when someone broke my heart, the best I could offer was to behave myself—so long as they stayed far enough away from me to let me be comfortable. Him being so close was uncomfortable because I once found myself lost in the warmth of his arms. It felt safe, like everyone else in the world faded away and my place was with him. Just the two of us against everything else that sucked. Then it turned out he sucked the most of all.

He picked up another egg and threw it at me. This time I grabbed it out of the air and treated it like a butterfly I didn't want to crush. There I stood, holding the ball as big as a car in one hand and an egg in the other. It wasn't the biggest challenge in the world, but it was a test of control. I smiled at him and threw the egg back his way. "I'd say I aced that one."

"Indeed." He smiled and threw the cloth back over the remaining eggs. "I had no doubts."

"Sure you didn't." I dropped the ball with a thud and put my hands on my hips. "Are we done for the day? I have things to do."

He arched his eyebrows. "Such as?"

"Such as not be here?" The truth was, my stomach was twisting with hunger, and the last thing I wanted to do was take another bite of him. He was sinful and delicious but in the worst possible way for me to try and resist. I wanted to do the bagged blood thing. The vampires had it set up perfectly for delivery and I wanted to ace that too. Grayson was delicious but my independence from him was even more important than his flavor.

"Just one more thing." He turned away from me and sauntered over to a door at the back of the training room. I hated the way his pants fit him perfectly, the way the muscles in his legs and ass showed *just* enough through his pants. I hated the confident swagger he had with each of his steps. Most of all, I hated the way I didn't hate it at all. From here I could smell his deep red wine scent. Resentment ran through my body. How dare he pique my interest without my permission.

He pulled the door open, and on the other side of it was an obstacle course the likes of which I'd never seen before. It was worse than the ones I'd seen on TV. It was the size of three football fields, and there was even more to it than I thought would be possible.

"This is one more thing?"

"Just a little something." He motioned for me to walk, and I fell into step beside him.

"I don't understand, I'm not training to be a power trooper." I looked at the rotating beams over a pool of water along with the platforms high above a pit of spikes. Further down, there were ropes hanging so far away from each other it'd be impossible to swing from one to the other. There at the very end of all of it was an open field with more streams of light shining down from outside. I could almost feel the warmth of sunlight from here.

"No, but you need to know what you're capable of." He turned and met my eye. "Piper, I need you to be ready for any situation. I need you to know yourself well enough to trust that you are now immortal and you can do *anything*. But even immortals have their weaknesses. And yes, if you never got involved with any of the drama, you'd live forever. But you're the closest thing to a new royal the world has seen in years. I'm afraid it has put a bit of a target on your back."

I could do anything but stop having feelings for him.

"Are you worried I'll be stuck in the middle of some war?"

He nodded. "There are things happening in the supernatural world of Evermore. Only a few weeks ago, I was in the middle of a battle between witches and warlocks. I've been in the underworld. I've fought with the Greeks. I've nearly died. There is too much happening for me not to worry about you."

My stomach turned in knots. This world was a lot to take in and get used to. As a human, all I worried about was making ends meet. Now, I had witches, warlocks, and all types of other things to contend with, so I would stick to the plan and learn as much as I could. He wasn't wrong. I did feel stronger than I ever had in life. Even now, my body thrummed with untapped strength. I knew I could run, jump, and lift whatever he had to throw at me. In reality, I wanted to get this done and get back to my room to feed and sleep. I'd show him what I was capable of and I'd leave.

"And once I master this, I'm done with training?"

He pursed his lips and crossed his arms over his chest. Then after a few long moments, he nodded. "Agreed . . . for tonight. Tomorrow, I will challenge you."

I didn't wait for directions. I just took off running. I hit the rotating beams first. They each twisted and turned in different directions, rolling over each other and making it nearly impossible to find my footing. Yet I leapt and twisted in midair, easily finding a place to step even though everything was moving too fast. When I reached the other side of the pool, I stood there smug as ever. He just waved me on, not even bothering to try and stop me from moving to the ropes. I leapt forward and wrapped my hands around them, letting my body swing there for a moment. I expected my hands to burn on the ropes, the muscles in my upper body to throb, and to feel like I couldn't hold on. What I got was the complete opposite. A chuckle escaped my lips as I climbed higher with ease. A cranking sound filled the air accompanied by a slight whistle.

Grayson learned his throat. "Pay attention."

A moment later, there was a boom and a wall of heat hit me a moment before I spotted the fireball. It shot right toward me, and I leapt for another rope. The fireball hit the rope I was on, instantly severing it with burning hot flames. The rope fell to the ground. I didn't realize how high up I'd gotten. I was at least thirty feet high. Another bang and I jumped to the next rope again, and again I climbed, slid, and dodged my way to the other side. By the time I let go of the last rope and dropped to the ground, the smell of burnt cinders clung to my hair and my hands were red from the rubbing of the rope. They quickly turned back to my normal pale color.

I headed right for the field of sunspots. I wove my way through them with ease, and yet I felt no fear coming this close to something I knew would end me. I was supposed to hiss and shy away from it, but there was warmth and light there. Though it'd only been a short time, I missed the sun on my skin, the smell of summer, and the lingering warmth it left on my skin when I stayed out too long. When I reached the end, I paused in front of a beam of sunshine. The different layers of light and colors fascinated me. I saw all the deepest reds, vibrant blues, enchanting greens, and an array of colors I never knew existed as a human. If I touched it, I wondered whether I would catch fire or if it would just leave a little burn. I reached my hand out toward it . . .

Grayson was there in an instant to yank it back. He held my wrist up and pulled me closer to him. "A fiery death is not in the cards for you, I'm afraid."

I pulled my hand from his grip. "I'm already dead."

He didn't have to let me go, but he did. "Technically."

"If you want to see how fast you can heal, then let's do it, but I warn you the sun is unforgiving. A burn will scar, and to submerge yourself means a fiery, painful death." He pulled a knife from his pocket and sliced it through the palm of his hand. His blood dripped and my stomach tightened for a taste of him. Visions of my fangs in his skin flooded my mind, and the desire was nearly overwhelming. Before I could sink my fangs into him, the wound healed up as though it never happened. I shook myself, forcing those tantalizing thoughts away.

"There are few things in this world that can hurt us. For one, certain poisons." He shuttered like he knew from first-hand experience. "Also, beheadings, and then there are a few other nasties hanging around. But for you, a made vampire, nothing is more dangerous than the sun and the ability to control your thirst. But just a simple cut? You will heal."

He grabbed my hand and sliced it before I could stop him. I was fast, but he was so much faster. I yanked it back and cradled it to my chest. The cut stung my hand and made my fingers tingle. The smell of blood filled my nose and I cringed away from my own blood. "Are you crazy?"

Grayson looked down at my gushing hand. His eyes widened for a split-second before they narrowed on me. "You haven't fed enough. Piper, this is serious. It should've healed by now. You have to learn to know your hunger, or you are going to hurt someone and yourself. The blood makes us stronger."

I pressed my hand harder to try to stop the bleeding. "You think I don't know that? I am trying!"

He shook his head. "You'll go feral, and you walking into the sun will be the least of our worries. Whatever you're doing, it's not good enough."

"Then please tell me what will be good enough for you, Your Highness, and I will be sure to comply."

"You don't mean that." He narrowed his eyes at me.

"I don't know. You're the king of broken promises. You tell me what's true or false, because from where I'm standing, it's all bullshit that comes out of your mouth."

His fangs extended in front of my eyes, and he nicked his wrist right in front of me. "Feed now."

That heavenly scent filled my nose, and I did everything I could to hold back from biting him. It was heaven

... sin ... I wanted it ... wanted him. "Is that a command?"

Grayson held it out toward me, and tiny drops of blood dripped on the floor between us. *Such a waste.* "A humble request."

"Then I humbly request for you to fuck right off." He was everything I wanted and nothing I could have. Why did he have to be so damn delicious, so damn overwhelming, so damn *him* ...

CHAPTER SEVEN

GRAYSON

I tried to follow as closely behind her as I could. She seemed to be moving faster and faster, running at a speed I barely hit when I was in battle. Yet around Piper, everything felt like a battle lately, and I hated every moment of it, even if it was completely deserved. I could hardly find the wherewithal to stay an inch away from her, let alone to keep the distance she deserved. Even as she ran from me, the blood pumped through my veins, forcing the animal deep within to stir. Her dark hair streamed out behind her and drops of blood fell from her hand with each step she took. Her honey scent filled my senses, and I wanted to catch her to pull her close to my body and feel her presence surround me.

Even when she was beyond irate with me, I found her to be sexy as hell—so tempting with her sassy mouth and fiery glares. When Piper was sweet, she lived up to her honey scent. But when she was angry and the sweetness disappeared, her fire called to me like waving a red flag in front of a bull.

"Piper, wait." I hurried after her, nearly catching up.

She growled in my direction and her arm shot out to connect with my shoulder. I soared through the air and slammed into the wall. The hard stone cracked under the force of the hit. My body rattled as I ricocheted off the wall and spun around to regain my footing. From here I could tell she was starting to lose it. She hadn't fed enough, hadn't taken enough from me. As a newly made vampire, she'd need more, and I should've given it to her.

"Damn it, Piper. STOP!" The hall was coming to an end, and if she made it to the stairs leading up, she'd be in the main castle and in the view of every single courtier . . . and my uncle, the King. The last thing I needed was any of them thinking I held a feral vampire in my keeping. I'd have broken about a hundred laws, and they'd chop off her head as quickly as possible.

The door at the end of the hall opened and a younger vampire walked through. I recognized him as one of the vampires who worked with the concierge service for vampires in the castle. He assured that all vampires in the castle had their every need met. He was smaller, too small for how powerful Piper was.

I waved my arm. "Get out!"

But it was too late. Her head tilted to the side like her eyes had locked on him, and she veered from one side of the wide hallway to the other. The man's eyes widened, and he dropped his little tablet when he turned to run in the opposite direction. Piper leapt up into the air and dug her fingers into the ceiling. She crawled across it, digging her hands into the stones like she was crawling across the ground and not the ceiling. Before he could reach the door, she dropped down in front of him. Her eyes were wild with hunger as she extended her fangs and hissed at him. He backed away from her slowly, trying to gain some distance, but she pursued him like a cat hunted a tiny mouse. Each of her steps were calm and haunting. Her direction never faltered, and at any moment she'd pounce on him. I ran faster than I ever dreamed possible.

She leapt forward and grabbed the man's shoulders, then yanked him to her. Before she could plant her fangs in his neck, I caught up to her and threw my arm in front of her mouth. Her teeth sank into my forearm and bliss shot through my body. I hurled my weight to the side, knocking the man out of the way a little too forcefully. He smacked into the wall and fell to the ground. He froze there, shaking for a moment, and I knew that to a vampire in the throes of thirst, he'd look like easy pickings.

"Hey!" I hissed at him. "Get a hold of yourself."

The man, who if he was human would look no older than eighteen, looked up at me with wide, dark eyes. Strands of his hair fell over this face in little greasy streaks. "I-I . . ."

Her eyes locked on him, and I wrapped my other arm around her waist and shoved her back, pinning her to the wall. "Go now!"

The man scrambled to his feet and straightened his coat. His mouth opened and closed like a shocked fish who'd just escaped the clutches of a shark. He gave me a half-bow out of habit and stared at her with wide eyes as she sucked blood from my arm. "Y-your High—"

"Speak nothing of this. Not a single word, or you will have me to deal with." I bared my fangs at him, assuring my point was made.

He staggered back and out the door he came through. The door slammed, and I was alone with her. I loosened my hold on her, but she kept those perfect little fangs in my arm. With the next pull, I groaned and let my head fall against hers. *Bliss.*

"Take what you need."

Her eyes were closed so tight, and I wondered if she was still with me, if only she knew I was here or wanted to be. Did she know I'd always give what she needed? Did she feel the connection I did? Suddenly, her eyes flashed wide, and she released me. Her arm shot out and she shoved me back. "What happened?"

"Your thirst took over." I took a step toward her, offering her my wrist. "You need more."

"Not from you." She pressed the back of her hand to her mouth and shook her head.

"Piper, you must. Your thirst is out of control. Of all the training and all the things you need to understand, this is the most important. If you don't, your life will be forfeit." I knew she hated me, and she had every right to, but I would not bloody survive in this world if anything happened to her.

Tears glazed over her eyes, yet she didn't allow one to fall. "You should've just let me die."

"Never." The word left my mouth on a growl.

She walked past me, heading back toward the training room. "I'm so sick of this."

"We will figure it out. Together."

She whirled around. "There is no together for us. What don't you understand about that? I've spent all my life figuring it out and fixing shit on my own. You cannot fix this. I will fix it myself, even if I have to meet the fucking sun."

Before I could argue, a dark shadow rose up behind her. I leapt forward, but it was too late. Atlas was there. With lighting speed, he pressed his hand over her mouth and shoved a needle into her neck and pressed the plunger down. Her eyes fluttered shut, and she collapsed into his arms.

"What have you done!" My heart pounded in my chest.

He sighed and rolled his eyes. "Drama is meant for times of ease and pleasure, and this is not one of those times, so I knocked her out."

"You wanker!" I tried to take her from his arms, but he scooped her up and turned away. "Give her over."

"Sod off." He looked me up and down. "Look at yourself, mate. You're so bloody daft to the situation at hand you can't recognize your own mistakes. You look like a right ponce."

"Come off it. I know what I'm doing."

"Do you?" He glared.

"I do."

"Riddle me this, your progeny is losing her bloody mind every time she needs a bit of a snack. Has it not occurred to you that something isn't right?" He adjusted her in his arms so her head lulled back and hung there, letting her long hair brush over the floor.

"We're addressing the issue." He wasn't wrong, things were slipping between us. She was so strong yet so susceptible to her thirst, why? In mere moments, she'd become a danger to everyone around her.

"There are so many bloody issues you are not addressing, and you call me daft?" he growled in my direction. "You've made a right mess of things. If you won't handle it, I will."

I didn't want to fight my oldest friend, but for her, I would. "And what are you going to do?"

"Toss her into the fiery pits." He gave me a withering, bored look. "Unless you've got a better plan."

He was right. I had to do something better than this. My mind raced and fought between wanting to keep things a secret for her safety and needing to figure this out once and for all. "Take her to the lab."

"Obviously." He rolled his eyes and kept on walking.

"I will follow." I wanted to be there every step of the way.

He shook his head. "No, you won't. You have other responsibilities."

Nothing was more important than Piper. Where she went, I would follow. "What of them?"

Sav paused and met my eye. His face turned deadly serious. "You've been summoned by the King."

Nothing was more important, except maybe that . . .

CHAPTER EIGHT

GRAYSON

I strolled down the hall toward the throne room with my mind a whirlwind of issues that just needed to be bloody solved. I shoved my sleeve down, hiding the bite mark on my arm. They were already healing, but Titus would see and assume something I *wish* were allowed to be true. I glanced over my shoulder, waiting for Atlas to appear. I needed to know what the hell was happening and how to fix it. Nothing was going right. Everything was a disaster of epic proportions. And I'd gone and stepped in it now. I could not do one thing right. I was accustomed to pissing off just about the entire royal family at one point or another, but right about now, I was entirely fed up with my own bullshit.

I moved closer to the throne room and tried to straighten my shirt, collar, and sleeves before I entered. Two double doors at the end of the hall were manned by two other vampires. As I approached, they grabbed the handles and pulled them back in a simultaneous move that looked choreographed. I'd seen it so many times that I'd gotten used to it long ago. Dark stone flooring and walls was the décor for the last few centuries. Wooden beams arched from the ground up to the ceiling where they met in intricate carvings that ran over the ceiling. Warm candlelight lit the way to the throne room. As I got closer, the normal nervousness I felt gave way and was replaced by cold determination.

The throne room was the centerpiece of the castle, with thirty-foot ceilings, wide-open space, and warm wooden beams going in all different directions. A single throne sat on top of a dais at the head of the room. Two flags hung on the wall behind it, both bearing the symbol for The House of Shade. It was a single silver sword with deep-red roses winding around it, and it sat on a black shield. The same symbol was made of a giant stained-glass window that took up most of the wall. The sunlight shined through it and projected the crest onto the middle of the floor.

Titus sat on his throne with the length of his dark velvet coat draped over the arms. He sat forward and glared at me the moment I entered the room. Annoyance ran off him in waves while he looked at me. The muscles in his jaw ticked, and he let out a long, slow breath like he was searching for the patience not to wring my neck this very second.

"Right, so we're off to a roaring start." I stopped just in front of him.

My mother stood at his side, wringing her hands in front of her. She looked from Titus to me and back again. "Darling, things have turned."

Titus didn't say a word, he just rose to his feet and rubbed his hand across his forehead. He squeezed his eyes shut and gave a heavy sigh. In the other hand, he held a piece of parchment that looked as ancient as he was. The sides were rough, and the color held a brown tint among the beige. The scrawled handwriting was thick and bold in a commanding way I didn't want to look at. Titus marched over to me and handed me the paper, then turned away and sat back on his throne. To say he was seething would be an understatement.

I groaned at the letterhead on the parchment. Black wings sat at the top of the page with two swords crossing them. A sprinkle of magic swirled around the wings and swords. It moved on the page, making it glitter as though the wings were flapping, and the magic swirling all on its own. Below that, the words were sprawling. It was the first time we'd ever received a letter from The Fallen. The fallen angels who ruled the supernatural world were ruthless in their decision-making. Empires tumbled under the weight of their anger. The last thing we wanted to do was draw attention to the vampires, and yet I had. In the worst possible way. I sucked in a breath and read the words with dread sitting heavy in my stomach.

House of Shade,

For over a thousand years, the family Shade has overseen the vampires. Do not make us regret the decision to allow this to continue. The laws are clear, and if you cannot uphold them . . . we will. Though we wish to keep our swords to ourselves, we have no hesitation to use them. The choice is yours. The thirst is both a blessing and curse to be managed. Vampires who cannot manage it must be dealt with accordingly, as we agreed upon all those years ago.

I swallowed hard and knew they were talking about Piper. My heart dropped into my stomach. I wanted to vomit. Even worse, the letter continued on.

In addition, I've got shit to do, so handle your own . . . or I will.

—Mika, The Fallen.

I marched up the two steps onto the platform where the throne sat and handed the paper back to Titus. I'd never been threatened by The Fallen before. It was unnerving, terrifying, and brought on a level of worry no one needed. Least of all me. I swallowed the ball in my throat and forced my face to be as impassive as possible. "Interesting enough."

He took it from my hand and glared at me.

"Here is where words normally occur in a conversation." I stood waiting, trying not to appear like I was holding my breath. We all knew who the problem was and how the rumor mill swirled within a castle of our size.

Titus' hand curled into a fist, and he growled as he crumpled up the paper in his grasp.

My mother stepped in closer, so close she was nearly between us. "My dear, it is clear The Fallen have taken an interest in what has occurred in the castle."

"Is there no privacy to be had in my own home?" Indignation laced my voice, even though I knew I'd gotten myself into a spot of trouble . . . or a touch more than a spot. This was bad. Very bad. This was more than just a sticky wicket or a deep hole. This was bad business I'd found myself in the middle of. I was in a bad way and there wasn't a damn thing that could be done to sort it.

"We are surrounded by staff and courtiers and all other manner of visiting species. You think any of us are entitled to keep a bloody secret?" Titus rose to his feet. "I have been patient."

". . . For four days."

"I have given ample warning."

"Hardly." I waved his words away.

He threw his arms up. "You never listen."

"I've got my ears on now, haven't I?"

"You're a right git."

"Oh, come off it. You and I both know I've always done right by The House of Shade."

He rolled his eyes. "So long as it fits your agenda."

"Oh, you mean ensuring our alignment with the most powerful factions in all of Evermore?"

"Right, the playboy Prince claiming responsibility for everything except what he's actually done."

"And what's that?"

"The Fallen are not to be trifled with."

"Like you need to clarify THAT. I'm not bloody thick, you know?"

"Oh, but sometimes I question if you are or not."

"Now who's the git?"

My mother stepped between the two of us. "Gentleman, let us not forget ourselves."

There was no other person in the world who could step between us. No other person who would dare. Yet we both took a step back. My mother cleared her throat and ran her hands down the front of her dress, straightening a ruffle that already laid perfectly.

"Now, The Fallen have sent us a warning shot. Your Majesty, what do you make of it?"

Titus gave a heavy sigh, but I could visibly see him find his calm for her. No matter what situation lay in front of him, he always gave my mother the respect she deserved as his brother's widow. She'd been his closest advisor ever since my father's death, and he allowed her the positions she handled so well.

"We need to heed this warning." He turned toward me. "Where is Piper?"

I wanted to yell and point this conversation in a different direction. *How do you know it's her?* But there was no one else in the court to stir the rumor mill like she could—the only vampire to be sired by a royal of The House of Shade and the only vampire who showed signs of being feral but still lived.

"I admit it was a rocky start."

"Where is she?"

"She's improving daily."

He arched his eyebrows at me. "Oh, you mean from thrashing her room?"

"A minor inconvenience at best." I waved away the fact she'd lost her damn mind earlier and would've likely killed someone had I not arrived. But was I going to tell him that? I wasn't in the habit of digging myself into a deeper hole.

"Where is she?"

"You know, I'm not quite sure. We had a difficult training session."

"So I've heard. Now, where is she?"

I crossed my arms over my chest. "And what do you plan to do with her?"

"How is that any of your concern?"

"She's my progeny. By our laws. She. Is. Mine." I had no intention of fighting with my uncle, but deep down there was a spark of desire to do just that for her.

He turned away from me, and his coat fanned out behind him. I stood waiting for him to turn back, but he marched away and walked over to the sideboard. He grabbed the decanter and poured himself a generous drink: his favorite blood spiked with bourbon. He turned toward me and narrowed those honey eyes at me. When he took a deep sip, he didn't break that deep glare.

"King. It all is mine."

I nodded. "Touché."

"The last thing I need is The Fallen breathing down our necks. We've got the year of the prophecy, the building of the underground, the Blood Borns up my arse, the Night Spawn clawing at me for attention, and a mysterious illness now plaguing the made vampires. We have no idea what the devil it is, and now thanks to you, Ophelia the psychopath of a witch who comes and goes as she pleases . . . do you have any idea how many people she's killed?"

I shook my head. When he gave me an exasperated look, I shrugged. "To be fair, I don't think anyone does."

He slammed his fist down on the arm of the chair and the loud bang echoed around the room. "Where is she?"

I swallowed just as the doors flew open and Atlas strolled through. He stopped when he took in the tension between me and Titus. His eyes ran over us quickly before he continued into the throne room. Usually, there were courtiers lingering about, but being alone made his walking in that much more dramatic. When he got to us, he gave a bow to Titus and then to my mother. Atlas never bowed to me unless he was being a sarcastic prat.

"Have I interrupted?"

Titus motioned to me. "Apparently, my nephew thinks he can saunter about not answering my requests. Because there are secrets in the castle . . . that he thinks I don't know already."

I moved to Atlas' side and waited for him to nod and assure me that Piper was safe. It was so subtle, but I caught that tiny movement. The dread in the pit of my stomach eased, and I faced my uncle with new vigor.

Atlas shifted from one foot to the other and lowered his voice. "Family is bloody complicated. Glad I don't have one."

"That's dark, mate. Even for you," I whispered back.

He shrugged. "They deserved what they got."

"Have I intruded on gossip hour?" Titus snapped. "Or can we handle the business at hand?"

I cleared my throat. "Apologies, Uncle. To answer your question, Piper has been sent to the medical lab."

"Has she?" He took another sip. "Why?"

"A minor hiccup during her training." I didn't know why I didn't just come out and say it but telling him she couldn't control her thirst felt like signing her death warrant. I didn't let her die in the street, and I wouldn't be the one to let her die now.

"After all these years, you think me a fool, is that it? Like I don't know your every coming and going?" Titus looked from me to Atlas and back again. "Atlas, report."

Atlas looked to me, and I knew in that moment it was either I tell Titus or he would. He was my best friend, but his loyalty to The House of Shade overruled any personal feelings he might have.

A groan escaped my throat. "Enough. She's had trouble with her blood intake."

"What?" Titus' brows furrowed.

"Whatever she drinks doesn't stay down. Essentially, she's only okay if she drinks . . ." I ground my teeth together, "... from me. And I haven't figured out how to help her yet."

My mother pressed her hand over her mouth. "How is that possible?"

"I'm not quite sure. But she's in the lab, and I won't let her leave until it's sorted. I swear to it, Uncle." I crossed my arms over my chest. "I will do whatever needs to be done to save her."

"And that's the concern, isn't it?" He walked back to his throne and sat down with that glass in his hand. He held it for a moment, swirling the blood around and watching it run down the sides. "You'll do anything to get it sorted... anything."

Atlas stepped forward. "Your Majesty, if I may—"

"—You may not." He swirled the glass and watched the blood move once more. "So, tell me, what am I to do with you? With her? With The Fallen? The kingdom is in jeopardy and on the brink of major change—change — might I remind you, that you have been instrumental in. To throw it all away on *her*? We do not sacrifice the many to save the one."

My mother sighed. "Why is it that men never see the solution right in front of them? And they call the fairer sex dramatic."

Titus snickered. "You have something to say, Moira?"

"Indeed. I do. Allow Grayson some leeway. You have deep ties with The Fallen and many favors to be had from them. Surely they can spare a few days to help a girl who is clearly very ill."

"Mother, thank y—"

"—And you, my darling, pull your head out of your arse and remember who you are. You have a duty to her, but you also have a duty to your people. To be king, you must learn to balance these things, and one day," she looked at Titus, "hopefully long from now, you will rule this kingdom. Steal yourself, my son."

Atlas pressed his lips together, fighting back a chuckle. "Moira called you an arse."

"Piss off." I turned to my mother and Titus. "I will do this. What say you, Uncle?"

"I will allow it, but my patience is running thin."

"Thank you." Before he could change his mind, I turned and headed out the door. Atlas was at my side, and we moved with our vampire speed from the room. There were only so many times Titus was going to show mercy, and I didn't want to give him the chance to take it back. We rushed toward the lab, but I couldn't wait until we got there. "What's happened?"

"It's not good."

My head was spinning from this day. Something had to give. Something had to work out at some point. For all the years I spent messing about, I was paying for it now. "How bad?"

"They don't know what's wrong with her . . . but it looks like she's slowly starving to death."

CHAPTER NINE

PIPER

The world came through in a hazy mess. I blinked, trying to clear the cloudiness in my eyes and groggy thoughts in my head. The side of my neck throbbed, and when I reached up to touch it, my arms were locked into place, stopping my movement. I squinted against the harsh overhead light and the stinging smell of bleach. The bed beneath me was soft and clean, with crisp white sheets that I could only associate with a hospital bed. I jerked my arms again, yet they were held down. The metal bed frame groaned as I tugged harder.

Ugh. Here again? I didn't like making a habit of waking up in hospital rooms. Yet my surroundings were all too familiar. The walls were a thick, rough rock, like the room had been carved from the side of a mountain. Stainless steel counters and equipment lined the room like a super modern hospital.

"I wouldn't do that if I were you." Doctor Stanbourn sat on a rolling chair with a mobile desk in front of him.

The laptop was open, and he leaned over it, staring at the screen. He straightened his glasses and rested his chin on his hand. He was an older-looking vampire, appearing to be in his late fifties rather than having that eternally youthful look. Grayson told me his sire made him when he'd been in his fifties in his human life. The change made him strong and fit, but he still held some maturity in his face and grey streaks in his dark hair. The wrinkles around his eyes were nearly smoothed out from the change. In that moment, I remembered I would forever be this age. I would never grow older or have grey hair. The wrinkles would never appear around my eyes. For some reason, it made me slightly sad.

He motioned to the thick metal cuffs around my arms and legs. "They're magnetic and now magically enforced so they can't be broken."

"Is this really necessary?" The heavy cuffs were cool on my skin and tight on my wrists and ankles.

Doctor Stanbourn turned toward me and pushed his glasses farther up his nose. He leaned away from the laptop and looked me up and down. "Until we understand what's going on with you, it is."

"What's up, doc?" A girl with long inky hair walked into the room.

Those pin straight locks were braided into a faux hawk down the center of her head. Her deep onyx eyes were surrounded by dark, heavy liner, making them look huge and all-knowing. She didn't stop walking when she got into the room, just simply hopped up on the foot of my bed and took a seat there between my ankles. She wore a black leather jacket, a burgundy turtleneck, and ripped black jeans. She swung her legs back and forth.

He gave a heavy sigh and took his glasses off. "Ophelia, I don't think the King will approve of you coming and going as you please."

She scoffed. "I do what I want."

"Indeed." He scrubbed his hand over his face. "Indeed, you do."

Vague memories of her danced in the back of my mind. I'd seen her before when I was in this very same position. She let her legs swing back and forth. "So, my spells are working, right?"

"Yes, it appears so." He motioned to my hands and legs.

"Did she kill someone this time?" She glanced at me over her shoulder.

I froze. *Did I?*

Grayson warned me so many times to control my thirst so I wouldn't hurt anyone. But lying here, I couldn't remember if I had or not. I remembered arguing with Grayson and leaving the training room, then . . . I thought I bit him . . . maybe. *Did I kill Grayson?* Oh shit. If I killed the cocky son of a bitch, I'd never forgive myself. So long as I lived, I'd never forgive myself.

"Not as far as I know." He turned back to his

computer and perched his glasses back on the tip of his nose.

A breath I didn't know I'd been holding escaped my lips, and I sagged back into the pillow. The relief I felt at not hurting him was both sweet and telling. *I shouldn't care about him or what he thinks or feels.* My annoyance with myself doubled.

"So why lock her up? She didn't kill anyone. She's harmless." Ophelia drew me from my thoughts. "If I were you, I'd let her go."

"She's one of the strongest vampires I've ever met. She's hardly harmless."

"How about you stop talking about me like I'm not here." I pulled my arms up and the metal groaned once more in reply before I let them drop to my sides.

Ophelia hopped off my bed and walked up closer to my face. She leaned her elbow on the rail next to my bed and met my eye. "You're not going to kill anyone, are you?"

"NO!"

"Pity." She shrugged and turned away. "Maybe if we sharpen your fangy fangs more, you could be totally inspired. Call me when you have something interesting we can do."

"But I don't want to kill anyone..."

She patted my head. "We're all killers . . . You just haven't met the right person yet."

"O, step away from the newly made vampire." Grayson sauntered into the room, looking cocky and delicious as ever. His hair was tousled in that carelessly perfect way.

Bastard. I needed a breath from him. To know him was to love him and to love him was to be eternally pining for him. "Must you be everywhere I am?"

"Until the end of time." He shoved the sleeves of his shirt up to his elbows, revealing two fading puncture marks. So, I *had* bit him. If I could throw my arm over my face, I would have.

Ophelia looked from his arm to me and back again. "Interesting. You may call me. I will put you on the list of potential best friends. Now, I will warn you the competition is steep, but you have mouth daggers and that puts you ahead."

"O, love—"

"—Mouth daggers." She lowered her voice and leaned toward him, cupping her mouth like she was going to tell him a secret. "I love daggers."

Before Grayson could say another word, she turned away from him and walked out of the room and back into the lab. Doctor Stanbourn gave a heavy sigh. "I shudder to think what she's playing with . . . or whom."

"Yes, I've heard she's taken to visiting that troubled female vampire we have quarantined off. The one addicted to her own blood." Grayson glanced toward the door she walked out of. "At least the lab techs are getting used to her."

"That's not concerning at all." He shook his head. "We

could mystically enforce the castle, but that'd be like waving a *try me* sign in front of her."

"Yes, she'd only get in another way . . . I fear it'd be more destructive than just letting her roam free."

Grayson walked over to the counter and lifted a remote. He wagged it at me. "Shall we free her? You're not going to claw at anyone or bite anyone, are you?"

I hissed in his direction. "Cocky much?"

"I'll take that as a *yes*." He pressed a button and the cuffs released from my wrists and ankles.

I sat up and sighed as I rubbed my wrist. "Why are we back here?"

"Because we have very little time to figure out what's wrong with you. You need to be healthy, and you need to feed properly to ensure your survival . . . and ours."

"Yours?"

He waved my words away. "Never you mind that. For now, let us figure this puzzle out together."

Together. It felt like such a lie when he said it like that, since he was the one who decided on us not being together. "Whatever. Let's get it done."

"I'll need to draw some blood." The doctor rose to his feet and retrieved whatever he needed from a drawer on the other side of the room.

Grayson crossed his arms over his chest and leaned back against the counter. He didn't take his eyes off me. "Worried about me?"

"No," I lied. I was hurt, disappointed, and all the other

complicated emotions that came with a breakup I didn't want or see coming.

He chuckled. "Liar."

"Ass."

The doctor approached me slowly. "It'll just take a moment."

I held my arm out to him. "Do what you gotta do, doc."

The needle prick came smooth and quick in my arm, and I looked away from him. I knew I was a vampire and all, but I'd always hated having my blood drawn. With my new and improved vampy powers, I could hear the blood filling the tube, smell it in the air, and practically feel it leaving my body. Still, I didn't look. Grayson kept staring at me in that unnerving way he had about him.

"What are you looking at?"

"Can I not watch you?"

"No."

He didn't look away from me, so I just pretended not to care, but in truth, I cared way too much. I felt his eyes linger on my skin almost like a touch. I couldn't understand why he'd cast us aside when he so clearly enjoyed our banter, and the flirtation between us. It was frustrating as hell, everything was: his secrets, his flirting, his need for me and the way he pushed me away. It was one big ball of messy emotions.

The doctor pulled the needle from my arm. Then he placed some of my blood on one of those little glass plates and moved over to a microscope on the counter. "It's fascinating. I'm sorry I didn't see it before."

"Yes, she fascinates me eternally," Grayson agreed.

I growled in his direction, and all the muscles in my body tensed. I was gonna hit him one day. Not today . . . but one day. I swore I would do it. The doctor tensed like he was getting ready to run from my little show of aggression toward Grayson. *Oh, if only he knew . . .*

Grayson gave the doctor a warm smile. "She'll be fine with you if *I'm* around for her to bite into."

I rolled my eyes. It'd be easier for me to have short visits with Grayson. Like if he wasn't everywhere I turned. It might've been easier for me to be around him on occasion. But he was everywhere all the time. "Talk about ego."

"Not at all. I just like being around you."

"If you'll both excuse me, I need to run to the lab with this for a moment." The doctor rushed from the room. Not that I could blame him. I wouldn't want to sit next to an aggressive vampire arguing with her ex either.

I sighed. "Well, get used to not being around me. We broke up, remember? Or are you into mixed messages? Because I can guarantee I'm not. So, you say it's over, and I agree."

Grayson groaned and scrubbed his hands down his face. "Then, perhaps a friendship?"

Friends . . . riiiggghttt. "You wanna be friends? With me? Just friends?"

"Yes of course I do."

Ouch.

"Friends give each other space." I didn't know why but —just friends— felt like a slap.

His eyes grew darker. "You know I can't do that."

"Why?"

"Because I can't be away from you." He shrugged. He'd said it so simply, like that's the way it was.

Today was gonna be the day I hit him . . . *had* to be the day. Anger threaded through my body, and it took all my self-control to not just take a little swing. "You make no sense. We're broken up, but you say you can't be away from me. But now we're also *just friends.*"

He shrugged, "I never said I was perfect."

Infuriating man. "I didn't realize doing the things you said you were going to do was asking for perfection. Just go. Okay? I don't need your help. Whatever is wrong with me, I will fix myself."

"We can at least talk about it." Why did he always come off as so calm and so smooth, like nothing could fluster him? All I ever felt around him was flustered. It was frustrating beyond words. I wanted so badly not to want him. I wanted to be as calm as he was . . . or at least be indifferent.

"Actually, I would love to talk about it. Are you ready to tell me why you seem to still like me, but claim to have duties that take you away from me, while at the same time manage to be next to me all the time?"

He pressed his lips together in a hard line.

"Excuses, excuses. I can't turn to you to help me fix it.

I can't lean on you. I have to learn not to do that. So, I will fix it myself like I always do." I shook my head. It was true. When it came to people, I was the one to pick up the pieces of myself. Well, and Dice.

The doctor cleared his throat as he came back into the room, "Actually, you can't."

I hopped off the bed and just wanted to leave. "Clearly you don't know me very well."

Grayson nodded. "You don't know her very well."

The doctor turned to both of us and pulled his glasses off his face. He held a clipboard in his hand and flipped the papers back and forth like he was re-reading his findings. "No, I mean you can't. When I test your cells with any of the blood from our blood banks, they begin to deteriorate. With a normal made vampire the cells fill, replenish . . . replicate. It's why even in death we all look so young and, for lack of a better word, healthy."

Nervousness filled my body. "What does that mean?"

He gave a heavy sigh and rubbed at his face once more. "Essentially, when you try to feed and the blood isn't compatible with your system, you continue to slowly die. And the first step to dying is going feral. Your vampire-needs take over, and you will hunt for survival. The problem is, whatever it is you're going to hunt or drink won't save you."

"I don't understand what the difference is between the bagged blood and Grayson's blood. Like, why is his so much better?"

The doctor sighed. "The bagged blood is from our

human donors. Vampires can live off of both human blood and vampire blood, but in your case, you can't."

Of course, leave it to me to be the fucked up fanger. "But why?"

"Well human blood is sustainable for us, but it's almost like being a human vegetarian. It's healthy, it sustains, it keeps us living eternally, but in some cases, it's not as strong or rich as blood from other vampires. Our blood is stronger, more potent, and higher in proteins." Grayson straightened his stance. His face fell and his eyes burned into the doctor's. "No, fix this. You hear me? You fix this. We will all bloody well stay here until you figure it out. No matter what the cost is."

"It's not about cost. It's about what she needs."

"So? Can't I use another vampire donor?"

A low growl rumbled in his chest. I shoved his shoulder. "Keep it together. It's not about you. Doc, please, there has to be another way?"

"My dear, you're one of the strongest made vampires I've ever seen. With that, you need something strong enough to fuel your power. In this case, you need one of the most powerful vampires to feed you . . ."

Grayson sighed. "And there's no other way to fix this?"

The doctor shook his head. "Actually, *you* are the fix."

Is this hell? Because it feels like it.

CHAPTER TEN

PIPER

No, this couldn't be the way. I ran down the hall toward my room. I had no place to go to have a moment of privacy. *How could this happen?* My luck had always been shit, but this was just badddd, bad luck, plain and simple. I'd never felt so trapped in my life. I'd gone from one insane moment to another ever since I met Grayson. Now I was tied to him like a ball and chain in the *till death do us part* kind of way—except I was already dead and now . . . now it seemed like we could never part. Even though it seemed that's what he wanted half the time.

My breath caught in my throat and my chest felt tight. I was trapped and bound to the one person I needed some serious space from. Courtiers all turned to watch me run down the hall, but I was a blur to my own vision. Tears pricked at my eyes, but I refused to let them fall. Crying could get me nowhere in this situation. It was impossible to move on and heal when I was surrounded by the scent of him, the taste of him, and the sight of him. I had nothing to my name. Everything that was supposed to be mine was *his*.

I hurried through the door and tried to slam it behind me. But he was there, right behind me, catching it before it slammed shut. My room was back to being completely immaculate. There wasn't any broken furniture, not one shattered piece of glass. All the clothing had either been hung up or replaced completely. I spun in a circle, sucking in deep, heaving breaths. Grayson stood there, silently watching me lose my shit.

"Why are you everywhere?" I ran my hands through my hair, tugging at the roots. I needed time. I needed space. I needed to be away from him.

"I live here."

"I can't believe this. You think you stopped me from actually dying, but instead all you did was slow down the process so I'm dying slower. You're going to have to put me down like a rabid animal."

Grayson walked farther into the room and sat on the foot of my bed. He rested one foot on the frame and put his elbow on his knee. "Now that, my dear, would be the greatest travesty of all."

I threw my hands up and turned away from him. It felt better to pace than to just stand there and talk to him. "Somehow I used to find you so charming, and now . . ."

"And now?" He held so still, like a statue.

"I've never wanted to be farther away from someone, and there is no escape." I had to get out of this. Was being locked in with an unrequited love really living? Was the hurt worth a life I didn't choose and hadn't even asked for? I wanted to live and explore the world, but to be attached forever to someone who didn't want the same felt like eternal punishment.

He sighed. "You really know how to hit a guy right in the bollocks."

"I mean it. How? How is this possible? I can only feed from *you*? Your blood is the only one compatible with mine. How is that fair? How can we live like this for eternity? And why would YOU want to be a blood bag for the rest of your life for ME?" I shook my head. "This . . . this is awful."

"I've faced worse odds." He shrugged.

I paused and sucked in a breath. He was calm . . . too calm. Like this wasn't a big deal to him. Was he . . . enjoying this? "Are you . . . are you *happy*?"

I narrowed my eyes at him. My hands shook at my sides. Here I was freaking out and feeling the walls trapping me in with someone who wanted to be *just friends*, and he was chilling like a happy little clam. I was drowning, and he was rolling in his fairytale life. How could he not see how far down I was sinking here?

"Happy is relative, Piper." He rose to his feet and took a step toward me. "I'm not happy. You drive me to madness daily. I can't control my mouth with you, my desire to have you pains me, yet there you are taunting my existence. Happy? No. I'm not bloody well happy. But I have a duty to my kingdom, and I will uphold it."

"At the expense of me? Is that it? You have a responsibility to all these other people but not to me? The one you got involved with. The one you made the most promises to. And now we are stuck like this for eternity."

"Could be worse things than being stuck with me, Sassy Creature." He shrugged and took another step closer, making me put my back to the wall. He lowered his voice. "I quite enjoy your little fangs in my skin."

His words sent shivers down my spine. The effect he had on me was worse than any I could imagine. How was it possible to both love and loathe someone at the same time? To both want to bang his brains out *and* throw him through the window? He had responsibilities to his kingdom, which made me low man on the list of importance. How could he seem so into me and yet cast me aside so easily? There was only one simple answer. I was important enough for him to toy with and be around all day long, but in the grand scheme of things, I was his entertainment, and the truly important things were his priority . . . not me. I never was. I'd always been an adventure for him and nothing more. Or perhaps a welcome distraction. Either way, I knew where I stood—as little more than a pretty pet locked in the cage he'd created.

"Do you know how much of an ass you are?"

He leaned down and his breath fanned across my ear. "You say the most loving things."

"How's this for love? Fu—"

He pressed his finger over my lips and the taste of his skin called to me. "How about we save the hate for later?"

I shoved him back. Hard. He flew across the room and gracefully landed just beside my bed. He wagged his finger at me. "Naughty."

I flipped him off. "It's time for you to leave."

"Aren't you hungry?" He brought his wrist to his mouth and let his fangs extend. He took a quick, sharp bite, and his deep red wine scent filled the room. My stomach tightened at the delicious scent of him. Yet the knowledge that I was just his entertainment hit me hard. His words said I was important, but his actions . . . they spoke for themselves.

I turned my nose up at him. "Give me death."

"While I do love dramatics, now is not the time for them." He dropped his wrist to his side. "This isn't a joke."

I might be better off. "Who said I was joking?"

"You won't feel that way when you kill someone over your stubbornness just to simply feed." He pulled his sleeve into place and shoved his hand into his pocket and pulled out a shiny brand-new iPhone. "This is for you."

"Gifts? Really?"

"It's so you can call me when you're ready to feed. We won't have you running amok about the castle." He handed it over to me. "My number is already programmed in there, along with Martin, the vampire concierge you met before, and Atlas, but only if you're in trouble."

The second he put that phone in my hand, I could only think of one person I wanted to call, and it wasn't Atlas or Martin. It certainly wasn't Grayson.

Dice . . .

"We monitor all the calls for newly made vampires. You cannot reach out to your old life. You'll only be putting her in danger."

I stared down at the phone. I wanted so desperately to hear her voice. He cleared his throat, calling my attention up to meet his eyes. "I know things aren't ideal right now, but it will get sorted. In the meantime, you cannot call her. Understand?"

Why did he have to be able to read me so well? I wanted to say no. But this life . . . this mess was not for the humans. How would I even react to her human blood? What if I got hungry around her? I wasn't safe to be around, and no matter how badly I needed her, the last thing I wanted was to hurt her. But once I learned control, I would go to her, and we'd figure it out bestie-style. I may not be able to rely on Grayson, but Dice was my ride or die bestie. She'd accept me dead or alive. I didn't even question it.

"Piper! Do you understand me?"

I nodded and slid the phone into the little pocket on the side of my leggings. "Understood."

"Now, about your feeding—"

"I'll feed when I'm good and ready. You've given me

very little choice since I died, even in my own death. I am not a toddler. You cannot force feed me." I walked over to the door and held it open. "So, I guess *I'll* call *you* when *I'm* ready."

Grayson's face fell and turned deadly serious. "Very well, but remember, blood on your hands is not something you want to live eternity with."

"Funny. I'm starting to feel the same way about you." I waved him toward the door.

Grayson smiled. "You're only fueling my fire."

"Yeah, well, keep it to yourself because your fiery charms have no effect on me."

... *So what if I lied?*

CHAPTER ELEVEN

PIPER

There was nothing worse than lying in bed and staring at the ceiling. I'd tossed and turned for hours. The day had been long and so much had happened that I still wasn't sure how to face. My mind raced with possible solutions and outcomes to all the situations around me. The only thing I figured out was my life was falling apart, and I had no idea how to fix it. I tossed onto my other side and punched the pillow. Feathers exploded out from behind my head and flew all over the room.

"Greattttt." I sighed and flopped onto my other side, which only managed to knot the blankets around my legs. It was both too hot and too cold in this room. Nothing would quiet my mind or make me feel comfortable.

I'd made the room pitch-black, and yet I saw everything perfectly, as though it were midday. I picked my phone up from the bedside table and checked the time.

Four in the morning should feel like a sleep coma, and yet I was wide awake, trying to forget my problems and feelings. But most of all, I wanted to ignore the hunger pangs in my stomach. I knew I couldn't ignore it. I didn't want to. It was just a pain in the ass to go to Grayson. But I refused to hurt anyone else. I would suck it up and keep moving forward as best as I could until another path opened to me. Something had to happen, something had to give. But for right now, I would go to him . . . even if I hated it.

I threw my blanket off and kicked the sheets away with all the frustration I could muster. A growl escaped my lips, and I straightened out my sweatpants and pulled my twisted cami back into place. I didn't bother putting on shoes or a robe. Instead, I walked out of my bedroom barefoot and headed down the hall. At this hour of the morning, I didn't expect to see any courtiers lingering in the hallways, but I was wrong. There they were in their well-pressed suits and long traditional dresses.

Their eyes lingered on me as I walked past. I looked bed-rumpled and not traditional at all. I didn't have a corset or flowing dress. My hair was wild around my shoulders and down my back. But I didn't care. If I didn't sate my hunger soon, they all would be on my very vampy menu. A woman with long blonde hair pinned into ringlets on top of her head narrowed her eyes and stuck her nose up at me. She fanned herself with one of those feather-looking things and looked me up and down like I was the smelly thing under her shoe. This was like working in a bar, and I knew the mean girls got unnerved when you showed no fear, so I stopped in the hall and stared back at her.

When it got uncomfortable, she stopped fanning herself and turned to me. "What are you looking at?"

She dragged out the word *are* so it sounded like *aaaarreee* in her very posh, very snobby accent. I took a step toward her, and she flinched back. A chuckle escaped my lips, and I hissed in her direction. She trembled as she stood facing me, but a man grabbed her elbow and dragged her back. "Have some sense."

"Yes, have some sense." I gave her a little wave and carried on my way. No one would make me feel like I was any less than they were. We all had fangs and bit the same way . . .

When I turned the corner and stopped just outside Grayson's door, about to knock, I heard voices coming from within. I froze and moved to the side, just listening through the door. It was amazing what heightened vampire senses could accomplish.

"It's not that bloody difficult to find a human girl. We've been over this." Grayson sounded genuinely annoyed.

"You know I've considered this intensely and I agree with Piper." Atlas' deep, calm voice sounded like it came from closer to the door, like he was standing just inside the room.

"Agree with her on what?"

"You are indeed an arse."

I pressed my hand to my mouth, holding in my laughter. At least I wasn't the only one who gave him shit on a regular basis.

"Piss off. I've got enough on my plate without the lot of you joining up together." The sound of him dialing numbers on a cell phone echoed around the room. "And the lot of you are bloody useless."

With my vamp hearing, I could hear the phone ring twice, then a rumbling male voice picked up. "Prince."

Grayson gave a humorless chuckle. "If we're to go by titles, Dark Prince Kylian."

The voice on the other end of the line chuckled. I could hear him clearly but faintly. "Fair point. What can I do for you?"

"Have you found the girl yet?" Grayson's voice didn't hold the usual calm I'd gotten so used to. He almost sounded concerned or nervous. It was a side of him I hadn't encountered before.

"No. I've searched the area, but the magic is thick there."

"It's Salem. Did you not expect it to be?" Atlas called across the room.

My breath froze in my chest. I pressed myself against the wall, not daring to move or breathe. SALEM? There was only one other girl they could be looking for. Only one other person who would've drawn their attention. But why would they go after her? Why would they hunt her? And why couldn't any of these great trackers find her?

"This woman, Dice, no matter where I go that she usually frequents, there's a thick magic around her." He cleared his throat. "We've tracked her cell, and it says she's at work or home, but each time I go there . . . no Dice."

"Is that supposed to be funny?" Grayson snapped. "I am paying you a hefty sum to produce what I want. I don't appreciate delays."

"If you think you could do better, then by all means, come and try to walk around magic this potent, leech."

Leech? Did people really call vampires leeches?

"Mind your tongue," Atlas warned, "or I'll cut it out."

Kylian chuckled. "You can try."

"Challenge accepted," Atlas growled.

"Shut it, both of you. Neither of you has been able to do what I've asked and produce me one small blonde human. She's outwitted the lot of you somehow, making fools of you both." He slammed his fist into something hard. "Find her now."

"I will update you as soon as I do." Kylian yawned. "Stop checking in on me. You're not my mother."

"Yeah, no one is as evil as that one," Atlas hissed under his breath.

"Should I take a page out of your book then?" Kylian snapped back.

Atlas scoffed. "You know nothing."

"I know enough."

Grayson growled at the two of them. "Enough faffing about. Do the bloody job I'm paying you to do."

He ended the call and sucked in a deep breath. I'd never heard him so exasperated, but I felt my own annoyance rise. Why was he looking for Dice? Was she in danger from the vampires? Did she know too much and he'd sent Atlas after her? I wanted to trust him, but I knew I couldn't. Our history made sure of that. He wanted me to stay away from Dice, and I knew I couldn't now. I would have, but now I had to get to her before any of them did.

... *or do I?*

The door flew open, and I startled. Atlas and I stood face-to-face. He let it fall shut behind him as his uncanny eyes bore into mine. "How long have you been standing there?"

"I just got here." I wasn't necessarily proud of my ability to lie on the spot, but it came in handy.

"I think it best to keep as much distance between you two as possible. So long as you have enough blood, I see no reason for you to share company."

"I couldn't agree more."

He tilted his head to the side. "Are you in earnest?"

What was it with the men around me that they just wanted to be annoying at every turn? "Trust me, I'd love to."

"Good, keep that in mind." He crossed his arms over his chest.

I mirrored his pose. "I like to think my anger is a superpower against any and all things."

A smile tugged at his lips. "Then play on, Scarlet Witch."

The door flew open, and Grayson stood there looking none too pleased. He nodded to Atlas. "Sav, best be on your way. You have important matters to attend to."

Atlas didn't say another word. He just turned and walked away, leaving the two of us standing outside the door. When he turned to me, he didn't give me that easy cocky smile. This early in the morning, he looked tense... And he should be. I didn't know why he was going after my bestie, but there was no way I was going to let him get near her. I had limited resources, but what I did have was a lifetime of experience at survival. Not to mention a bestie who knew me well enough to understand any hidden message I could get to her. We were born survivors. It was always the two of us against the world. I'd be damned if I let anything happen to her now. I just had to get out of this castle and get to her, and there was only one person I knew of who could do both of those. I made my face impassive as the plan formed in my mind.

Grayson leaned against the doorjamb and forced a half-smile to his lips. "Sleepless night?"

I bit my bottom lip, letting my fang pop out ever so slightly. "I hate to admit it, but... I'm hungry."

He backed up a step and crooked his finger at me, inviting me into his room. I strolled by him and stopped just before the huge bed. It was hard to believe we'd been tangled up in each other not that long ago. Somehow, we'd now gone from lovers to enemies. Deep down it hurt, but the pain fueled my inner fire to survive and thrive. Grayson closed the door behind us and strolled to stand in front of me. He rolled his sleeve up and held his wrist out to me.

"Take what you need."

I leaned in closer to him, playing as innocent as I could. For what I had planned, I needed this to be quick and semi-painless. "I'm starving. Is this the best way?"

He unbuttoned the top three buttons of his shirt. "If it's a feast you want, then the neck is best."

I laid my hands on his chest and went up on my tiptoes. "Are you sure this is okay?"

"I'm here only for you, Piper."

Yeah, I bet you are. I let my fangs extend and I struck hard and quick, piercing and letting my lips brush over his skin. His warm tangy blood filled my mouth, and when I swallowed, that delicious first drop of energy burst through my body. It was like being on a sugar and caffeine high all at the same time. He tasted like rich red wine and chocolate.

I swallowed him down and took another pull. His hand wound around my back, and he pulled my body closer to his. I could feel his excited reaction to me, and my body warmed to the idea of us. This wasn't just the taking of blood. It was hot and dirty . . . like forbidden fruit. I let my body lay into his, pressing every inch of myself against him. There would always be fire between us, a fire that I felt low in my stomach and made goosebumps run over my skin whenever I thought about the two of us together. I knew it would be all heat and passion—the kind that was deeply addictive and would be hard to say no to. I didn't want to be dicknotized, but with his sinful body, it was difficult not to be.

But I had to stay focused on my little mission. This was Dice, and he'd crossed a line. The breakup I could take. No one should stay in a relationship they didn't want. But to go after my bestie, my sister from another mister . . . No, just no. I sucked his neck even harder, taking his blood into me and letting it run through my body, giving me strength.

A groan escaped his lips, and his voice rumbled in my ear. "There now. Not so bad, is it?"

He stumbled forward, and I held him there. I pulled my fangs from his neck and licked my lips. "Are you all right?"

"Never better." He wavered on his feet.

"You are delicious."

He blinked. "Are you sated, Little Creature?"

I blinked up at him with my best sheepish look. "Still a bit nibbly."

He leaned his neck back, giving me more space. "Then by all means."

I turned my head to the other side of his neck and struck hard. A moan seeped from his lips as I let his warm blood fill my mouth. He tasted like sin and felt like hell. I didn't know if Grayson was the best or worst of his kind, but he was the most alluring. I drank him down until my stomach felt sloshy and my body felt like it was buzzing with strength. When he finally passed out and sagged into me, I caught him and lowered him to the floor. I swiped my hand across my mouth and stared down at him. There was no doubt about it, Grayson Shade was fine as fuck. This was the most twisted relationship I'd ever been in, which made it more like a situationship.

I searched his pockets and pulled out his phone. I turned his head and held his phone over his face for ID and it opened. I flipped through the call log and groaned. Zinnia, Astrid, Tabi, Nova, Serrina . . . *My, my, he has a long list of ladies at his disposal.* Even if we weren't together, jealousy wasn't my prettiest side, but my green monster was always lurking under the surface.

"Quite the list you have here." I didn't believe in kicking a man while he was down, but I considered it . . . only for a second. But I didn't have time to waste on my feelings. The bestie needed me, and I wouldn't fail her. Without further hesitation, I went to the app center and downloaded a social media app—one I knew Dice would have. A few questions answered, a selfie, and I had an account ready to use.

I made my name POL: Proof of Life. It was the one thing we always said to each other when we went out. Send proof of life, no matter where we were, to let the other know we were okay. I knew her well enough to know that if I sent her this one message with a selfie and an address, she would understand. Most besties spoke their own language and we were no different.

Meet me at the place with the best curly fries.

She would know, and I knew there was only one place with the best curly fries around. I sent the message, then deleted the account. I glanced down at Grayson. He was still out cold. *Maybe I took too much?* His chest still rose and fell with even breaths, so I wasn't too concerned. It would just take him a moment to come to. If a moment was all I had, then I needed to get the next part handled like a boss bitch.

I scrolled through the names on the phone and found the one I was looking for. If he didn't answer, then this whole plan would go to shit. I only hoped Grayson's name would force him to answer. Three rings later and the phone clicked over.

"I'm not cool with impatience."

I cleared my throat. "Hello?"

"This isn't the leech."

"No." Well, not the one he expected.

"The lack of accent and female tone intrigues me." I heard the bedsheets rustle around him.

"I have a proposition for you." I tried to sound as calm as I could.

"Seeing how you got the leech's phone and got to me, consider my interest piqued." His voice was thick with sleep.

"The girl you're looking for, Dice, I can tell you where she'll be." I held my breath.

"What's in it for you?"

"Get her, unharmed and I'll make it worth your

while." I didn't have money, but I had a mountain of jewels and gifts in my room that would fetch a pretty price.

"Define *worth my while?*"

"I'll pay you twice the amount he will . . . in jewels. Plus, you get to piss him off, which I feel would be fun for you."

He chuckled. "I like the way you play. So, what do I do once I've got this Dice girl? Grayson had a plan. Do you have a plan?"

Shit. I didn't think it'd go this far . . . but I did need a better plan. "Just call me once you get to her. I'm guessing if I give you my number, it won't be restricted for you."

Kylian sighed. "Nothing is restricted for me."

What was it with the men in this world. They just oozed confidence, and they all had the swagger to back it up. "Are you always this confident . . . this cocky?"

"Not cocky when it's the truth."

I rattled off my number and was practically bouncing to get this done. Grayson would wake soon, and I had to be as innocent to him as I was when this all started. "Do we have a deal or not?"

Kylian gave me a deep chuckle. "Deal. I kind of like you, Piper."

I sucked in a sharp breath. "How'd you know my name?"

"You'll learn that I know lots of things."

CHAPTER TWELVE

PIPER

I squatted down next to Grayson, just watching him while he slept. Or should I say, recover from me knocking him out? There wasn't a physical thing I could pick apart about Grayson. His face was perfection, his lips were meant for mine, and when he looked at me with those mahogany eyes, he could melt me from the inside out. If I was being honest, what bothered me the most was that I'd fallen for Grayson Shade hook, line, and sinker. He had me, all of me, wrapped around his little finger.

What gave me the audacity to believe in happily ever after for myself? I wasn't the kind of girl that happened to. Yet I reached for it, wanted it, and pictured it in my mind. Sitting next to him now hadn't cooled my feelings toward him. Not to mention this weird thing he had going on with Dice. I wanted to trust Grayson, but in my heart of hearts, I felt I couldn't. It made it easier to try and just let these feelings go, or as I liked to do, bury them down deep until they died an irreversible death.

Once he was awake, I would leave. It was taking too long though, and my patience for this was on empty. My hand snapped out and I smacked his cheek. "Wakey wakey."

His eyes fluttered open, and he blinked hard. A slow smile spread across his lips. "Am I that delicious then?"

I rolled my eyes and shoved his shoulder. "If you can't take the heat, get out of the kitchen."

Grayson rolled onto his side and rested his head on his hand. "I'd love to be in your kitchen all the time."

I groaned and popped to my feet. I dusted off my hands and straightened my outfit. "You can't just do that?"

Grayson hopped up like he'd never been knocked out. "Do what?"

I crossed my arms over my chest. "You can't just break my heart and then flirt with me afterwards like nothing ever happened. I hope it was worth the sport for you."

Grayson ran his hands through his hair. "You were never just sport for me."

"Yeah, well, you could've fooled me. From now on, let's just figure out a way to live with this until it can be fixed and I can get gone."

Grayson's face fell. "How long can you hate me?"

My lips pulled up in an evil grin. "Until all the stars in the universe turn cold."

CHAPTER THIRTEEN

DICE

*N*ervous bubbles filled my stomach, and my heart hammered in my chest. This was the first real lead I'd gotten since finding Piper in that grave and watching that video. I knew she was alive but also in trouble. Wherever she was, I had to get there too. We were family, and family stuck together. When I'd gotten that weird message early in the morning, my stomach almost evacuated itself. I missed my bestie, but most of all I wondered what the hell happened. I didn't sleep for the rest of the night, just waiting for morning to roll around, and now it was two in the afternoon—the exact time Piper told me to be here.

So here I was at a diner just on the outskirts of Boston. It was a little hole in the wall place that we found on a drunken night spent barhopping. They had the best curly fries from here to Salem. The place was old school with red and white vinyl booths and Formica tables. A long shining counter ran across the back wall, where people could sit on stools and get a milkshake or dessert. The doors to the kitchen had those little portholes to look through. The waitresses all wore light-blue polo shirts and black pants with their little black aprons.

One came up to my table and smiled down at me. "What'll it be, hon?"

She was older, with salt and pepper hair pulled into a high bun on her head. Thick bangs fell over her forehead, covering some of the wrinkles. She was slim and wore heavy makeup on her cheeks and deep-red lipstick. I smiled up at her, knowing she was a permanent fixture in this place. She had restaurant-lifer written all over her.

"I'll take a coke please, extra ice, and an order of curly fries."

"You got it." She scribbled my order on her pad, then motioned to the seat across from me. "You waiting for someone?"

I didn't want to hope, didn't want to believe that Piper would just stroll through after all this time and sit in front of me. Even her picture didn't look like her. She was more sultry, sexy even. Piper had always had that way about her, but now it was more pronounced. Her lips were redder, her eyes a brighter green. Even her arm looked muscular in the photo. Something had happened, I just didn't know what.

"Yeah, well, kind of."

She gave a humorless laugh. "Say no more. But take

my free advice, pretty girl like you should wait for no man."

I smiled up at her. "I couldn't agree more."

She winked. "I'll get right on that. Shouldn't be long."

I ripped at the paper napkin next to me and crumbled it into tiny balls. What if this was all wrong? What if it was a set up? What if someone was messing with me? Human trafficking was a real thing. I bit at my bottom lip and glanced at the door. Each time the little bell went off, my eyes shot there looking for her, like this was a blind date and I was waiting for the guy to show up. Except this was Piper and she was my sister. I didn't need to be nervous, but I was. More so than I'd been in a while.

I never used to carry my dice around with me, not since Piper and I moved in together and I knew they'd be safe at home. But lately I kept them with me in every outfit. I pulled them from my pocket and rolled them in my hand. They always warmed to my touch and brought me comfort, even if they hadn't told me anything about Piper when they usually told me everything about everyone. I took the pair out and squeezed them in my palm. Heat instantly bloomed in my hands, and I squeezed them tighter. Sometimes they grew so hot I thought they'd burn me, but they never did. It was almost like the heat washed away my inner turmoil, kind of like taking a hot shower after a hard day and washing away the stress of it all.

The waitress walked by and dropped my drink in front of me. "Still no sign of him?"

"Not yet." I didn't bother correcting her. She'd see soon enough who I was waiting for. If people didn't think you were in a relationship with your bestie, were you even really besties?

Christmas music piped in over the speakers overhead and everyone was dressed in their winter gear with hats and gloves. The smell of fried food and hot cocoa filled the air. It was one of Piper's favorite holidays. The snow was coming down outside, and I missed bitching about the cold to her. She'd tease me about how I loved the summer. My mind lingered on the Christmases we'd spent together. They weren't much but they were great. We'd spoil each other with presents under the tree and pig out on our favorite junk food—all the while sitting in the dark with only the glitter lights of our Christmas tree lighting the room.

The constant ache I had in my chest from missing her spread throughout my body. Without Piper, I had no one. I refused to believe she died, not when there was video of her walking out of that morgue. She had to be alive. Because if I was going to be honest with myself, I didn't want to live without her. I let the dice roll across the table just to see if they would tell me something beyond what they'd been saying for weeks now. The interior of them glowed a sapphire-blue and were surrounded by metal shapes. Each one held a different meaning for me. And when I looked at them, I just got a feeling. It wasn't like tarot where each card was set up to have a meaning and each flip of the card meant something. There was no book for my dice. I'd been abandoned with them as a baby and just had to figure it out.

But then they stopped rolling across the table. All they told me was that harsh, rapid, and violent change was to come. It was so vague I nearly wanted to throw them across the room. Never had I not gotten so little from them. I scooped them up in my hand again and held them so tight that surely this time they'd burn me. But when they didn't, I let them roll once more. One stopped right in front of me, and the other headed toward the edge of the table. I reached my hand out to catch it when a bigger hand beat me to it.

He caught the dice before it hit the floor and raised it up to his eye level. "Dice, I presume?"

My breath caught in my throat. This man was the most beautiful man I'd ever seen. His eyes were like a light green crystal. They were so vivid they nearly sparkled all on their own. Straight black hair fell in front of his eyes and around his face in damp, inky strands. Snow covered his broad shoulders and sprinkled down the sleeves of his dark leather jacket. They'd yet to melt against his pale skin. This guy had the face of the Devil. It was too chiseled, his lips too full, his cleft chin too bold. Even the black sweater he wore under his coat was too perfect. Just the look of him had all the red flags going off in my head.

Hard no.

I extended my hand out toward him. "Yeah, that's my dice."

He slid down to sit in the booth across from me and turned his body, leaning against the wall and bending one knee. He rested his arm over his knee while he turned the dice over in his other hand, examining all the sides of it.

"Interesting piece you've got here."

There was a huge red sign flashing over his head: *Do not trust! Do not trust! Danger! Danger!* I wiggled my fingers at him. "I'll take it back now."

He turned and faced me, fully meeting my eye. "What do I get in return?"

"To keep your balls right where they are." I snatched it from his fingers and shoved the dice back into my pocket. They were mine, and I didn't like people touching them, especially sexy as fuck walking red flags.

"Oh, I fully plan on doing so anyways." The smirk he gave me showed his perfect white teeth. "You can keep your little dice . . . for now."

"And you can keep yours." My Dice-o-meter was at a negative zero, which meant I definitely did not like him. I waved him away. "You can go now."

He snored. "Aren't you an entertaining little human."

"As opposed to what? Being an entertaining little dolphin?" I glared at him. "So, about you leaving."

"Oh, I'm not." He said it so simply. Not a threat, just a calm matter-of-fact thing.

The waitress came by and dropped my fries down in front of me. "There now, he showed up. Aren't you dashing?"

The guy lifted his eyebrows at her. "Am I?"

"You are." She nodded.

"I don't think she agrees with you." He motioned to me.

"I don't." I looked him dead in the eye.

The waitress chuckled. "Anything I can get you, hon?"

"Chocolate milkshake please." He flashed her a smile and her cheeks heated to a bright red.

She scribbled across her pad. "Right away."

"I'm waiting for someone, in case you haven't guessed by my not-so-subtle hints." This guy was ruining everything. I needed to talk to Piper and see her. We had shit to figure out.

He reached across the table and took one of my fries and popped it in his mouth.

"So, you're just gonna eat my food like I'm not talking. Great. Love that for me." I groaned and picked up my drink and fries. I slid from the booth and moved to the booth across from him.

He outright laughed. "Your fries are delicious."

I rolled my eyes. When the bell above the door binged again, I glanced up, waiting for her. He moved into my booth and blocked my view. "I'm Kylian."

"I really don't even care." I froze, a memory prickling at my brain. "Kylian, you say?"

"Yep."

"Do you know Maze and Tilly?"

He groaned. "How do you know them?"

"I don't . . . I mean, I do . . . kind of." I wasn't making any sense at all, but all the warning bells were going off in my head. They'd shown up that night and said his name. I was sure of it.

"Yeah, I know them." He didn't say anything else.

"Any reason they wouldn't want me to know you?"

He popped a fry in his mouth and smiled. "None that I can think of."

This guy was bad news. The kind of guy who was pretty and knew it. The kind of guy I always avoided. I liked them bad, a little dark, and a little twisted, but this was dark, twisted, and bad times ten.

"And you are Dice."

I froze and glanced around. "I didn't tell you that."

"No, you didn't." He took another of my fries.

The waitress walked over and gave him his shake. "You moved, I see."

"What the lady wants the lady gets."

She playfully smacked his arm with her pad. "Charming, isn't he?"

"No." I knew Maze and Tilly didn't want me near this guy, but Piper obviously did.

"She'll come around," she whispered to him, then winked and walked away.

I leaned across the table. "How do you know my name?"

Another fry. "I'm who you're waiting for."

I crossed my arms over my chest and pushed the fries toward him. They were his now. "Unless you've grown a vagina and a pair of tits to die for, you aren't the person I'm waiting for."

"You're funny. Your friend Piper sent me." He pushed the fries between the two of us and motioned to the plate. "Have some."

"So, you're telling me she's alive?" I narrowed my eyes at him. It seemed too good to be true.

He paused. "I'd say so. She's also an interesting one. Your friendship makes sense."

"Thanks?" I didn't want to be excited. I also didn't want to believe him right away. "How do I know you're not lying?"

He pulled his phone from his pocket and dialed a number. He hit the speakerphone and let it ring. She answered after the second ring. "Kylian? Do you have her?"

I'd recognize that voice anywhere. My heart stopped in my chest and tears pricked the back of my eyes. *She is alive! I knew it!* In my gut, I knew my bestie still walked this earth. I reached for the phone, and he snatched it back and took her off speakerphone.

"What do you want me to do with her?" He took a sip of his shake and coughed, nearly spitting it out. "You want me to take her there? You're sure?"

I waved to him for the phone. "Let me talk to her."

He held his hand up. "I can get anywhere."

"No, I need to hear her voice."

He put his hand over the bottom of the phone. "She

said *proof of life soon enough.* Does that make any sense to you?"

I swallowed. "Why the secrets?"

"You'll find out soon." He turned back to the phone. "Screw the price. I'm doing this for fun now."

He hung up and faced me. "Believe me now?"

"I knew she was alive." For the first time in weeks, the heavy weight that pressed down on me was finally lifted. There was an end in sight to the overwhelming sadness that strangled my existence. My heart hammered in my chest, and I felt like I could bounce out of this place and run miles. My bestie was ALIVE. I needed to see her, to get to her. Why all the secrecy? Why not come herself? Why use this guy? Shouldn't he have sent her shady-radar off?

Kylian scoffed. "Sure you did. But the look on you face tells me you're pleasantly surprised."

"Where are we going?" I wanted to burst out of this place and get to her now. I didn't care how or when or where, but it had to be this second.

"I can't tell you." He sat back and met my eye. "You sure you still want to go?"

For Piper, I'd do anything. She was alive. That's all that mattered. We'd figure out the rest later. "Hell yes."

"I knew I'd like you."

"I still don't like you."

CHAPTER FOURTEEN

PIPER

*P*ace. Pace. Pace.
Turn.
Pace. Pace. Pace.

The audacity of me. Who was I? A nobody who just got a bounty hunter to agree to take her best friend to a psycho . . .

What the hell was I thinking?

I was taking my life back in little pieces. I didn't know why, but for some reason deep down, I knew Kylian would take her right to where I wanted. Dice was one of the biggest pieces of my life. I would figure out how to get back. All I had to do now was figure out how to fix my thirst madness and be on my freaking way.

Maybe I'd turn her into a vamp, and we could just chill out living forever together. Who knows?

There were worse things than just hanging out with the bestie for eternity. I could get behind that and be here for it. I could even see making more friends to chill with for a while. *Yeah, yeah. This could work.* I'd rebuilt so many times before. This wasn't anything new. Suddenly, it all didn't look so bad. Forever twenty-two... I had all the time in the world to see the world and experience every adventure. I would problem-solve the hell out of my little blood thingy and then I would gather myself up and make an awesome life. Everything seemed a bit brighter from this perspective. I was super powered, superhuman, or even better... vampire.

Three quick knocks drew my attention right to my door. No one beside Grayson came to my room, and I was about done seeing him.

"Please go away."

A curt throat-clearing and three more quick rasps on the door told me it might not be him. "Ms. Piper, it is Martin."

I pursed my lips. *Possible first friend... Here we go.*

I walked over to the door and yanked it open. "Martin, Hi. Come on in."

Martin was always perfection. He was a bit shorter than Grayson, with bright-blue eyes and slicked-back blond hair that was parted to the side. He was slim and tailored to perfection in a navy three-piece suit, with a pressed white shirt, burgundy tie, and polished brown shoes. He held an iPad in the crook of his arm. His lips curled up in a smile, showing me his perfect white teeth. There wasn't one thing about Martin that wasn't tailored.

"You look lovely, Piper. I'm here on behalf of the King."

"The King?"

"Yes." He glanced around and looked me over. His eyes were sharp and observant. "Did you need something from me first?"

I sighed. "For lack of a better word, I need a friend."

"Oh, say no more. I'm glad you decided to take me up on my offer." He sauntered into the room and hopped on the foot of the bed.

"What about the King?" King Titus had let me stay and insisted on my care. I both feared and respected the shit out of him.

"We have five minutes exactly," he waved me on, "so use your vampire speed and talk superfast. I'm an expert at keeping secrets."

I was willing to bet Martin held all the secrets of the castle in that little tablet of his. But most of all, I needed someone to talk to, and there was no one else, so Martin was it. Sometimes a girl just needed to vent and to let things out. I'd had no one and nothing. Normally, I wouldn't just spill so easily, but loneliness had a funny way of making people do things they normally wouldn't . . . like deciding he was going to be the perfect friend and then emotionally unloading on him two seconds later. But here I was, and he was a set of ears. I sucked in a deep breath and let it all loose, everything that'd happened from the beginning to this very moment. It felt good to tell someone the whole truth about Grayson and me.

As I let it all go, he sat there fully attentive. But the more I spilled, the more his jaw dropped. When I finished, he pressed his hand to his chest and sucked in a deep breath. "Let me get this straight."

I waved him on. "Go ahead."

"So you met and he was all I'm human, but noooooo he's a vampire."

I nodded.

"Then you all spicey tango all over the hot spots, wined and dined and . . ." he looked me up and down, "Sa-tis-fied . . . but nooooo he plays the ghosty ghost game."

"Yup."

"And thennnnn *wham* you get hit by a car and . . . dead." He leaned forward and sucked in a dramatic, gasping breath. "But noooo, he bit you and now you're a vampire . . ."

"I know, right?" I crossed my arms over my chest.

"But wait, there's more. He's all lovey, but then he's all *noooooo we can't be together*. And then after that, *I can't help myself*."

"Annoying, right?" I felt myself getting all riled up again.

"Very. So now you're all *get away from me. I'm not a toy you can take out and play with* . . . Respect." He gave me a nod of approval. "But noooo he's all flirty, and now to top it all off, you can only drink his blood for some fucked up *the universe is messing with you* reason."

"That about sums it up." It was frustrating as hell. "I didn't mean to unload on you like this. I know you serve the King but—"

"—Do I serve the King? Absolutely. But that doesn't mean I can't be a friend or someone to rely on. I've kept the secrets of every vampire who's walked these halls. It makes me good at my job. The way I see it you're not hurting anyone but yourself. If I thought you'd hurt The House of Shade I'd be obligated to say something. But you're not, I think you might be the only one hurting here."

He wasn't wrong I felt completely alone and trapped and he'd been the only one who was actually nice to me and helpful. "I just don't know what to do now. I don't know the world well enough. But you do and I was hoping you'd help me."

He hopped up off the bed. "Well, if that's the case, then step into my office because we have all the solutions any jilted love would need."

"What do you mean?"

He pulled his tablet out. "Look, I'm not without my talents. Like I told you before, whatever you need, I can get . . . including a place to stay outside the castle."

My heart leapt in my chest. But I was deflated as quickly as I was excited. "But what about the whole needing to drink from only him thing?"

"I think a little distance will do him some good, don't

you? And it would be educational for his highness to enter our donor program where he can donate blood. We can have it bagged and sent right to you—all at the very good cost of keeping your sanity."

I wrapped him in a tight hug and kissed him on the cheek. "You're a genius."

"I know." He tapped some things into the tablet. "Now, about housing, you're still too fresh to live alone."

"I was worried about that too, like I still need to learn this world and all I can do and what it has to offer."

He lowered his voice. "The castle is beautiful, but there are other places a vampire can go and be welcome."

"Like where?" I didn't know what he was talking about, but I wanted to go, and I wanted to go now.

"Night Spawn City." He wagged his eyebrows. "All made vampires are welcome there, and you'd be safe."

I clapped my hands together. "How are you just the best ever?"

He did a fake hair flip because his was too short to get the effect. "Years and lessons in people crossing me. Though, if I can say something..."

I waved him on. "Please do."

"I've never seen Prince Grayson do anything like this before, and I've been around for nearly as long as he has." He rose to his feet. "Something is off."

"But what?" I refused to let any sort of hope bloom, but my curiosity was triggered.

He pursed his lips. "I don't know. But we're running out of time."

"Oh shit! The King!"

"Don't panic. It's only been five minutes, and we've got at least seven before he comes looking for us."

I headed right for the door. "I don't want to keep him waiting."

"As you shouldn't." He was at the door before I got there and yanked it open for me. "Leave it to me. I'll get you all sorted."

I pressed a quick kiss to his cheek. "I can't thank you enough, Martin."

"Thank him for what?" Grayson appeared just outside of my door.

I groaned and sighed. "Stalking me much?"

Grayson's eyes lingered on my face. "More like admiring."

"I see what you mean." Martin passed between the two of us and gave Grayson a daring little side-eye. "See you soon, Lady Piper."

Before I could even thank him, he was gone, leaving me alone with Grayson. Grayson leaned against the wall. "Back to admiring you."

I walked past him. "Do it somewhere else."

Grayson chuckled and fell into step beside me. "Thought you might be hungry."

Arrogant ass. I snickered. "Thought I wore you out last time."

"My turnaround time is fairly quick, if you recall." His lip turned up in a smirk.

I shrugged. "Not that memorable."

I lied he was completely memorable.

Grayson sighed. "And yet you're completely burned into mine."

"Is there a reason you're following me?" Now that I had an out, I was ready to jump. There wasn't a thing holding me here, and suddenly I felt lighter. I just had to make it okay with the King. If I had his blessing, then no one could stop me but Grayson.

"We've both been summoned by the King. I simply thought I'd accompany you."

"I don't need your company. I have a good memory now, and surprisingly enough, two legs that work perfectly."

"I happen to think your legs are one of your best features, especially when they're wrapped—"

I whirled around and my hand shot out before I knew what I was doing. It cracked across his cheek and his head snapped back. My hand stung as I shook it out. Grayson pressed his hand to his cheek, and his jaw dropped. "What was that for?"

I paused just outside the double doors to the throne room. "To knock some sense into you."

He rubbed at his jaw and adjusted it. "Consider me sensed."

I didn't feel an ounce of guilt about it. In fact, he'd had it coming for a while now. "Now, remember I am here to learn how to be a vampire, and once I figure that out and don't need your blood, I am out of here . . . for good."

Grayson nodded. "Noted."

"Good to hear." The King's deep voice came from right behind the both of us.

Even with my vampire senses and hearing, I hadn't heard him or felt him move in closer to us. I fumbled a bow I hadn't quite mastered yet and bobbled to stand up straight. "I didn't know you were listening, Your Highness."

Titus was taller than both of us, with an imposing presence I hadn't gotten used to yet. I wasn't sure I ever would. It was as if the man himself just commanded respect by standing there. He made a show of looking all around our surroundings and at the two guards outside the door. "Yes, well, the walls have ears in the castle. As do I."

Was this my moment to get his permission to break free? "Your Highness, if I may, did I hear you correctly? If I can leave, you'll let me go?"

He pressed his lips together and glanced at Grayson and back to me. "No one has the right to hold you anywhere you don't want to be, my dear."

Excitement fluttered in my stomach, and I fought not to takeoff down the hall, find Martin, and begin packing.

"Uncle." Grayson stepped in closer to him, giving him a warning tone.

Titus held his hand up, stopping him from saying anything else. "The BBA is here. He is insisting on meeting Piper."

Grayson sighed and ran his hands through his hair. "On what grounds?"

Titus waved for the guards to open the doors. "On the grounds that Marius has already met her."

He turned away from the two of us and walked into the room. The doors fell shut behind him, and he left Grayson and I standing there as though that was explanation enough for the new vampire in the room.

"What is a BBA?"

Grayson groaned, "Blood Born Ambassador. Basically, the representative for natural born vampires."

Vampire politics confused the hell out of me daily. "What does that mean?"

"It means we have a dinner to attend."

CHAPTER FIFTEEN

GRAYSON

*I*f ever there was a time when I wanted to just pack it in and leave, now would be it. Boredom seemed to be the order of the night, and I usually liked to avoid that like a cat avoids bath water. Chamber music drifted from the throne room out into the hall as I waited for Piper. Even I had to admit she was being a good sport about all of this. The BBA would be a long, boring event that I'd rather not attend. But for the sake of vampire politics, I would do my duty, and they were right—Marius, the representative for the Night Spawn, had already met Piper. It would be a great offense to the Blood Borns if they too didn't get the opportunity to meet her. In truth, I hated putting her on display like some kind of sideshow.

But there hadn't been a made vampire sired by The House of Shade in forever. It was a rarity, and not one I wanted to parade about like I'd done some great thing. In truth, I'd done a very selfish thing. Still, I wasn't sorry. I ran my hand down the front of my suit coat, then tugged the sleeves until they were tight and straight.

"You always look like perfection, darling." My mother glided to my side and paused. She reached out and cupped my cheek in the gentle way she always did.

"And you as well. I can't think of a more beautiful vampire." I bent down and pressed a light kiss to her cheek. My mother was the constant hostess, and as such, she always looked the part. Tonight, she had a delicate diadem on that drifted across her forehead and tangled into the dark strands of her wavy hair. It was a rose gold that matched her pink flowing dress and light glittering makeup. If Titus hadn't been King, I would've thought her every bit the queen of the vampires. Yet she was only his closest advisor, while I remained the Prince and heir to the throne.

"You flatter me, darling." She ran her hand over her dress. "I do hope this goes well tonight."

I always felt so warm and at ease when my mother was around. "One can only hope so, under the circumstances."

She dropped her hand to her sides. "I think you're doing well enough. Remember who you are and remember who *they* are, and all will go well for all of us."

"I just want all to be well for Piper. These things aren't the easiest to sit through."

"And yet I have total faith in her intelligence." My mother gave me a light smile. "You chose her, after all."

"Are we talking about me?" Piper moved toward us with a slow, deliberate grace that many new vampires had a hard time mastering.

Usually their movements were too quick, too jerky. Yet as she walked, her dress flowed perfectly around her. Her dress wasn't the traditional sort I'd grown used to seeing with the Blood Borns. They liked their corsets and poofs. This dress had flow but for a whole different reason. The top was strapless and fell into a neckline that showcased her curves perfectly. It fell to the ground in long silky material that caught the glowing Christmas lights in the hall. The material was smooth and gave her olive skin an even warmer tone that made her look like she glowed from within.

"We were, yes," my mother admitted freely.

Piper stopped by my side and gave me a sideways glance. "All good I hope."

My words had yet to find my mouth. She was utterly stunning with deep-red lips, bright-green eyes, and her hair pulled high on her head while strands of the wildness fell all around her face. When I said nothing, my mother continued for me. "Always good, my dear."

When I still didn't have the words, my mother elbowed me with a quick shot to the ribs. I coughed and winced at the pain in my side. "Of course. Always good."

"Riigghhttt." She glanced down at her dress and began to fiddle with an invisible string.

"Piper, you look lovely. More than lovely." I cleared my throat, trying not to look like a daft fool.

"I'll just be inside. I'll see you in there." My mother drifted away from us, leaving only Piper and me to have a moment alone.

We stood there for a few moments in pained awkward silence that made me want to rip my guts out. The distance between us was deafening. "Look, I —"

"Grayson, we—"

We both spoke at the same time. I pressed my lips together and waved her on. "Please."

She swallowed. "Grayson, I don't want to hate you."

"I don't want you to hate me."

"Whatever happened between us, it was lovely. But you have duties I don't understand . . ."

When I opened my mouth to try to drum up some explanation for her, my uncle's power burned in my throat, stopping me from saying a word. Even so she held her hand up, cutting me off. "It doesn't matter anymore."

"It doesn't?"

She shook her head, sending those loose strands flowing around her face. "No."

I hesitated, unsure what to say next. "No?"

"Look, after this dinner, let's talk about something, okay?"

I didn't know why she seemed so calm, but it sent off warning bells through my mind. Calm was like preparing for a storm. Calm was never a good sign when it came to females. Calm was like *prepare to be shot at a moment's notice*. I knew she had every right to be angry at me. I'd miss led her and she needed time to forgive and herself for that.

"Right then."

When I didn't move, she arched her eyebrows at me. "Something to add?"

I glanced around to assure no one was lingering in the hall. "This dinner tonight is a bit of a quandary."

She leaned in closer. "Explain that."

Courtiers started to drift down the hall toward us, and I didn't want them to hear me. I wrapped my hand around her elbow and steered her toward the throne room. I lowered my voice as we walked through the large double doors. "There's a political battle going on in the vampire world now, and tonight I need you on my side, Piper."

She gently removed her elbow from my fingers but didn't move away from me. "Are we on the right side?"

"Yes, always."

"How do I know I can believe you?"

It was a fair question given what we'd been through. I motioned toward the head of the throne room where Titus stood with my mother at the front of the room waiting for the ambassador to arrive. I headed toward them, and Piper remained at my side, distant but there. To his credit, Titus gave Piper a wide smile as we approached and even looked pleased to see her.

"Piper, you look lovely as ever."

She gave him a bow that was seamless compared to how she started out. "Thank you, Your Highness."

"Uncle, I'm trying to give Piper a bit of background on the BBA and what's to be done at this dinner."

Titus gave a little sigh but stepped in closer, tightening up our circle. "There are those in the born vampire world that would like to hold status over all others, especially those who are made vampires. It has been our goal to close the gap between the two vampire factions and create peace."

"And some of them don't want this peace?" Her brow furrowed in confusion.

"Some are stuck in their old ways, where only born vampires are allowed privilege in our world." Titus shook his head. "Grayson and I are working toward total equality for all."

When she looked up at me with admiration in her eyes, it nearly brought me to my knees. I didn't deserve such a pure look from her. Sure, I'd done right by all others, but I certainly hadn't by her. Piper wrinkled her nose. "So, why are we having dinner with them? I mean, they sound stuck-up as hell."

"They're not the only ones. Marius would have the same split but would love to see the Blood Borns fall." It was a tenuous situation to say the least, one my uncle and I were trying our best to resolve without having everyone kill each other.

Piper sucked in a breath and blew it out. "You know, I've always hated politics."

Titus chuckled. "You and me both. It'd be much easier if people would just do what was right rather than what personally benefited them."

"I agree. So, you all need me to be on my best behavior and on your side?"

My mother shook her head. "No, we need you to be yourself, my dear. Grayson has all the faith in the world in you. As do I."

Piper turned to Titus. "Is there anything you'd have me do, Your Highness?"

Titus looked taken aback for a moment. Then a slow smile spread across his face. "Aren't you lovely? I'm just pleased you're feeling well enough to attend this dinner, and hopefully it'll all turn up well."

Before anyone could say anything else, the doors filled with a large group of people. At the center of it all stood Clive Cristiano. He oozed privilege and smelled like money even from over here. It was like the ponce rolled in dollar bills before he left his mansion. His dark hair was combed back from his face with about a pound of gel or oil. He had a thin mustache and small triangular patch of hair under his lip that pointed downward. He was tall and regal, with a straight nose and sharp cheekbones. Even his clothing was of the old ways.

Where Titus and I favored a more modern look with pressed suits and straight shirts, Clive preferred the uptight style of the old ways. He wore a light blue Victorian style vest with swirling silver embroidery. His white shirt was also of the Victorian era, with plume sleeves that cinched in at the wrists and a cravat tied around his neck that tucked into the top of his shirt. His trousers matched his vest perfectly and were fitted around his hips, falling in a straight line down to his polished shoes. He held his arms out wide.

"My King." He gave a flourishing bow with his arms out to his sides and one foot poised in front of him.

Titus gave me an exasperated look for a split-second, then forced a smile in place. "Clive, it is good to see you, as always."

Clive rose from his bow and in a blur of movement and shoved his way between Piper and me. He grabbed her hand and held it up. "My, my, you are lovely, aren't you?"

Piper's lips pressed together for a moment, and I waited for her to throw him back in his place. Instead, she took a deep breath and took her hand back from him. "You must be the Blood Born Ambassador."

"Indeed I am." He reclaimed her hand once more, this time pressing his lips to the back of it.

I placed my hand on his shoulder and pulled him back. "You forget yourself, Clive."

"Prince Grayson." He let go of Piper and turned to fully face me. "Are you with us for the duration or will you be flitting off to new ventures soon?"

I looked past him to Piper. "I think my interests lie closer to home at this point."

"Clive!" Eloura bellowed across the throne room and everyone turned to look at her standing in the middle of the doorway.

Eloura was an interesting Blood Born. She was older than most, wealthier than all, and liked to move forward with the times. She was a heavy supporter of The House of Shade and was outspoken at most events she attended. Many avoided her for her brash ways, but generally I liked her way. She wore a dark burgundy corseted dress that complimented her dark skin. Her hair was twisted in neat rows back from her face and flowed down to the middle of her back. A gold headband was threaded through the twists and shined in the candlelight. She didn't need a walking stick, but she liked it. She took a few steps into the room, and it clicked against the stone floor.

"Must we remind you that personal space is a thing? Especially when a lady peels her fingers from your slimy grip."

Clive snapped to attention and forced a smile. "I was merely showing my respects to our latest addition to The House of Shade."

"Really, Clive." She rolled her eyes. "The art of brown-nosing was mastered by you."

A burst of laughter escaped my lips at the same time Piper pressed her hand over her mouth to hold in her own chuckle. Eloura hurried to our little circle and poked her walking stick between Clive and Piper. "Space, man. Space."

She chased him back like an old woman chasing bratty kids off her porch with a broom. Once he was exactly where she wanted him to be, she smiled at Piper. "Well, now, there you are."

Piper looked down at herself and then back up. "Yes, here I am."

"You've made quite the stir, young woman." Her dark-eyed gaze was strong and direct as she met Piper's eye. To some it would be unnerving, but Piper seemed to enjoy the directness.

"Should a young woman do anything else besides make a stir?" Piper beamed at Eloura.

"Quite, my dear. Quite."

The dinner gong sounded through the room and a set of double doors off to the side opened wide, showcasing a long table laid with golden China and crystal water goblets. The room was slightly smaller than the throne room, with The House of Shade flags hanging every few feet. Christmas garland wrapped around the wooden beams and glowed with gently twinkling lights. Red ribbons flowed through the garland and were covered in sparkles. Aside from Eloura and Clive, he'd arrived with a dozen of the highest pure born vampires in our world. Their families' bloodlines were old and well-established. They owned things in both the vampire and human world that allowed for their influence to be felt for centuries to come. Governments rose and fell under the weight of these families.

Piper leaned in closer to me and whispered, "I think I like her."

"One thing you need to know about all of this," they began to filter into the other room, leaving me and Piper behind for a split-second. "No one here is your friend..."

CHAPTER SIXTEEN

PIPER

He wasn't lying. No one here was my friend. I wasn't even sure if *he* was. "Does that include you?"

He gave me a sly smirk. "We will be the best of friends. You'll see."

Best of friends . . . righttttt. How would we be friends once I left here? Would he forgive me, or would it further the rift between us? Either way, *friends* felt like an insult or a line drawn in the sand between the two of us. "Friends. Right."

When an ex called me a friend, it either felt like a stab in the heart or a happy farewell. And this was not a happy farewell sort of feeling. *Just breathe through it all, Piper. Friends, friends, friends. Right . . . Friends is a good thing . . . My ass.*

"Shall we?" He offered me his arm. I took it. If we were going to find a balance here and he was going to let me go, we had to find a way to function. I wasn't lying. Did it all still hurt? Yes, so much so it seemed hard to breathe sometimes. But I excelled at picking myself up, and I'd started that tonight.

"Yes." I took his arm and let him guide me into the hall.

As I walked by, I felt like I was on display. Every one of the highbrow vamps stopped and stared at me. I didn't know if I was more like a sideshow or a welcomed guest. It was difficult to say. There was one thing for sure: none of them seemed like allies . . . so far. Grayson pulled my chair out and stepped to the side. I made my way to my seat and let Grayson push my chair in as I sat. I let my dress fall around the chair and settled in. Judging by how many plates and how much silverware was laid on the table, it was obvious I'd be here for a while. I'd spent enough time in restaurants to know that all that silverware came with way too many courses.

Grayson settled in between me and Titus, who sat at the head of the table. Across from us sat Moira and Eloura. The two seemed to get along like old friends who'd spent many years together sitting through dinners neither of them wanted to attend. They ducked their heads together, gossiping and chuckling in hushed tones. On the other side of me, Clive took his seat and gloated at the others. If I wasn't on my best behavior, I'd roll my eyes. I was just me, just Piper.

"So, Piper, do tell me, how is it now being a vampire?" Clive turned his attention to me.

"It was a shock at first, but I think I'm getting the hang of it." The waiters moved in unison as they filled everyone's goblets with blood. I placed my hand over my glass so they wouldn't fill mine. The last thing I needed was to lose myself to the thirst in front of the upper crest of vampire society.

"Come now, as the only vampire to be sired by The House of Shade in ages, it's got to be . . . thrilling." He smirked at the rest of the table, then turned back to me. I had to admit, Clive was full of himself, but at the same time, he liked to put on a show—always keeping the others looking by making eye contact with them all, then turning back to me . . . the prize of the night.

I cleared my throat. "Um, well, considering I didn't know that vampires existed up until I was one, it's been an adjustment."

"Opulence isn't easily won in our world, and you just stepped right into it." He motioned to the beautiful room around us. "A life of privilege at your fingertips, and as a made vampire too . . ."

"That way of thinking is exactly what we're working to change, Ambassador." Grayson took my goblet and placed it in front of himself. He pulled a knife from somewhere within his pocket and sliced his hand, then held it over the goblet. His warm red wine scent hit me, and my stomach tightened. My tongue tingled for the flavor of him.

He squeezed his hand into a fist and held it over my goblet until it was full, then he took a cloth napkin from the table and held it over his cut. Everyone just stared at him. Without so much as batting an eyelash, he handed me the glass. "For you."

I lifted my chin and took it. This was, after all, the world of blood and decadence. I would live the role . . . for now. "Thank you."

The Ambassador's mouth opened and closed a few times before he forced a smile across his face. "I'm not sure why anyone should have to give up their birthright."

"We're not asking anyone to give up their birthright." Titus lifted his glass and motioned to me. "To you, Piper."

I smiled at him and returned the gesture. When no one else followed suit, Titus just held there, waiting. One by one, they lifted their goblets in the same fashion. When all had followed, Titus made a show of taking a sip. My throat burned for just a taste of Grayson. I tipped the glass to my lips and let his warmth slide over my tongue. I forced myself not to sigh at the taste or lick my lips . . . or even chug the glass like I was some kind of frat boy doing a keg stand.

"Thank you, Your Majesty."

After everyone placed their glasses back on the table, the first course came out in a line of servers all holding plates covered with little silver domes. They all placed them down as if it was some kind of coordinated act and lifted the lids in unison. The smell of warm food hit me, and I suddenly missed the ability to eat. Grayson had told me that I would regain it one day, but for now I'd have to remain on a liquid diet.

Clive lifted his fork and held it over the tiny portion of scallops with a red wine drizzle. "Dazzling, is it not?"

I nodded. "It is indeed."

"Do you miss food?"

"More than I could tell you." I sighed. "But Grayson assures me it won't be long until I can once more."

"Ah, yes, it might take some time to join the world of civility. Such is the way for The Night Spawn."

"Civility? So you think because I'm on a liquid diet or a Night Spawn made vampire, I'm not civilized?" I placed my goblet down on the table and faced him fully.

He paused, seeming to consider his words. "The Blood Borns have spent many years making accommodations for vampires such as yourself. I'm of the belief that at some point these accommodations need to end and The Night Spawn must fend for themselves."

"Correct me if I'm wrong . . . and I may be . . . but aren't Blood Born vampires responsible for making Night Spawn? It was an entire race started by yourselves, correct?"

"It's been so long. No one really kn—"

"—You'd be correct," Titus interrupted.

"Also, I understand your positions coming from birth, but you've been alive for hundreds of years, and no doubt your fortunes have been passed down from generations. I would think someone with that level of wealth, such as yourself, would see the benefit in lifting up those who are new to the life."

Grayson chuckled. "This is the exact argument I've been making for the past fifty years. Brilliant little creature, isn't she?"

Eloura took a bite of her scallops and nodded. "Considering the top one percent of the world's wealth is sitting in this room, I quite agree. We have a responsibility to our people to better their lives."

Half the table remained silent while the others all nodded with her. Grayson didn't touch his food. He just let it sit there, as if in solidarity with me. "I couldn't agree more, Eloura."

"So we should squander our fortunes as The House of Shade has squandered theirs?" Clive scoffed. "Only a foolish man would do so."

"Squandered our fortunes?" Titus outright laughed at his words. Grayson and Moira joined him. Titus waved away his words. "Even with building the underground city, the expansion of the blood banks, and the investments into vampire health, I can assure you our fortune is still triple what you claim yours to be . . . and I'm being cautious with that figure."

My eyes widened. I knew Grayson was wealthy, but that kind or wealth was beyond something I could comprehend. I was used to taking extra shifts just to be able to scrape together enough for Christmas presents for Dice.

The ambassador waved his words away. "If that's

accurate."

"I like to think of The Night Spawn as an investment." Grayson sighed. "The future should be bright for the newer generation."

Clive held his drink to his lips and scoffed. "You've spent more than us all."

"So?"

"So, I fail to see how a prince who spends so frivolously can be trusted in matters that concern a whole kingdom." Silence fell over the entire room at the insult Clive left sitting on the table. "There are many prominent houses in the vampire world who'd assure the lines are preserved, as well as the status."

Grayson swirled his drink and gave him that half-smile. "I would think The House of Shade has proven its worth for centuries. Let us not forget we've pushed the vampire community forward and have kept all of you in the station you value so much."

"Grayson," Titus warned.

But he kept going. "You forget, Ambassador. If you're not moving forward, you're dying."

Clive sat up straight. His eyes widened. "Is that a threat?"

"Hardly." Grayson met his eye. "If I wanted to threaten you, I would, and it would not be veiled."

Eloura chuckled and raised her glass to Grayson before taking a sip. "Prince Grayson, a pleasure as always. Your words have a way of landing right where they should. Even Clive can see he's pushing buttons when talking of messing with the line of succession. There are no better rulers than The House of Shade."

"In your opinion." Clive motioned to the rest of the table. "There are those who might see it otherwise."

"Then let them speak it." Eloura glanced at the other vampires, waiting for someone to say something. After a few moments, she took a bite of her scallop and nodded. "That's what I thought."

"I think what my son is trying to say is that forward progress is what keeps us all relevant in this world. We have to move forward and assure the survival of us all while also remaining in the shadows as we always have," Moira said calmly, with that easy tone she used to disarm others so well.

The truth was, I hated politics down to my core. It was part of the age-old question: do the haves support the have-nots. Though I didn't see The Night Spawn as the have-nots. The ambassador dropped his fork on the plate with a loud clank.

"And you, a kept vampire in this castle, are one to have an opinion on this, Moira?" He rolled his eyes. "Oh, please."

"Watch yourself," Titus growled.

"Apologize now," Grayson demanded.

"Hey! Manners," I snapped.

The three of us had all replied at the same time. There were people at this table who could take an insult, even I was thick-skinned enough to deal with a slim like him, but Moira was perfect to any and all who met her. The ambassador's eyes swung over the three of us before they landed on Moira.

"Apologies."

A low rumbling growl sounded in Titus' chest, and his fangs descended. "Like you mean it."

Clive looked to the King, then swallowed hard and composed himself. "I apologize for my tone with you, Moira. It wasn't warranted."

Damn straight.

Moira gave him a polite smile. "Apology accepted."

But it seemed he wasn't finished yet. He leaned in closer to me and muttered. "You're one to lecture about manners when yours aren't up to par."

I sighed and rolled my eyes. "Can you not breathe on me? You smell as old as you are."

"Perhaps he should stop breathing altogether." Grayson seethed at my side, but I waved him off. This was a political dinner, and I knew they'd want a reaction from Grayson. Any reaction at all would only prove The House of Shade wasn't right for the throne.

"I got this."

"By all means." Grayson waved his hand toward Clive, who'd moved a few inches back from my face.

"Though my time has been short here, there are a few things I could tell you about your society."

Clive motioned to the other aristocratic vampires at the table. "Please enlighten us. We've only been around for a few thousand years."

"And in those thousands of years, your thinking has

closed. I haven't seen many Blood Born vampires around. The made vampires will soon be outnumbering you. And while you all have your own special blood magic gifts, sometimes numbers are all it takes. If that's the case, why not invest in the numbers and eventually make a profit? Furthermore, your society is a secretive one, I hardly think any of the made vampires volunteered for this life, so you've taken people from their real lives and moved them into this—where they're expected to lose the only family and friends they've ever known and start all over . . . alone."

They all fell silent, pausing and watching me with wide eyes. "I suppose none of you have considered this. Most people, in my opinion, want a life and want to move forward. So, I think the only right thing to do is to make that transition easier."

"You presume to know much," Clive spoke through thin lips.

"I can only speak to what I see." It was all true. Grayson and Titus would bring the vampires into the future. Not only by helping them but by also making sure it ran smoothly and organized it all ways. Everything was meticulous down to the last drop. I didn't want to side with Grayson, but the right thing was the right thing.

The others began to grow tired with Clive's attitude. I could tell by the way they shifted uncomfortably in their seats, looking from me to him and back again. Clive turned three shades of red as Grayson chuckled under his breath. When I turned to look at Titus, he smirked into his glass. Moira and Eloura both nodded in approval. Even some of the other vampires found my words to ring true.

"You know little of our world. There is no place for you to comment on such things." His lip curled into a sneer.

I held my breath for a moment, wanting to curse this guy out, to tell him he needed to pull his own head out of his own ass, but that wouldn't help here. It wouldn't change his mind or facilitate the conversations that needed to be had. Was it my job to help The Night Spawn? No. But if I was put on the spot like I was now, I'd speak my mind. I'd lived in enough places and known enough people to see the world through a view they'd never seen before.

"On the contrary, I'm probably the only one here who can comment. I'm the only one who's transitioned, the only one who did it recently, the only one who has experienced both the high life and the average. If anything, you should be asking me, Clive, because my point of view isn't as dated as yours." I lifted my glass and took another sip. The blood warmed me from the inside out and filled me with satisfaction.

Eloura snickered. "She does have a point, Clive."

I sat there watching the array of emotions cross his face: anger, confusion, arrogance, and finally, contempt. I'd seen the look before many times in the face of men. It was the look when they realized that I was smarter and more well-equipped to handle an argument. It was the look of knowing I'd be difficult to win against. It was a look I'd grown bored with. Like I said, politics and I didn't mix.

"Rather brilliant. You didn't think I wouldn't choose wisely, did you?" Grayson said, breaking the awkward silence. "That's why you're here after all—to see my choice of progeny."

Clive sucked in a deep breath and blew it out. He narrowed his eyes at me. "Yes, I dare say she is."

The waiters came out with another round of food, and I felt stifled in this room. How many courses would I have to endure? I felt a bit like a caged animal being watched. I'd made my point, given my impression, and I couldn't eat yet. How much longer would I have to sit here playing tit for tat? I turned to Grayson. "May I go?"

"Of course." He rose to his feet. "I think you've satisfied the curiosity of the masses for now."

Clive shook his head and motioned to the others. "We've not yet finished."

"I think we're finished." Grayson gave me his arm and I took it. I wasn't going to fly out of the room the way I wanted to. My life was fucked up enough without adding the weight of the vampire world on it.

I didn't say a word to him as we left the dining hall and walked through the throne room. Once we were out through the double doors and they closed behind us, I dropped his arm and hurried toward my room. Grayson stayed at my pace. "Piper, wait. You did so well."

"Thanks." I shoved my door open and tried to slam it

shut before he could walk in, but he was too quick and was suddenly in the room with me.

"Piper."

"I can't do this." I spun around to face him.

"Do what?"

"I wish I had it in me to be the friend you need right now, but I need to take care of me for a while before I can attend things like this." I sucked in a breath, feeling so shitty even though I knew he did me wrong. I wanted to help. "Look, I believe in your cause and the things you're doing here, but I can't."

I turned away from him and went to the closet. This dress was too much. The shoes were too much. I hadn't meant to tear the dress off, but my frantic movements left it in pieces on the floor at my feet. I grabbed a pair of jeans and shoved my legs into them, then threw on the first fuzzy black sweater I saw. At the back of my closet stood a suitcase that hadn't been there before. I wanted to kiss Martin in that instant. I knew he'd gotten the suitcase for me. I slid my feet into a pair of black Uggs and pulled the suitcase out from the closet with me. I threw it on the bed and opened it wide.

Grayson arched his eyebrows. "What are you doing?"

"Leaving." I turned back for the closet and walked right past the line of fancy dresses and grabbed some sweatpants, jeans, and leggings.

Grayson stood behind me and followed me back out to my room when I started throwing stuff into the bag. "Have you forgotten you'll go mad with thirst?"

He wasn't wrong. But I needed to breathe, to have some freedom. "Then put me down. Feral vampires do not live. Or go down to the lab and donate the blood I need to survive. You made me. It's something you'll have to live with. I'm sure Martin will arrange for it to be delivered wherever I am."

Grayson shook his head. "No, I won't allow it."

"It's not about allowing. I need to breathe, to figure out who I am as a vampire. I can't do that here with you so . . . close." I ran in the closet and pulled all the comfy sweaters and tank tops off the hangers. With this level of speed, it was easy to have them all folded and in the bag within seconds. "Sometimes a girl just needs to find her own space."

"No. Absolutely not." He crossed his arms over his chest.

"It's funny you think that'll work on me . . . It's like you don't know me at all."

There was a light knock at the door a moment before it swung wide open. Titus filled the doorway with his massive body. "Piper, I've come to thank you."

He paused, taking in my packed bag. "What's this then?"

Grayson motioned to me. "She thinks she's leaving."

"I am leaving," I snapped at Grayson.

"And I said no." Grayson's annoyance rose to meet my own. "It's bloody madness to let you go under the circumstances. I will not allow this."

Titus sighed. "You *can* allow this and you *will*."

A wave of shock jolted through my body, and I froze not knowing what to say. "Thank you, Your Majesty."

"It is I who should thank you. I'm quite impressed by how you handled yourself at that dinner tonight. A lesser vampire would've been overwhelmed, but you seemed poised."

"You've clearly never bartended on a Halloween that falls on a Friday night in Salem. That was nothing." I brushed away the thought of Dice and me on that crazy night. We'd made a killing in tips and even had a blast with all the madness. It was a simpler time. Way simpler than this.

"No, clearly not." Titus chuckled and took a step closer, getting my full attention. I craned my neck to look up at him. He placed his hand on my shoulder. "You are always welcome here, but I wouldn't contain a bird that's meant to fly."

I could only smile up at him. "I will be eternally grateful for your kindness."

Grayson turned away from us and started pacing back and forth. "This is not to be done. I won't allow it."

Titus dropped his hand from my shoulder and stared at Grayson like he'd sprouted eight heads. I sighed and zipped my luggage closed. "You keep saying that like it's going to make a difference here... and it doesn't."

It felt kind of good to take back some of the power he had over me. Deep down, I wanted to make him happy, to stay where he might need me. But all that made me feel was angry at myself for being so pathetic as to hang around someone who clearly didn't want me. Sure, he flirted with me, but his actions told a whole different story. So, I needed this. I needed space. A break. A way to take back the little pieces of myself that I'd given him.

Titus ignored Grayson's words completely. "Go to the lab and make arrangements to get Piper the blood she needs."

"Have you both gone mental?" Grayson's voice rose in anger. "Where will she even go?"

"To start with, The Night Spawn Headquarters." I pulled the bag off the bed and extended the little handle to drag it along.

"Excellent idea." Titus nodded, agreeing with me. "I will allow it. Why don't you go to the lab, Piper. My nephew will meet you there."

I didn't hesitate to take my chance to get out of there. I headed to the door and pulled it closed behind me. I wanted to run to the lab to get there before Titus changed his mind. But something held me there, listening to them through the door. A loud crash sounded through the room like the bed had been split in half.

"Was that necessary? We've already replaced this bed once this week."

"It was bloody necessary . . . Made me feel better anyways." Anger snapped in every single one of Grayson's words.

Titus sighed. "You need to let her go . . . for now. Sometimes we lose the battle to win the war. We can keep tabs on her at Night Spawn City. And you know she will be looked after. You designed that system yourself. Now you must trust it. In the meantime, you must deal with things at hand."

Grayson gave a pained groan, and I could almost picture him tugging at his hair in frustration. "What's that?"

Titus' voice grew low and serious. "You will fall. . . soon."

"And? What of it?" Grayson's voice was heavy with tension.

"You didn't spend months wandering around with The Fallen, witches, and warlocks for no reason. You've made your powerful contacts. It's time to use them."

"Indeed. It's time."

Powerful contacts?

Fall?

What was happening to him?

How could so much be happening all at once and I had so little knowledge of it? *Right because he never told me, even when I asked.* There was one thing for sure, I wasn't going to get my answers within the secretive walls of the castle. It was time for me to find out about this world, about vampires, and about what in the actual fuck was going on with myself, and though I hated to admit it . . . with Grayson.

CHAPTER SEVENTEEN

PIPER

Walking into the lab with my bag packed felt like an open declaration of my leaving. In some ways it was. But the lab assistants were in a buzz, zooming around the lab from holding room to holding room. I'd never seen it so packed. Even since yesterday, it'd gotten chaotic. It reminded me more of an inner-city ER than an underground lab for vampires. Around the perimeter of the room were holding rooms with thick glass walls where everyone could keep an eye on the vampires who were kept there. Usually it was older vampires who'd started to lose their minds or made vampires who didn't handle the transition well. But now there were younger vampires struggling to deal with this mysterious sickness and the effects it had on them. Down the center of the room, there were lines of tables where the lab assistants did their work. But today all of the chairs were empty.

It was overflowing with made vampires who were showing the sickness I'd heard so much about. A male vampire lay strapped to a gurney on the other side of the lab. Trails of blood from his eyes and nose streamed down his pale skin. He fought against the restraints on his arms and legs. His eyes were completely black, and blood sweat beaded his entire body.

"I can see it all! Everything is clear! BLOOD ON THE STREETS! BLOOD ON THE STREETS!" He fought against his restraints as three of the lab assistants piled on top of him. Doctor Stanbourn ran across the lab with a syringe in hand. He dove on top of the vampire and jabbed the needle into his neck.

The vampire's eyes rolled into the back of his head, and he fell limp onto the gurney. The lab assistants didn't look like the types who could handle things like this. Most of them were made vampires, and though they likely had the strength and speed, so did the infected ones. Sweat rolled down the doctor's face, and he pulled a handkerchief from the pocket of his lab coat and rubbed it over his head. He shoved his glasses farther up his nose and gave a heavy sigh. He motioned to an empty holding tank at the end of the line of them.

"Put him in there. I'll see if I can't get Ophelia to calm his mind." He gave a heavy sigh and closed his eyes, like this was the longest shift in the history of shifts. I kind of felt bad for being in the lab when he clearly had so much more going on.

I turned to face one of the rooms only to find a girl

standing at the glass. She was just staring at me. Her face was void of all emotions. Her hair hung down the sides of her face in matted, soaking knots. She wore a hospital gown that was soaked and clung to her naked body. Drops of water fell off it one by one, and the glass looked like it'd been doused with a hose. I stepped in closer to the glass, and her deep, brown eyes tracked my movements. Something felt off about her, about them all. I couldn't put my finger on it, but deep down I knew it in my gut—this wasn't just some kind of virus, it was something else.

"No . . . no . . . no." She backed away from the glass to stand in the middle of the room. She shoved her hands into her hair, yanking at the knots. A terrified scream ripped up her throat, and water began to pour from her skin.

"Holy shit!" I turned to the doctor. "Help! Somebody help over here!"

She looked like she was melting from the outside. She looked at me with pleading eyes. "Make it stop!"

Her entire body burst into water and fell to the floor in a puddle. I jumped back from the glass as lab assistants rushed into the room. The water expanded out toward them, then slowly seeped back until it reformed into the girl once more. She lay on the floor curled into a ball on her side. Sobs wracked her body, and she shook from head to toe. I sucked in a sharp breath as the two lab assistants picked her up off the floor and put her back into the cot in her room.

"It's awful, isn't it?"

I jumped at the sound of the doctor's voice next to me. I couldn't take my eyes off her. "What's wrong with them? All of them..."

Looking around now, there was a man who burst into flames every few minutes setting off the sprinklers in his room. Next to him was another man whose veins turned dark-black and threaded over his body. His eyes turned blood-red and he fell to the ground in a seizure-like fit. The doctor gave a heavy sigh and took his glasses off.

"If I'm being honest, I've never seen anything like it before. On a cellular level, they all appear to be normal. But cells don't account for half of what's happening in our world these days." He folded his arms over his chest. "Take, for example, a born vampire... the cells are nearly identical, and yet the abilities are far different. The blood magic is stronger when passed from birth. Made vampires don't have that kind of blood magic, but this looks like magic gone completely wrong."

"What does Ophelia say?"

"Very little. She comes and goes. Tests her potions and mostly they help, but it's no cure."

Something inside of me knew there was more to this. It was darker and deeper than anything they could imagine. My mind lingered on Titus' words to Grayson.

"Do you think they've been cursed or fallen to something worse?"

"It would take one hell of a witch or warlock to pull

off something of this magnitude. None that I have ever known or come to memory could do it."

Grayson appeared at my side.

When I gave him a sideways glance, sadness settled over him. He didn't smile or have a playful air about him. Deep down, I felt awful for upsetting him, which in turn just made me angrier at myself for caring that he was upset when he'd hurt me most of all. It was a cycle I needed to break before it got worse and I stayed for him... and just kept ruining myself.

"What are you going to do?"

"We're doing all that can be done right now. But we have O looking into it."

"What does it say about me that I have all the confidence in Ophelia on this?" The girl was a complete loose cannon, and yet I had faith she'd help somehow.

The doctor groaned. "My dear, I feel the same way."

We all stood there in silence for a moment, taking in how dire everything was. I felt selfish doing this now, but if I didn't do it now, I might never. I just didn't know how to start this conversation or even make it feel like a natural transition. I hated trying to find the right moment to chime in on times like this.

As if Grayson could read my mind, he turned toward me. "Ready to do this?"

Not at all. "Yeah, I'm ready."

The doctor looked between the two of us. "Ready for what?"

"We need to set up a way for me to donate my blood to Piper and get it shipped to her in a timely manner."

His words fell like a hammer between the three of us. The doctor shoved his glasses back on his face and clapped his hands together. "Right, well. Okay then. This way."

He pointed toward an empty exam room on the other side of the lab, and I dragged my suitcase right for it. Grayson followed behind me, and when I got to the room, I wasn't the one who would be sitting on the table. I stepped to the side and let him hop up on the table. His legs dangled off the bottom of the gurney.

He met my eye and rolled up his sleeve. "You sure about this?"

Not at all, but I have to try. "I'm sure. I can't live like this anymore."

The doctor pulled a needle with a tube attached to it from one of the drawers. At the end of the tube, was an empty blood bag. He didn't speak as he wrapped a rubber tie around Grayson's arm and pulled it tight, making the veins pop. Grayson still didn't look away from me. "I want you to know I'm truly sorry."

He'd already apologized, and really how many more times could I expect him to? I knew he was sorry. I knew he had his reasons. But his reasons logically didn't make sense to me. If what he said was true, and how he said he felt about me was true, then why would it be totally okay for us not to be together. "We could've been great. We could've been so much more."

The doctor jabbed the needle into his arm, but Grayson didn't flinch. Instead, he hung his head. "I know."

"This is the way it has to be." Even saying the words were hard. When silence fell between us, I knew there was nothing left for me to say to him. Not now at least. I didn't know why but this felt like a second breakup, like somehow me leaving made it so much more permanent. My heart squeezed in my chest, and it felt hard to breathe. The pain of leaving would come, but it would be far less than the pain of staying so close yet so far out of reach.

The doctor filled up four bags of blood so quickly I hadn't even noticed him switching the bags. It was only when he snapped the rubber tie off Grayson's arm that I felt the end of our time together. He pulled the needle from Grayson's arm and rose to his feet. "You'll have to come by every day to assure she has the right supplies."

"Whatever she needs." His words were almost a whisper, and I still couldn't look away from him. Fire and pain burned between us, and my breath caught in my chest.

Before I could find the words to say, Martin strolled into the room with his tablet in hand. He moved between me and Grayson, breaking the moment. "Okay, Miss Piper, I am all set to transport you to Night Spawn City. Your accommodations have been arranged. Are you ready to go?"

"I'm ready."

"Be careful." This time when Grayson spoke, he couldn't even look at me.

I wrapped my hand around my suitcase and popped to my feet. "I can take care of myself."

Grayson gave a humorless chuckle. "Oh, I know."

"I guess this is goodbye." They were words I'd never thought I'd speak to him.

He stepped around Martin as if he wasn't there and got so close to me that I could feel the heat rolling off his body. His warm scent wrapped around me, and for a moment, all I could picture was the two of us wrapped up in each other surrounded by a tangle of sheets. The heat, the passion, the feeling that I'd found my other half all flashed through my mind. He grabbed my hand and held it to his lips. He gave it a lingering kiss, then let my fingers drop.

"With you and me . . . it'll never be goodbye." And then he was gone, leaving me there with my luggage and bag full of feelings.

Martin blew a low, long breath. "That man is like quicksand. Before you know it, you're sunk."

I sighed and took a step toward the door. "That man is the name of my sorrow."

CHAPTER EIGHTEEN

GRAYSON

*G*oodbye was not a word I ever thought I'd utter to Piper. Not when I'd met her and certainly not when I changed her. She consumed my thoughts. It was the most acute kind of torture. I both loved and hated it. The pain made me feel alive, like the constant ache of not having her reminded me why I was here and what I was doing. Titus had said it was time for me to use my contacts, and he wasn't wrong. It was high time I reached out, so here I was starting at the top of the food chain in our world. It was presumptuous of me, but when had being timid gotten anyone anywhere?

The last time I was here, the leaves had just turned, flurries had barely started, and the air was only just crisp. Now, winter had set into The Pine Barrens of New Jersey. The leaves had all fallen and the branches looked like fingers reaching into the grey sky. Snow gathered on the empty limbs and piled on the ground. The eerie silence that came with fresh snowfall would freak some people out, but I found the purity of it refreshing. There wasn't one footprint to be seen, nor even an animal print. Here, this close to The Fallen Compound, there would be none. No one dared travel this close to where they lived . . . No one but me.

Desperate times, desperate measures.

As I approached the imposing gate, I stood there waiting. The mechanical sound of something moving drew my attention up to the top of the gate, and I froze. Cameras all turned in my direction. The Fallen were cautious as ever. Those who came up against them would meet an early end. There was no doubt about it. But I was here for a favor . . . and favors from The Fallen weren't easily given. When the gates began to swing open for me, a jolt of surprise flitted through my body. I thought I'd come out here only to be turned away. The gate swung wide, and I walked into the property. I took my time, letting them see me every step of the way.

The Fallen Compound was as impressive as ever. Some people would expect a castle in a mountain like that of the vampires, but this reminded me of an old sprawling southern mansion. Thick white columns rose up from the ground floor to the roof. Balconies surrounded each of the three floors. French doors lined each of them, as though every room in the house had access to the outside. It made sense, seeing how they all had wings.

Black shutters framed the windows and doors. They

stood out against the white exterior of the house. The grounds extended in all directions, with wide, snow-covered lawns running to the perimeter fence. When I glanced up at the rooftop, I saw multiple cameras all pointed in my direction. We were only days away from Christmas, yet I didn't see a decoration in sight . . . just a single red bow on the front door, and even that hung a little crooked. There were no lights or garland or even figurines. It was sparse at best, though I didn't know what I'd expected.

When I walked up the steps to the porch, I held my breath and reached to knock on the door, but it swung open. I stood there, frozen, with my hand lifted in front of Mika's face. I dropped my hand down to my sides. It was hard not to shift uncomfortably under this scrutiny, but I held myself still. His eyes were an uncanny emerald-green with a vivid honey color around his irises. His hair was a dark, nearly brown, blond that was parted down the middle and fell just above his shoulders and around his face. He wore black trousers and a dark-red button-down shirt that let his tattoo peek from his collar. He held a crystal glass in his hand. It was filled with a golden liquid that smelled like bourbon. A light smile played on his lips as he leaned against the door jam.

"What brings a young vampire to our door?"

"I've got a problem, and I'm seeking some advice." I didn't know how else to give a synopsis of the situation without going into detail.

"Who is it?" Matteaus barked from somewhere deeper inside the house.

"Baby vamp," Mika called over his shoulder.

"Handle it." I saw Matteaus walk behind Mika and go down the hallway that led farther into the house. I'd always been intimidated by the fallen angel. He was big and well-muscled with a fuck off attitude to match. His hair was a wild array of colors that went from dark brown, to blond, to red depending on the light and who was looking at him. He glanced at me with those piercing sapphire eyes and shook his head. "This place is turning into a madhouse with visitors."

He threw his head back and bellowed toward the ceiling. "Drew, can't you take us off the grid or something!"

He disappeared down the hall and out of sight. The feeling that this was a bad idea started to sink in, but I had no other choice. The curse loomed. I felt myself stepping closer each day. If anything, the dinner and Piper reminded me that I had to be around for other vampires and for her. Mika chuckled and shook his head.

"What's up, vamp?"

He stepped back and motioned for me to walk into the compound. White marble floors extended out from the foyer, all the way back toward the hallway Matteaus walked down. A set of double stairs bowed up in a U-shape to the second floor. I tilted my head back, looking up to the third and fourth floors. Dark iron railings ran around each of the levels, separated by large marble pillars. White double doors were closed tight on each of the floors. A free standing three-tiered fountain stood in the middle of the foyer. My brow furrowed at a very beat up GIANT dog bed beside the fountain.

The Fallen didn't have a dog . . . that I knew of. My brow stayed furrowed. "I've got a problem."

"I figured. Social calls aren't a thing for us." Mika stopped just before the fountain and crossed his arms over his chest.

I swallowed. "The curse of The House of Shade."

His eyebrows shot up. "My condolences."

"I'm hoping to avoid my own funeral. That's why I'm here."

"You know our rules are strict . . . We do not interfere in the matters of mortals. You all have to live your own lives. We're here for the higher purposes." Mika slapped his hand on my shoulder. "It's regrettable, but fate is fate."

"I'm aware of the rules." I lowered my voice. "But a helpful tip wouldn't go against those rules."

A wide smile spread across his face. "You're a smart one."

Before I could reply, a huge black lion strolled into the foyer and flopped down on the dog bed . . . *lion* bed. Mika groaned as Aidenuli, Taliam, and Tristan all walked into the foyer after the lion.

Taliam crossed his arms over his chest. He wasn't as bulky as Aidenuli or Matteaus, but he was long and lean with silvery hair tipped with a deep emerald green. He wore a white T-shirt with some kind of rock band on it and loose-fitting leather pants.

He hauled back his thick boot and kicked the corner of the bed, then hunched over, getting in the lion's face. "It's been two weeks. It stinks like big cat in here."

A lizard zoomed out of Taliam's pocket and ran up his body to settle on his shoulder. Its tongue darted from its mouth a moment before it turned a silvery color with green stripes, nearly blending in with Taliam's hair. The lion roared at him and settled back onto the bed with a dramatic flop. "I don't give a shit. Change back, Collias."

Another roar and Aidenuli chuckled, sending long strands of his black hair over his face. He was the largest of The Fallen and the most intimidating by far. I found it odd that my thoughts weren't my own when he was around. Most believed he held all the secrets of the world. Truth was, I thought so too. He was dark-haired, dark-eyed, and scary as hell.

"He said to go fuc—"

"—I know what he said. I speak lion," Taliam snapped back at Aidenuli. "Just because he's your best friend doesn't mean he gets to wallow and have you translate."

Tristan shook his head. "Taliam is right. You can't just walk around like this, Collias."

Another lion groan and Taliam's face turned stony. "My animals are at least clean and are polite when they communicate."

Collias, in all his lion glory, dragged himself to his feet and prowled down the hall toward the back of the house. The three started after him when Mika cleared his throat and called out, "Hey, Tristan, got a sec?"

The angel left the other two to follow the lion and strolled over to where Mika and I stood. Mika motioned to me. "The vamp is in trouble."

Tristan shoved his hands in the pockets of his suit. He looked me over with those light-blue eyes, and I felt he saw my every desire when it came to Piper. "Tread carefully. The threats of the past are very real."

I sighed. "So I've been told."

"Man, that was a shitty night. Do you remember that?" Mika froze and looked at Tristan with wide eyes. "Of course you remember that. I didn't mean to bring it up."

Tristan nodded. "Forever burned into my mind."

I stiffened. "Wait. You were there?"

"Yep." Mika nodded.

"The night my entire family line was cursed, The Fallen were there?" I didn't know why I was so shocked, but in my mind, it'd always been this thing that happened in a dungeon somewhere and no one knew how it came to be.

"Asking a second time doesn't make it any less true." Tristen cocked his head to the side, his blond hair falling around his face.

I tried to force away my surprise. "Apologies. I just . . . the curse has been a plague on all of us."

Tristan's all-knowing gaze ran right through me. "And yet you play with fire with your little vampire progeny. I can assure you it is not worth it."

How could this be? There were songs written about

love. People lived for love. They died for it. It made kingdoms rise and fall. It was what was supposed to make the world go round or a life worth living, and yet I'd found nothing but cynics. "The fallen angel of love says love is not worth it?"

Tristen reached up and fiddled with the broken locket around his neck. A haunted look glazed over his eyes. "Love is both a blessing and a curse. For most people, the curse outweighs the blessing. In your case, the curse could be your end."

I shook my head and ran my hands through my hair. I was getting nowhere. "All a matter of experience, I suppose."

Tristen let the locket fall back on his chest. "There isn't one person in this compound who will tell you it's a blessing. Perhaps keep that in mind."

How could I forget? "I will."

Tristen shook his head and shared a chuckle with Mika. "You won't. The naïve never do."

"You're the second person to call me stupid lately. I'm starting to feel a bit daft for even trying. Why not just lie down and let what's destined to happen just happen? You lot are as downtrodden as the rest. Can no one say they've found love and lived a long, happy life?"

Tristen chuckled. "Love is one thing that no one can claim intelligence with."

"And no, happily ever afters are for movies and songs." Mika rocked back on his heels. "We've lived long enough to know that."

"Say I don't throw in with you lot and I reach for the impossible, how would one go about beating a bloody centuries-old curse?"

Mika and Tristan shared a look for a moment before Mika spoke. "Curses aren't really a Fallen thing. You might want to check with a source closer to that kind of magic."

He turned and walked away from us, leaving me alone with Tristan, who leaned in and lowered his voice to a whisper. "Start at the beginning."

CHAPTER NINETEEN

PIPER

"You ready?" Martin stood at my side in front of a full-length mirror in a room at the back of the castle. I knew vampires traveled by mirror sometimes, but I still hadn't gotten used to the idea. As a human, legend told that vampires avoided mirrors because they wouldn't have a reflection. The fact of the matter was that they could walk right through them and get anywhere they needed to be.

"I'm ready." I wanted to start fresh, and the excitement of that nearly drowned out the fear I felt at going to a new place. This would be my home until I got my shit together and figured out the next steps. Martin pressed his finger to the mirror, but nothing happened.

"Shit." He looked down at his hand, then rubbed it over his pants. "Just a sec. It takes some time to make this thing work."

He raised his hand again and nothing. He smiled at

me. "Well, that's a bloody shame. I could call a car around, but it'd take some time as the sun hasn't fully set yet."

I was ready to go now. Sometimes the anticipation could be worse than the event, and I wanted the event over. I stepped up to the mirror. "So, what do you do? Just, like, touch it?"

"It's super simple blood magic. Even *some* made vampires can do it on occasion. All you have to do is press your hand to the mirror and think about where you'd like to go." He pressed his hand to it once more, but still nothing happened. "I'm telling you, I had it last week."

"It's not a big deal. We'll figure it out." I wasn't sure what made me want to try to touch the mirror or why I thought it would work, but when I pressed my fingers to the cool surface, it rippled under my touch.

Martin's head snapped around, and his eyes darted from the mirror to me and back again. "Okay, miss thing. Since when can you do that?"

I pushed my hand farther into the mirror, and it gave way under my touch. It felt cold and goopy against my skin. "Since now, I guess?"

"Well, let's not waste time." He took my suitcase from my hand and motioned for me to walk through. "You have to lead the way now."

"So, are you telling me I can get anywhere that has a mirror now?" I pushed farther and the mirror drifted across my skin like a gooey slime, yet it didn't leave a residue in its wake. On the other side, I felt a cool air and nothing else.

"I mean, technically . . . yes. But it's only recommended to travel to places you've been before. Otherwise, you might walk into someone's living room and . . . you know . . . get stabbed. Or worse, you could expose vampire secrets to the humans, which would be bad for all involved." He gave me a little push between my shoulder blades, urging me forward.

I stepped into the mirror and let it run all over my body. At first it felt like walking through mud, but then when I kicked my other leg through the mirror, it peeled back from me and gave way, letting me step into a long and narrow hallway. It was dim and cold like a damp basement. I glanced to my left and to my right, and it looked like it could go on forever. Martin staggered through behind me with my bags and looked around.

"Impressive." He turned to the right and started walking. "This way."

"How do you know? It all looks the same to me." I fell into step beside him and kept on going even though this felt like some kind of endless matrix.

He pointed to the end of the hall. "See that white speck all the way at the end?"

"Yeah?"

"That's our destination." He hurried his pace. "Come along."

Had I still been human, it would've felt like miles. But

as a vampire, it was only a second until we reached the other mirror. I froze, staring at it. "Same thing?"

"Bit easier once you're on this side. Just push through."

Simple enough. I placed my hand on the portal. *Push through.* I shoved my energy forward and the mirror exploded outwards. Drops of silvery goop flew in all different directions and a smoky tar smell filled the air. When we peeked through the opening, all the vampires in the lobby of The Night Spawn Headquarters stood there covered in shimmering goop—all staring at me.

I gave them a little wave, feeling like I wanted to crawl back to where I came from. "Sorry. My bad."

The interior was chic and clean, or it was before I got there, and it was very London-punk. The walls were painted a matte-black finish, but there were brightly colored paintings everywhere . . . and now silver goop. The floors were black wooden planks laid in a herringbone pattern. Bright, funky furniture was spread throughout the lobby, and there were vampires lounging everywhere. Most still stared at me and my disastrous entrance. It was funny to think I used to believe this was a seedy place with humans lying around being bitten. I loved that I was wrong. I loved that it was so much more —even if everyone looked annoyed at me.

I stepped through the mirror with Martin right behind me. He pulled my luggage through. And his eyes widened at the mess I'd made. "That's one way to make a bloody grand entrance."

"I was kind of hoping to keep it more low-key," I whispered to him, as if every single vampire couldn't hear what I was saying.

"Maybe just clean it up?"

"How the hell would I do that?"

"Perhaps make your intention more known and the mirror will respond?" a deep masculine voice said from one of the seating areas in the lobby. When I turned toward it, I sucked in a breath.

"Theon, it's um... good to see you."

He rose to his feet and gave me a devilish smile. "You mean when our Prince isn't throwing me across a room for breathing the same air as you?"

I shifted from one foot to the other. "I'm so sorry about that."

He shook a glob of the liquid mirror from the sleeve of his leather jacket as he approached the two of us. Strands of his blond hair fell around the sides of his face to his chin, and his sage-green eyes seemed to sparkle in the dimness of the lobby. "No need to apologize. I enjoy a bit of action every now and then."

I tried not to think of what'd just happened only days ago, or how that night had ended with Grayson and me. I motioned to the mirror to distract us both. "Umm, how do I..."

"Fix it?"

"Yeah."

He strolled up to me and wrapped his fingers around

my wrist. He pressed my hand to the frame and let his hand rest over mine. His touch was warm yet totally unfamiliar. "Just think about your intention and see if that helps."

Just go back so I can stop embarrassing myself. All at once, the globs lifted into the air and soared across the room. They smacked into the frame with a wet slapping sound one by one until they were all back in place and the mirror was once again whole. When I tried to pull my hand from his, he held there a moment longer and caught my eye.

"Well done, Piper."

"Ew." Martin smacked the back of his hand. "Do try to control yourself. I know she's a beauty, but really."

Theon dropped his hand and shoved it into his pocket. "Apologies."

"Let's just call it even now." I didn't want to make a fuss on my first night here. My idea was to keep my head down and try to blend in. But when a light round of applause began in the lobby, all I wanted to do was melt into the shadows.

He motioned for them to quiet down, and they all went back to their own conversations. Theon stepped to the side and gave me space to head to the front desk. I found it so odd he'd been in the lobby at the exact moment I came through the mirror.

"Were you here waiting for me or something?"

"Yes," he said simply, without explanation.

My brow furrowed. "Why?"

"We like to make sure we welcome all new vampires into The Night Spawn properly."

Martin groaned. "Oh please, they're just nosy and wanted to see what you're about."

He walked between us and ran the suitcase over Theon's foot as he dragged it along. When we approached the front desk, a female vampire I recognized almost instantly stood there. Her outfit was everything punk and amazing. She wore blue denim shorts, fishnet stockings, black combat boots, and a ripped black T-shirt that showed her hot-pink tank top under it. The whole thing was topped off by a leather jacket with silver zippers everywhere. The makeup around her eyes was dark and dramatic, along with her dark-red lips.

"Amanda, hi. I'm Piper . . . Do you remember me?"

She gave me a warm smile. "Of course. You're looking well."

Martin seemed to whip his tablet from out of nowhere. "Amanda, hi. I'm Martin. Everything should already be arranged for our Piper here."

"Wait . . . stop." She held her hand up. "You're Martin?"

He didn't look up from his tablet. "I am."

"*The* Martin?" A smile broke out over her face.

"I am." He looked up from his tablet. "And you're Amanda."

"You know my name?" She practically bounced on her feet.

Martin glanced at me, then back to her. "I do. Piper just mentioned it."

She deflated a bit. "Oh right."

Theon leaned on the desk. "How do you know Martin?"

Amanda brightened. "He's kind of a legend in the service industry. He can literally get anyone anywhere at any time and can totally get the ungettable. There's no one more connected than Martin."

The three of us all looked at him at the same time. A light-red color tinted his cheeks, and he looked back down at his tablet. "It's an acquired talent. Now, if you'll look at your screen, I believe you'll see Piper's arrangements."

Amanda looked down at her screen, and her eyes widened. "How did you . . . Never mind. See? I told you, he can do anything."

I chuckled. "I didn't realize you were famous."

He gave me a little elbow. "Not like you, the only made vampire from The House of Shade."

I elbowed him back. "I won't tell if you won't."

"Deal."

Theon chuckled and shook his head. "I'm afraid that probably won't work . . . for either of you. News travels fast in the underground."

Amanda pressed a few more buttons on the tablet. "Okay, you're all set. You're in apartment 1410. Your fingerprint will open the door for you. No key needed.

Everything you need should be there, as per Martin's arrangements."

Martin grinned at her. "Lovely, Amanda, thank you."

"You're so welcome."

He took a step toward the hallway behind her, then hesitated. "If ever you'd like to be moved to my service, I'd be happy to have you."

Amanda practically fell out from behind the desk. "Yes! Absolutely yes."

"Lovely. I'll arrange for your replacement." He didn't say another word as he walked down the hall with my bag dragging behind him.

"I guess this is where I follow." I gave Theon and Amanda a small wave and turned to follow Martin.

Theon fell into step beside me, and suddenly it felt awkward. "I don't need a bodyguard, you know?"

"Oh, I know. I just figured it'd be nice to welcome you properly and see if you like your accommodations." He kept his pace with me, and I couldn't decide if this was nice or if I wanted him to leave.

"Umm, okay."

Martin shot me a *what the hell* look over his shoulder and continued down the hallway. It wasn't that I minded Theon hanging out, but I didn't want to bring any more attention to myself. I just wanted to be me . . . Piper . . . not this House of Shade princess.

The hall was long and had multiple doors. Each of them was made of frosted glass and thick black metal. The doors opened and closed automatically as vampires walked in and out. We walked by the salon I'd seen before, and I still wanted to stop in there. It was modern and chic with black chairs, black counters, and bright hot-pink walls. But there weren't any hairdressers. Instead, men and women all stood behind their clients with magic swirling around them. With a flick of the wrist, magic of all colors flew from their fingers and around the heads of their clients, changing their hairstyles completely.

"Martin?"

"Yes?"

"Can I get my hair done in there one day?"

He smirked at me over his shoulder. "A single word from you and it shall be done."

"Sweet." That looked like one hell of an experience that I did not want to miss.

The farther we strode, the more impressed I was with The Night Spawn Headquarters. As we walked, I peeked into restaurants for vampires who could eat, bars to hang out in, shoe stores, clothing stores . . . everything anyone could want was right here so close to the lobby. When we reached the end of the hallway, it opened to a huge area with a stained, glass-domed ceiling. The glass showed pictures of sights all around the world: London, Paris, the pyramids of Egypt, Niagara Falls. Every scene was more beautiful than the next.

Dim light glowed from the stained-glass, sending wild colors around the wide-open area. I tilted my head back, taking it all in. "Isn't it kind of dangerous to have a window like that?"

Martin chuckled. "It's just lighting behind the glass to mimic the different times of day."

"That's brilliant."

Everything about The Night Spawn called to me. It was almost comfortable and familiar. We walked a bit farther toward a railing, and when I looked over it, there were so many levels going deeper into the ground. They looked like dark, golden rings descending straight down into darkness.

"This is intense. How deep does it go?" I glanced over to Theon.

"Right now, it goes down fifty floors. But it's expanding in all different directions." He grinned at me, then pointed down the pathway to the left. "We'll go by tram."

Just as I was about to say *what tram,* a sleek-looking shiny silver train pulled into a dim pathway off to the side. It was so quiet, not like the trains in Boston, and unlike the subway cars of New York, it was sleek and clean. The windows were mirrored on the outside, and a single red stripe ran down the side of it. The doors slid open and vampires flowed out from the tram, going about their business.

Martin crooked his finger at me, then pointed to the tram. "This way."

The three of us stepped onto the train, and it all felt so normal. Seats lined both sides of the car, and there were poles spread throughout that we could hold on to. When Theon motioned for me to take a seat, I shook my head. I didn't want to say I was too excited, too curious, and too nervous to sit still. I wanted to walk all those flights down just to burn some energy off. In Salem, it was easy to constantly walk and brush off any excess emotions or energy.

Theon wrapped his hand around one of the poles. "You might want to hold on."

I wrapped my hand around the pole just below his and the tram shot forward. My body rocked with the motion. I'd never ridden on anything that moved so fast. When I looked out the windows, everything flashed by in a blur. The tram didn't run in a straight line, it dipped and twisted like a roller coaster. My stomach went up into my throat and then back down to my toes. My grip tightened on the pole as the tram took a hard right turn and then a hard left. The metal groaned under my grip and dented with each of my fingers. Theon arched his eyebrows at me.

"You okay?"

I peeled my fingers from the pole and shook them out. "Yeah, I bet that happens all the time."

"Not really, no. Everything is reinforced for vampire strength." The tram came to a screeching halt, and I fought to keep my balance. He nodded toward the little dent. "Impressive though."

"Sorry." I hadn't meant to do it, and here I was thinking I'd gotten control of my strength.

"It's not a problem." Martin tapped on his tablet. "It'll be fixed by tomorrow."

The doors slid open, and we walked out onto the platform full of people. When Theon appeared, they all seemed to pause for a moment, staring at him. They weren't as awestruck as they were with Grayson, but Theon drew attention in his own way. Female *and* male vampires swooned ever so slightly as he walked by with that air of confidence he had. It was like he was almost famous among The Night Spawn. He strolled with his head back and shoulders straight. It was almost cocky, but not quite.

As we walked away from the platform through an archway, the walls opened up to a wide-open lobby the size of a mall. The walls were a dark brown that looked like different hues of sand all over the walls and floor. Seating areas were spread through the wide-open space with oversized, brightly colored furniture that matched the lobby above. Doors slid open and closed, giving me a peek into little dorm-like apartments. In the lobby area, there were small carts that dispensed blood of all different types and flavors like a coffee cart. We stopped just in front of my door, 1410.

Martin motioned to a little black box on the side of the door. "That's how you'll open and close your door. Just place your finger on the keypad. It's a bio-scanner, so your fingerprints will open the door. It can also sense your blood type and match it to your registry."

"Oh, so we're fancy?" I placed my finger on the pad and the door slid open.

It was no palace suite, but it reminded me more of home. There was a small kitchenette right when I entered the room, as well as a two-person table. Farther back, there was a queen-sized bed with a thick black comforter and a mountain of pillows. Off to the side was another sliding door that led to the small bathroom. It wasn't as big as the one I had in the castle, but it was nice enough, with white tiles and dark countertops. I loved it instantly. It was cozy and warm with just the right about of space.

Martin walked over to open the closet and inspect everything there. Gone were the extravagant ball gowns, and in their place were jeans, sweaters, T-shirts, and seemingly any other kind of comfy clothes that I could think of. "Everything looks good here."

Theon chuckled and looked at me. "It really does."

"Ew, don't be that guy, Theon." A girl with a curtain of straight black hair that fell to her hips walked into the room. Her hair was loosely braided down her side and she wore a bright red long-sleeved shirt, dark jeans, and a bright scarf with different-colored glitter. Her skin was a dark, rich brown that matched her eyes and hair.

Theon sighed. "Always good to see you, Prisha. Where's your other half?"

"I'm here." Another girl sauntered into the room and crossed her arms. When she stood next to Prisha, they looked almost identical, except this girl's hair curled at the ends in soft waves and her eyes were a vivid emerald-green that stood out against her dark skin.

"Piper, may I introduce you to the Gupta sisters, Prisha, and Sanchita."

I held my hand out to them. "I'm Piper. It's nice to meet you."

Sanchita was the first to take my hand and shake it. "Piper, where are you from?"

I wanted to say *all over* because as a kid I had moved around a lot. "Salem."

She arched her eyebrows. "Ah, the land of witches."

"I suppose so." I chuckled. "And you're sisters?"

Prisha nodded. "Originally from India, but now we call London home. I was changed first, then I took her down with me."

"We couldn't be separated." Sanchita glanced at her sister. "It was too difficult."

My heart panged at the thought of not having Dice. But now that I was here, it brought me one step closer to her . . . and maybe to changing her. These two seemed so down to earth, like the kind of friends I would've made back home. "I totally get that."

"Are you two always getting into whatever's happening around here? I'd like to know how you get your info." Theon crossed his arms and leaned back on the wall.

"Like we'd tell you." Prisha's beautiful accent rolled over each letter as she spoke and shook her head at him. Her hands moved with all the attitude she clearly felt. I nearly chuckled at the lack of influence Theon seemed to have over them.

Martin snickered. "I'd like to know too."

"Wouldn't we all," a deeper voice came from behind us, and we all spun around to find Marius filling the door. He was tall and slim with dark, spiky hair cut close to his head on the sides. His face was strong and angular, with plump lips and a thin goatee around his mouth. Though the rest of us were in everyday attire, he wore tight, dark, gothic pants, a loose knit black sweater, and a modern trench coat that stopped just at his ankles.

Martin and I glanced at each other in a moment of *what the fuck*. Marius was the ambassador to The Night Spawn, and essentially, he spoke for all of them when it came to policies and ways of life in the underground city. There was no reason for him to be here . . . now . . . with me.

"Marius." I tried to make my voice sound calm and passive. "It's nice to see you again."

He walked into my little apartment and looked around. "This is pleasant. You have one of the nicer apartments for a Blood Born. The others are far less . . . accommodating. I believe you'd call them slums."

That didn't seem right to me. From what I knew about Grayson and Titus, they wouldn't let anyone live like that. But I was here to lay low and not make trouble. I'd already argued with on ambassador, I didn't need to argue with another. I chose my words carefully. "Oh, I had no idea."

"Yes, I'll take you to see them if you like. In fact, I'd like to take all of you to see the rest of The Night Spawn underground city."

"Oh . . . I . . ." How did one turn down an invitation for a tour? Though, I would've rather explored with Martin or even the Gupta sisters. "I was thinking about walking around with Martin and maybe Prisha and Sanchita if they wanted to go."

"We'd love to." Prisha beamed. "There are some really cool places to see."

Marius waved to the door. "Why don't we all go? I'd love the opportunity to get to know everyone better. Wouldn't I, Theon?"

"Of course." Theon gave us that easy, agreeable smile.

I hesitated, feeling like I was being put on the spot. I didn't want to be rude and say no, but I also didn't want to have to deal with more vampire politics, and with Marius around, I knew that's what it would be. When they all turned and looked to me, I forced a smile to my face.

"Sounds like fun." *I am really getting good at lying in this world.*

CHAPTER TWENTY

DICE

"Look, I'm not sure where you're taking me, but yesterday you said we were going to find Piper, and today I feel like you're yanking my chain. Was that really her on the phone or just someone who sounded like her?"

Yesterday with Kylian in the diner was suspect, but today was even more so. He'd gotten me on a flight from Boston to New York. The flight was an awkward one for me and a silent one for him. I'd fidgeted the whole time while he pretended to sleep. He stopped in front of a thick metal gate that reminded me of something you'd see on the front of a castle. It stood at the center of a gothic-looking brick building. There were no windows and only the single door. On the corners in the front, it looked like a tower stood at each point.

The sounds of New York surrounded us, and I didn't know why, but I found comfort in all the noise: the beeping horns, the racing cars, the loud music and sounds of people coming and going. The street was lined with cars and the smell of restaurants down the street. Everything about it was familiar. I knew where I was and how to get home if I had to. I knew there were ways for me to get where I felt more comfortable. It was all so fishy, and my red flags were waving.

"You should just trust me."

"Yeah, I'm sure that's what Dahmer said to his victims before he munched on their parts." I glanced around the street, making sure I was in view of other people.

Kylian's head snapped around and his crystal-green eyes met mine. "You think I'm going to kill you . . . then eat you?"

I crossed my arms. "You never know with you people."

"You people?" His brow furrowed.

"Yes, you know . . . the good-looking guys who can't be trusted."

He chuckled and strands of his inky hair fell over the side of his face. "Don't know if I like being considered a *you people.*"

I shrugged. "I'm sure you've been considered worse."

"I'm sure I have." He pulled his cell phone from his pocket and held it to his ear. It barely rang once when a voice came from the other end. Then Kylian responded, "Yeah. You got it?"

There was a moment of pause, then he nodded. "I'm

outside. Nah, I'm not coming in. I can't bring a normal behind those walls. Yeah, see you in a second."

He hung up and slid the phone back into his pocket.

I narrowed my eyes at him. "What's a normal?"

"You are."

I didn't know why, but that sounded like it should be offensive. "Oh."

"Relax. It's not a bad thing . . . you're just *you*."

"Why does that sound like an insult?"

Before he could answer, the front gate creaked open and a tiny person in an oversized hoodie and holding a big pillow popped out. Kylian smiled down at the person, and when she pulled her hood back, I froze for a second. She was otherworldly. Her skin held a slightly green tint to it. It wasn't sickly, it was more like she'd lived her life in nature. A shining scale print ran around her right eye and down her cheek. Scales covered her neck and shoulders, but they were so delicate and glossy in an entirely beautiful way, like a mermaid trapped on land. Her short black hair stood in soft spikes from her head and a single long braid ran down the side of her head and over her shoulder. Sweeping bands fell across her forehead and curled around the side of her face. Her silver eyes glowed in the mid-afternoon light. I couldn't tell if her makeup skills were just that on point or if I was losing my damn mind.

She yawned and barely glanced at me. "Why this one?"

He shrugged. "Kind of intriguing, don't you think?"

"Meh, I've seen weirder." She looked at me sideways.

"Umm. Hi, my name is Dice . . . not *this one*." I waved my hand at her.

Kylian snickered. "Soto, this is Dice. Dice, this is Soto."

"Nice to meet you." I held my hand out to her.

"Yeah, I don't like to be touched." She looked at my hand like it would somehow kill her and held her pillow a little tighter.

"Okayyyyy." I shoved it back into my pocket.

She cupped her hand around her mouth as though she was going to tell me a secret. "You never know who might try to kill you or steal your bed."

My eyes widened. Was she joking? *I mean, I worried about my stuff when I was in the foster care system too. Nothing was safe.* "Yeah, that's a legit problem."

"You have what I need?" Kylian cut in.

Soto nodded and pulled a small vial with clear liquid from her hoodie pocket. She shook it up, then handed it over to him. "Should get you where you need to be."

"Drugs . . ." I groaned. "You brought me here to get you some kind of drug? Really? I need to get to Piper, not run all over the city to feed your addiction." I turned to walk away from him.

His hand wrapped around my upper arm, and he pulled me around to face him. Kylian towered over me. His breath fanned across my face, and his chest was flush against me. "I don't do drugs . . . but I *do*, do my job."

I tried to pull my arm free, but his grip only got

tighter. Even through my jacket, I felt the pinch of his fingers. "Let go of me. I knew this was a bad idea."

He dragged me across the street and between two buildings. He dropped the vial down at his feet, then stomped on it. A shimmering vaper rose from the cracked vial. "In you go."

"I'm not inhaling that shit."

He rolled his eyes. "No one asked you to."

When I yanked at my arm once more, he shoved me into the vapor and I stumbled forward, tripping from the momentum. Kylian's hand disappeared from my arm as I landed roughly on my hands and knees. The pain vibrated up through my palms and into my arms. My hair fell over my face, and I already knew there were scrapes on my hands.

"You're such an ass." I threw my hair out of my face and popped to my feet. I held my fist up, ready to swing at him. I'd had enough of this shit—the mystery, the weird travel . . . the being with a stranger and being forced to trust him when I really didn't freaking trust him.

I froze and backed up. When I looked at Kylian, it was as though he stood on the other side of a doorway with a softly glowing outline. He was in the street we'd just been on in New York, but I wasn't there. I staggered back and looked around. I stood in an older historical looking room. The walls were high and made of stone that matched the ceiling and floor. On each side of me there were cells with no bars. Each cell had something different in it. Some overflowed with wild plants while others held shelves of vials with colorful liquids in them.

"What the fuckkkk." My heart raced, and a tremor ran through my body.

Kylian stepped through the window doorway thing. "Sorry to drop in."

He looked over my shoulder, speaking to someone behind me. I spun around to face a small woman with straight black hair and even darker eyes. They were huge and round and glistened in the dim lights of the room we were in. She sat upside down in a throne-like chair with her legs crossed and stretched vertically up the back, and her hair fell straight toward the floor.

"Did you make an appointment?"

Kylian crossed his arms over his chest. "No."

"How did you even get here?" A man just as big as Kylian and even meaner-looking melted from the shadows beside the woman in the chair. His hair wasn't nearly as long as Kylian's, but it was oil-black and fell to his chin. His eyes were like molten gold as he glared at Kylian.

"Stole a portal potion."

What the hell was a portal potion?

The girl spun around in the chair to sit up straight. "The one on the shelf in my room?"

"I don't know, O. Probably." Kylian shifted from one foot to the other, looking exasperated.

A wide smile spread across her face, and she turned to the guy with golden eyes. "Pay up. I win."

A groan rumbled in his chest as he pulled a long weapon from behind his back. It looked like two knives strapped together with a handle in the middle. Burgundy smoke spilled from somewhere and wrapped around the knife. It shot from his hand right at her. It was so fast I lost track of it until she just suddenly caught it. She looked it over in her hand, staring at how the candlelight glinted off the blades.

"Mine now."

"Like you need another." He rolled his eyes.

Her head snapped up. "When it comes to weapons of destruction, there are never enough. Never. Enough, Cross."

They all seemed so comfortable together, like this was an average day and I hadn't walked into some kind of messed-up world. "Does someone want to tell me WHAT THE HELL IS GOING ON HERE?"

All their gazes swung toward me. Kylian was the first to speak. "Piper told me to drop you off here."

"And where is *here*? Where is Piper?" For December, the air was thick and humid, like being in Florida. It was some kind of castle but unlike anything I'd ever seen before.

The woman they called O popped to her feet. "Hi, I'm Ophelia. Welcome to my island. Formally, the castle of Alataris, but he's dead, so it's mine now. Don't worry I didn't kill him . . . At least not all the way."

I turned to Kylian. "Is she for real?"

He nodded.

"You brought me to an island, wherever here is, from New York?" This wasn't real. He put my face in that vapor shit, and I was tripping balls right now. That was the only possible explanation. "How is that possible?"

He shrugged. "Magic."

"Magic? Yeah, right." I shook my head, trying to get rid of the effects of whatever he'd done to me.

Ophelia chuckled. "I love it when they figure out there's more to the world than the boring shit they know. It's like watching a baby deer learn to walk."

She opened her hand and gray smoke poured from her palm. "There is indeed a world of magic."

"I'm kind of surprised you don't believe that . . . given what you've seen." Kylian bent down and placed his hand on the stone, and a piece of the stone rose up and formed into the shape of a small snowflake no bigger than the size of a dime.

My eyes widened, and I took a sharp breath. I'd lived in Salem long enough to know there was more to the world and that it lurked in the shadows, but this . . . this was a lot. "So, I'm on an island? Surrounded by magic?"

Kylian nodded. "And on that note, my job is done here."

He stepped backward through the window thing. I ran toward it, hoping to dive through to get back to a world I knew, but it closed up before I could even get close. I stopped short of where he'd just been. I stuck my hand out to reach for the window, but I knew it was gone.

"Are you gonna freak out? Because if you are, Ophelia has a potion for that." Cross, the larger guy, sat down on the stairs leading up the throne and kicked his legs out. "I'm not real good with freak outs."

I swallowed down my panic and tried to focus. "I'm not going to freak out. I've seen some shit over the last few weeks that I can't explain. I didn't lose it then, and I'm not gonna lose it now. Besides, I've almost killed someone."

Ophelia wrinkled her nose and shook her head. "Almost?"

"Yeah." I lied, hoping it'd make me seem more formidable.

She lowered her voice to a whisper. "We don't advertise our failures."

It definitely hadn't worked. I glanced from Ophelia to Cross and back again. "Are you going to kill me?"

Ophelia broke out into little fits of laughter. "If I was going to kill you, you'd already be dead."

"Truth." He nodded.

Ophelia didn't stop laughing. "Why are they so touchy about the stabby stab? This one with the almost killing and Piper with the I could have killed—"

"—You saw Piper?"

"Yep." She twisted in the seat so her legs hung over one arm and she slouched on the other side.

"Can you take me to her?" Hope bloomed in my chest.

"I can do whatever I want." She shrugged seeming board with this conversation.

I had no doubt of that. "Will you take me to her?"

"Probably." She sighed and kicked her legs back and forth while cleaning her nails with the tip of the blade.

"Is she . . . is she like you now?" I *knew* there was something wrong with Piper. For her to be alive for this long and not find me or tell me what was going on wasn't who she was or who we were as besties. There was something keeping her away. Maybe this was it.

"She wishes she was as cool as us," Cross mumbled as he pulled out his own blade and started sharpening it with a rock he pulled from his pocket.

"Then what is she? Why is she staying away from me? Why so much secrecy?" The questions I'd been dying to ask tumbled from my mouth one after another. I'd been holding them in for so long, and this was the first time I'd even gotten close to someone who might have an answer.

Ophelia glanced at Cross, and he shook his head. She rolled her eyes and turned to face me. "She's . . . other. You know, kind of like you."

My breath left me in a rush. *Like me? What the hell am I?*

CHAPTER TWENTY-ONE

PIPER

I walked from one mess right to another, and I hated being stuck into issues I had no business being in. I was here to figure out how to live in this new world, and somehow I'd gotten dragged into another disaster I wasn't ready for. Marius strolled beside me. We were so close the smell of his cologne blocked out the scent of anything else surrounding us. The walkways were crowded with vampires of all shapes and sizes. They moved like traffic during rush hour, all jammed together like fish caught in a net.

They all seemed so dazed and unhappy. The air was thick and even hotter this far down. This part of the underground city looked more like the rundown parts of Boston where violence was high and it wouldn't be safe to walk at night. The vampires looked defeated, dirty, and forlorn.

"Why is this like this?" With all the cool things

happening above, I couldn't fathom why it'd be like this below.

Marius gave a heavy sigh. "This is what I've been working to resolve with The House of Shade. The Night Spawn are grossly mistreated."

When I glanced over my shoulder to the Gupta sisters, they had their eyes down and walked without any of the life they'd shown before. Even Martin was stiff and uncomfortable with his movements. Something wasn't right down here. I didn't know why, but it wasn't sitting well with me. Grayson would never let this happen to anyone. No matter what Marius said I knew Gray well enough to know that this was a set up. Marius wanted me to believe The House of Shade would let vampires live like this, but I wouldn't, not for one second.

"You don't think they're doing enough?"

"Hardly, my dear. Honestly, they look down upon all of us." He glanced around. "I believe we're all created equal."

"It's just a shame they don't." Theon moved to my other side, and I felt like I was being surrounded. I didn't dare show an ounce of discomfort. Something nagged at me to stay and find out what exactly was happening.

After sitting at that dinner and having witnessed all the things Grayson worked for, I found it hard to believe Marius. "I'm not sure I agree."

He paused, stopping in the middle of the crowd, and held his arms out to his sides. "This is evidence of their care, their work. We live in poverty while they dine on many courses each night. They live in castles, and we rot underground."

When I had nothing to say in return, he turned from me and started to stroll, waiting slowly for me to catch up. A slow smile spread across his face. "I suppose as a human you're used to the difference in living situations. Your world is a cruel one as well. You must be desensitized to it all."

"Hardly. But I like to see things from all angles before I make a decision about anything." He wasn't wrong. Things were in a sad state this deep in The Night Spawn City. What would Grayson think if he were here? I knew what he would think. He'd be pissed that his people were left to live like this.

"See? I told you she was brilliant, didn't I?" Theon smirked at me.

I narrowed my eyes at him. "And that doesn't feel condescending at all. How old are you again?"

He pressed his hand to his chest. "I was changed when I was twenty-five."

"And how long ago was that exactly?"

He hesitated. "Hundred or so."

"Careful. Your age is showing." I sighed. "But you're not wrong, I am brilliant, which brings me to my next question: why are you showing me all of this? I came here to learn about being a vampire and to figure out who I am in this world, not to be used for political agendas."

Marius placed his hand on my shoulder. "No one will

dare try to sway you in either direction, my dear, but we always like to offer a different perspective to what one has known."

"I'm not sure you know what I've been through to be able to determine what perspective I should be taking."

He dropped his hand from my shoulder and glanced around like he couldn't believe my audacity to have my own thoughts. "And your opinion on the sickness?"

"Well, what is happening? Does anyone know? Do you? Until we all know what's happening, the only thing that could be said is that it's awful and a solution needs to be found."

"I suppose you are correct. But I would think The House of Shade would be more involved."

"I'm pretty sure they are very involved." Images of those poor vampires inside the holding cages in the lab played in my mind.

He took a step back. "Well, if you are ever in need of anything . . . I am at your service."

Marius gave me a low bow, then turned into the crowd surrounding us. Martin moved in closer to me. "What is it with you and people wanting your attention?"

"I have no idea. I'm a nobody." I watched as the crowd closed in behind Marius, making him disappear.

"You're not nobody," Theon whispered. "You'll soon see."

Did he know something I didn't, or was that his way of flirting?

Prisha hooked her arm through my elbow. "This was the weirdest shit I've seen in quite some time."

"I know, right? Marius among the common people." Sanchita chuckled. "Cold day in hell."

"You both have no idea what you're talking about. He's busy trying to make things better for the lot of us," Theon snapped at the two of them.

The sisters shared a look, then both busted out into fits of laughter. Prisha flipped her hair off her shoulder and gave my arm a little tug. "Come on. You want to see something fun? I'll show you something fun."

Of all the things I thought would happen tonight, this was not it. I didn't know that I'd find new friends so quickly, get dragged along by Marius, or end up in parts of the underground I didn't know existed. "Where are we going?"

Sanchita hooked her arm on my other side. "To see the future."

CHAPTER TWENTY-TWO

GRAYSON

Whenever I entered Evermore Academy, it felt like stepping back to when things were simpler. I found comfort in the bustle of the school. It was all so innocent. Mostly. So different from the wars, magic, and plotting that defined my life now. I felt more at home here at Evermore than I did even in my own castle. I didn't realize how much light Piper had brought to the castle in her short time there, but I looked forward to seeing her—even if she loathed me with the fire of a thousand suns.

As I strolled through the courtyard, I huddled into my coat and pulled the scarf around my neck a little higher. Snow crunched under my feet and fog blew from my mouth with each breath I took. The cool air pricked at my cheeks. Sometimes it astounded me that the weather I enjoyed in London was so similar to that of New York.

Christmas here was as chilly, merry, and bloody bright as it was home. Within the castle, garland hung around the railing of the second floor of the courtyard and wound around each of the beams and columns.

The water in the fountain trickled lightly and gave off little clouds of steam in the way a heated pool would in the winter. The fountain glowed from within, illuminating the area around it. Bright-yellow caution tape surrounded it, forcing the students to give it a wide berth. I chuckled at the way Matteaus hoped to save the damn thing that was destined to be destroyed at every opportunity. I walked past it and headed under the balcony to one of the hallways off the courtyard. I turned and went down a set of stairs off the hallway. This used to be an abandoned part of the school where the secrets of a hidden cast of witches remained hidden until the Queens of the Witch Court united with the warlocks and unlocked their hidden connection.

Now the abandoned underground wing was alive and bustling with power. I felt it running over my skin—the power of new warlocks and experienced ones. Even walking down the dorm room corridor and glancing into rooms as I passed, I saw bright, sparkling pink magic fill a room and move all the furniture around like a tornado. Another room filled with a plume of green magic, and a bunch of frogs began flooding from the room and into the hallway. I turned down another hallway and stopped in front of a door I'd walked through a thousand times before to help others. This time I would be the one asking for help.

I wrapped my hand around the doorknob and shoved the door wide open. In the center of the room was a huge wooden table with thick legs and an even thicker tabletop. A map of the world was spread out across it with red pins in all different places. Queen Zinnia stood in the middle of the room and at the center of the table. Her midnight hair was wild around her face, hanging in thick tatters. Her sapphire eyes snapped up to mine.

"What happened?" Zinnia was the most powerful witch in the world, with the ability to siphon off magic from anyone or anything and use it against her enemies. Though she was deadly, she never abused her power. She wore a hoodie and black jeans and topped the whole thing off with a thick gothic crown. It was very un-royal by vampire standards.

"Why do you immediately assume something happened?" I asked. *What gave me away?*

Serrina, the Queen of Desires, looked me up and down. Strands of her full blonde hair fell around her shoulders. She too was very low-key in a red turtleneck and blue jeans. She held more pins in one hand and a phone in the other. "Your pants are wrinkled."

"So?" I looked down at them.

"I've never known a time when you weren't pressed within an inch of your life, with not a hair out of place. And now, well, you kind of look like . . . shit."

I rolled my eyes. "Says the woman who's the personification of desire. It's like perfection telling you you're bloody imperfect."

"Aww! He thinks I'm perfect." She winked and blew me a kiss.

"He's not wrong." Ashryn, the Elf guardian, spoke softly from the other side of the room. She was sitting on top of a table with one of her legs dangling and the other curled to her chest. The tips of her ears poked out from her sandy hair. Her all-knowing forest-green eyes looked right through me and sent a chill down my spine.

"Oi, don't look at me like you know everything in my soul. Bit much today."

She smirked. "Oh, but I do."

"You're worse than Maze." I glanced around. "Where the hell is the bloody psychic?"

Zinnia sighed. "That one marches to his own beat and does his own thing. And now that Tilly, his soulmate, has been saved things have been weird with them. She's showing some new powers and we still haven't figured out what the hell it means."

"At least she's still alive." I found it hard not to keep the bitterness of my own situation with Piper out of my voice.

Zinnia tilted her head to the side, watching me, but she said nothing. The door flew open and Tucker, her soulmate, walked in with Tabi, Queen of the Elements, and Logan, the most posh bastard alive. A smile spread across Tucker's face.

"Gray, about time you resurfaced." He shook my hand

and brought me in for a quick pat. The smell of burning embers filled my nose as he stepped back.

"Had some sorting to do back home."

Zinnia rolled her eyes. "He's lying. He's got girl problems."

Tuck scoffed. "Gray doesn't do girl problems, right?"

When I didn't answer, he met my eye. "Right?"

I ran my hand through my hair. "You might want to sit down for this. I need . . . I need your assistance."

He motioned to the door. "Let's go somewhere we can talk."

"No. I mean," I looked to Zinnia and the other Witch Queens, "I need all of your help."

They all froze, staring at me, and Tabi moved in beside Zinnia. Her hair stood on edged and fanned around her face in tight, wild curls. Golden sparkles glittered on her cheeks and stood out against her dark skin. Her eyes were intense and only focused on me.

"So, it *is* a girl problem."

I groaned and ran my hands through my hair, tugging at the strands in frustration. I backed up and leaned on the table against the wall. "Yes and no."

"Hold on. We're going to need more for this." She scribbled something on a piece of paper and held it in her hand. "Little help, Tuck."

He shot a flame from his hand, and it lit the edge of the paper on fire. Zinnia's silvery magic wrapped around the paper as it disintegrated into ash and fell from her fingers to the floor. "I know just who to call."

A moment later, a swirling bright blue portal opened at the back of the room, and one of my best mates, Beckett, strolled through with Astrid, his soulmate. Beckett and I had hit it off almost instantly the first time we met. We were complete opposites in looks. I was dark-haired and dark-eyed, and Beckett was blond-haired and blue-eyed. When he strolled through, a wide grin spread over his face.

"Gray, what's going on?"

I sighed. "You might want to sit down for this."

Astrid, Queen of the Occult and manifester of all things imaginable, stood at his side. Her wild auburn hair looked like it'd been whipped about in a wind tunnel. Her emerald eyes sparkled, and she arched her eyebrows at me. "Are we going into another world to battle monsters?"

"Not that I know of?" My brow furrowed. "It's not on my agenda as of late."

"Very well." She walked into the room and moved to stand on the other side of the table with Zinnia, Tabi, and Serrina. The power in the room was overwhelming, and for a moment I had a fraction of hope that I might somehow find an answer on how to fix the shit-storm whirling around me.

Astrid looked around at the others while Beckett sat on a tabletop on the side of the room next to Logan. The smile had dropped from his face as he watched me like a hawk. He motioned to me. "You have the floor, vamp."

I sucked in a deep breath. Titus had forbidden me

from telling Piper or anyone in the vampire world about my plight, but my friends were either of those two things. "I've been cursed."

Their voices rose all at once.

"What the fuck?"

"Who would do this?"

"I'll kill them."

"No way!"

"We can take it off."

Zinnia held her hand up and everyone stopped. "How do you know you're cursed?"

"It's a family curse on The House of Shade." I threw my shoulders back. "It's been a bloody plague on us all, and now it's coming for me."

"But, like, how do you know?"

"Because the curse killed my father." It was like I'd dropped a bomb in the room. Everyone fell silent.

"Gray, I'm so sorry." Zinnia's face fell and she looked like she was about to come around the table to give me a hug. But I didn't want it. I didn't want their sympathy. I wanted a room full of killers who would go to any length to get what they needed.

I shook my head. "He was lost before I was born. But that brings me to this . . . I'm sure his fate will soon be mine."

Astrid leaned her elbows on the table. "Tell us why?"

They were words I remembered but never wanted to recite.

"Mark these words, avenge thy crime,
Bound by blood in space and time.
From kin to kin one wretched vine,
A wicked curse seals a shaded line.
What was denied shall now be taken,
For when thee love thee turn forsaken.
Deep in thee veins thy soul will burn,
Forever more thy thirst shall yearn.
Breath by breath thy mind unwound,
To madness now thy life is drowned.
And if fate shall deem thy love requited,
Don't speak the words or curse the blighted.
For if on the wrist thy souls entwined,
Death shall call and forever find."

Serrina shook her arms out and made a gagging noise. "Does anyone else have chills?"

"I think we all do." Tabi glanced around the room at the others. "Whatever that curse was, it was powerful and strong as hell. Even now the words feel like a layer over my skin."

"Write it down for us." Astrid flicked her hand and her golden power soared across the room to float a pen and a pad of paper in the air in front of me. "And avenge thy crime? What did your family do, and who did they do it to?"

I grabbed the pen and paper and started scribbling. "That's the thing. I don't know, and Titus doesn't remember, so I suspect the curse is older than he is. If I knew who cast it, that might help . . . but again, we don't know."

Zinnia walked around the table and took the paper from me. Her eyes roamed over the writing. "Bound by blood in space and time. From kin to kin one wretched vine. A wicked curse seals a shaded line. That bit seems obvious, the curse holds for any member of The House of Shade. Someone very powerful did this, Gray. To curse future generations would take ancient magic. Dark and ancient magic."

"You think Alataris could have?" I didn't want to grasp at straws, but if anyone knew curses and this magic, it would be the people in this room.

She bit her bottom lip. "I'm not sure. It's a possibility. We'll have to research it."

The paper disappeared from Zinnia's hand and appeared in Astrid's in a flourish of golden magic. "For when thy love thee turn forsaken. Deep in thy veins thy soul will burn, forever more thy thirst shall yearn.

"What does that mean?"

Serrina met my eye. "When a member of The House of Shade falls in love, the curse will take effect."

All eyes swung toward me, and I shifted from one foot to the other. I wasn't much for talking about the bloody ins and outs of my feelings. But I trusted everyone in this room. I sucked in a deep breath. "I'm fighting it with every ounce of my being."

"Awww, Gray, you're in love." Tabi clutched her hands over her heart and smiled. "It's sweet."

"I can bloody well assure you it is not sweet." I spoke the next lines of the curse. "Deep in thee veins thy soul will burn, forever more thy thirst shall yearn. Breath by breath, thy mind unwound, to madness now thy life is drowned. And if fate shall deem thy love requited, don't speak the words or curse the blighted. For if on the wrist thy souls entwined, death shall call and forever find."

Zinnia's eyes widened and she lowered her voice. "If you fall in love, you'll be driven to madness, forever walking in the vampire thirst."

"And thinking of nothing else, and I would . . . I would . . ." I couldn't say the words. Couldn't think it. Didn't dare to speak it.

"You'll try to kill her," Beckett finished for me.

When I gave a silent nod, they all stood there staring at me. No one spoke, no one breathed, the curse hung heavy in the air between us all. I didn't want to descend into madness. I didn't want to try to kill Piper. She was . . . everything.

"Hold up. So, you're telling me you have a lady friend and we've never met her?" Logan scoffed. "That's cold."

"You're one for keeping secrets." I didn't mean to snap at him or bring up his own sins in this conversation. The pressure of it all was starting to get to me. "I'm sorry, mate. That was uncalled for."

Logan had been a pretty boy when I first met him, but it'd never actually been him. Once they got the real Logan back from weeks of torture and imprisonment, he'd turned into something . . . darker and more twisted.

His blond hair was longer and he had a constant five o'clock shadow. Before he was tailored in the latest fashions, much like myself, but now he wore torn jeans, ripped shirts, and worn-in flannels. He waved my words away.

"You're not wrong."

"Well, to answer your question: yes. I wasn't looking for Piper, but somehow fate had other plans. We found each other." I felt my lips turn up in a smile. "You lot would like her. She hates my guts at the moment."

Beckett chuckled. "What'd you do?"

"I love that you assume it was him who made the mistake." Astrid smirked at him.

"I've learned." He winked at her, and it gave me hope that if those two could figure things out, then maybe Piper and I could too.

"And you'd be right." I didn't look at them. "Any number of things, I suppose."

"Spill, leech." Tucker crossed his arms over his chest.

"Well, I've lied. I nearly got her killed and was only able to save her by actually killing her and turning her into a vampire. I find her damn near irresistible, which makes me have to be close to her while at the same time pushing her as far away as I possibly can so I don't, you know, become another one of the besotted cursed."

Zinnia shook her head. "So you messed it up?"

"Yep."

"Any chance of fixing it?"

Even if there were, there was only one thing I could do to assure there would be. "I'm hoping if we break the curse, I could repair things."

"And if that doesn't work . . ." Serrina narrowed her eyes at me, ". . . beg."

"That's the backup plan, love." I clapped my hands together. "So, how do we break it?"

The queens all looked at each other. None of them said a word. Finally, Zinnia was the first to speak. "I think we need to speak to The Fallen."

"I already did, and they said, and I quote, *start at the beginning*, end quote."

Tabi rolled her eyes. "Super helpful."

"That's what I said." I'd hoped they'd help me more, but deep down I knew they couldn't interfere with us—no matter how much they wanted to.

"Okay, then we'll start with that." Zinnia sighed and let her eyes roam over the map with all the pins in it. "Everything else we can pause for a bit."

"Excellent, because the sooner the better. Piper needs me."

Tabi arched her brows at me. "Why would she need you? She hates you."

"She struggles to control her thirst, and in the vampire world, that's a death sentence. I don't know how to help her, but I'm trying to figure something out. Plus, she can only drink from me."

She shook her head. "Excuse me? Controlling much?"

"Oh, come off it, Tabi. Like I'd try to control her. She gets very ill if she drinks from anyone but me. I just can't figure out how to help her control it before she gets to the point of losing control."

She walked from around the table. "I've got an idea to help her with that. Come with me. Beckett, I'll need a portal please."

"You got it." He didn't hesitate, and his smoky blue magic began to seep from his palms.

"Hold on now. I'm here to break the curse. I've got to help the others." I wasn't just going to be off without having so much as a helping hand in my own fate.

Tabi wrapped her hand around my elbow. "You're of no use here. You'll only pace back and forth driving them all nuts. Right, guys?"

Serrina, Zinnia, and Astrid were unanimous. "Right."

Zinnia glanced around. "Astrid, we'll need to gather the others. Can you get Tilly and Maze?"

"Yeah, but they've been up to something lately, and I have no idea what it is." She began to scribble something on a paper and then set it on fire in her palm. "That should get to them."

"It'd be nice if the bloody cell phones would work in this part of the castle." I glanced around at the rest of them. "Where's Ophelia and Cross? I haven't seen them about in some time."

"She's got some kind of new pet distracting her and you know Cross never leaves her side." Tabi yanked at my arm. "Beckett, portal."

It opened up in front of us in a wild, swirling blue mass. I couldn't fight the queens or how they wanted to do things. If they wanted me gone, I would go. I trust them with my life, so I let her tug me along. "Well, I hope that pet survives. She'll either smother it in love or smother it period."

CHAPTER TWENTY-THREE

PIPER

"Piper, come on." Prisha dashed ahead of me and ran toward a giant crane standing at the edge of the city. Her long hair streamed out behind her as she leapt up onto its treads and stood next to the driver's seat of the crane. It was bigger than any other I'd ever seen, reaching high up into the open underground.

I paused and tilted my head back, looking up at it. "Where are you guys going?"

Martin and Sanchita had already started climbing the boom—the part of the crane that held the rope and swinging ball. It was composed of thick metal bars that crisscrossed each other. They leapt from one bar to the other like Tarzan swinging through the jungle. Prisha waved me toward her. "You'll see."

There were no other vampires in this area. It was completely empty and silent. The smell of freshly dug-up earth filled the air and mixed with other smells like metal, rock, and wood. It was dark everywhere, and we'd taken some kind of abandoned hallway to get here, which consisted of us climbing over some fences and ducking under a few roped-off areas.

"I don't think we're supposed to be over here."

Theon glanced around. "I know we're not."

"No one invited you." Prisha hissed. "You followed along, which means you get to keep your mouth shut."

I chuckled and gave him a sideways glance. "I mean, she's not wrong."

"Last one up is an old blood bag." Prisha started climbing, and I shook my head. When I pictured myself making new friends, trespassing wasn't in the game plan. But if Dice were here, she'd have already started climbing.

I started walking toward the crane. "Is that like calling someone a douchebag?"

"Worse." Prisha's voice came from even higher up.

Theon placed his hand on my shoulder. "We shouldn't."

I brushed him off. "You can keep your feet firmly on the ground, but I'm going to have some fun."

I jumped up and reached for the first bar, easily pulling myself up. I kicked my legs out and swung to the next bar. Like a gymnast, I glided, twisted, and flipped my way to the top of the crane. When I stopped at the top just next to Prisha, she wagged her eyebrows at me. "Didn't know you were that good."

"Just normal vampire skills." I shrugged.

"Whatever you say." She rolled her eyes. "That was pretty amazing."

"Thanks." I felt my cheeks heat, but I didn't actually know if vampires blushed.

Theon stopped just below me, and I chucked. "You're the last one up."

"So does that make me the empty blood bag?"

"It makes you some kind of bag . . ." Martin quipped.

"Ohhh, shots fired." Sanchita's light, tinkling giggle filled the air. When she smiled, two dimples formed at the corners of her mouth.

Theon sighed. "He's just got himself in a strop because he's a Royal vampire elitist through and through."

"And you're just a right git because you think anarchy is the answer when we all know it's not," Martin shot back.

"Hey, guys, shut it," Prisha cut them both off. "We're here to show Piper something amazing."

She pointed out into the darkness. "Check it out."

At first I didn't see it, but then, when I let my eyes take it all in, I sucked in a sharp breath. It was city for as far as my eyes could see. The buildings were built of beautiful stone that'd been carved into intricate designs and shapes. It was a mix of the beauty of an ancient Roman design with all the modern touches of twisted metal, carved stone, and pristine roadways. There were apartment buildings that rivaled the resorts I'd seen in Florida. A makeshift river flowed around the city, and many of the balconies overlooked it. I could hear the sound of the trickling water. Other buildings that had pointed steeples were spread through the city, and tiny shops were at the ground level with big windows to peek into.

"Holy shit."

Prisha nodded. "Pretty amazing, right?"

"I'd say." The entire ceiling, which stood a hundred feet over the city, was made of the same technology as that smaller dome I'd seen before. It was bright and showed the stars, each one twirling and shining down on the empty city.

"It's almost finished," Sanchita chimed in. "It's for us. Well, all the Night Spawn vampires."

After the dinner I'd sat through with Clive and then the times I'd met Marius I'd felt they only wanted to pull me in both directions. Both sides blamed The House of Shade when really *they* were the ones making all of this happen. "It makes all the crap with Clive and Marius from before seem like bullshit."

Prisha's eyes sparkled as she looked out over the city in progress. I knew that look. It was the look of hope, of excitement for something new. She leaned her cheek against the metal pole. "Marius has some ideas about The Blood Borns, but they're not all like that. Titus, he cares about us, even if Marius is so blinded by the glamor of the old immortal money. But if I were a hundred years old, I'd be rich too. Titus makes that possible."

Theon scoffed. "It's looking at the world through

rose-colored glasses. The rich hold all the power in our world."

Martin rolled his eyes. "Have you taken the time to think for yourself? Open your eyes and look around. They built an underground park filled with night-blooming flowers and bioluminescent things to give to us. That isn't thinking about themselves. They want us to love it here."

Theon pressed his lips together. "I can think for myself."

"You kind of sound like Marius." Prisha spoke so softly. "Look, I know there are some made vampires who didn't choose this life and they're bitter about it. They want more. But somehow, fate brought them here and brought you here."

"Sometimes fate is a shitty thing," Theon grumbled, and I fought not to smirk at how much he sounded like me sometimes.

"Yeah, but Titus is not a shitty king." Martin straightened his jacket and looked down toward Theon. "I've known shitty kings, and he's not one."

"Yeah, he's no Alataris." Prisha pretended like she got the shivers. "Now, *that* dude was evil."

They all paused for a moment of silence. I wanted to know who Alataris was and what that had to do with our world, but they were dishing about more important things I wanted to know about. It felt like I'd only seen the inside of the castle and now this with Marius. But I wanted to know what they all thought—the real people who lived through the power struggles. "What about Grayson? What do you think of him?"

Sanchita swung back and forth like a little kid spinning around a pole. She smiled and wagged her eyebrows. "You mean Prince Grayson? He's the most different of them all."

He seemed to have that effect on everyone. They all thought he was the most wonderful thing. At one time, I did too. But I couldn't stop from rolling my eyes. "He seems like a typical guy to me, human or otherwise."

Prisha scoffed. "The whole city is his design, Piper. Every building, every park, every restaurant, even the fun things like the river and the pools around the city. The night-blooming flowers were his plan too. Grayson puts more into us than any other Royal."

Martin chuckled. "Yeah, add in the fact he kind of saved the world . . . twice . . ."

"Hey, who's side are you on?" I teased him.

"Yours. Always yours." He blew me a kiss.

"Is it hard being his progeny?" Theon asked, surprising me with his question.

"Is it hard being Marius'?" I countered.

"Sometimes I feel like I have to be swayed in his direction because he made me. Other times I agree with what he says. Then there are times when I feel like I need to move in my own direction to discover what I really want from this life."

Theon's candor threw me off guard. I expected him to say something along the lines of how great it was being tied to such an amazing vampire. Instead, I got a version of the *truth,* or a very light sprinkling of it. I could appreciate that. It made me wonder what happened to Theon. How or why Marius choose him? And was he happy in it? Did he find this life as jarring as I had?

"Yeah, it's hard being his progeny. I don't know where I fit, and I have to figure that out." When he gave me a warm smile, I couldn't help but return it. "I guess that's why I'm here with you all. I want to find myself and figure out the kind of vampire I want to be. You know, on my own."

"I understand your lot in life more than you know, Piper." He jumped up onto the rail next to me. "I'm not all that bad really."

"But you are," Prisha blurted out, and we all started laughing. It was a moment that broke the open connection I briefly felt with Theon. Nonetheless, there'd always been something about him. I just didn't know if it was something I could trust enough to be friends with.

When the laughter died down, Sanchita motioned to the city. "Don't you see, Piper? Grayson's giving us the stars. And tomorrow he'll give us the closest thing to a sunrise on that ceiling. People who had the light once but never will again... that's making a difference... to us all."

CHAPTER TWENTY-FOUR

GRAYSON

The wind whipped around me, sending my jacket and scarf to float around my body. The air was cool and chilly. The smell of sea air filled my nose, and a fine salty mist gathered over my skin. A wave crashed against the rocky cliffs below, and the cold water sprayed up in front of us in foaming white bubbles. My clothes started to dampen just as I stood there. Clouds rolled across the darkening sky and lightning forked out as thunder rolled in the distance. The rain hadn't begun yet, but the air smelled of it, warning me it would start at any moment.

"Right, so you want me to dive in there . . . You know I'm a vampire, not a bloody mermaid."

Tabi rolled her eyes. "Technically, I think it's merman."

I motioned to my legs. "I haven't got a bloody fish tail, have I?"

"You're so dramatic." She was completely at ease, even this high on the cliff, with her hair whipping in the wind and the water spraying up with each crashing wave.

"I hardly think a land creature refusing to dive into the depths of the ocean is dramatic. There's a megalodon down there waiting to have me as an appetizer and end my immortal life." I folded my arms.

"Do you want to help Piper or not?"

"Without question."

"Then to do that, we have to go talk to Poseidon, because the trinket you're looking for will do exactly what you need it to and he has it . . ." she motioned to the ocean, ". . . in his castle."

"Oi! Why can't you just magic one for me?"

She rolled her eyes. "Something cannot just be magicked for you, Grayson—kind of like your curse."

"Low blow, love." I looked over the edge. "Right, off we pop then. How do we do this?"

She held her hands up and golden ribbons of her magic surrounded my head. I felt the air pressurize around me, and I sucked in a deep breath. When she let her magic drop, there was a wobbly bubble around my head. I shook my head back and forth.

"You want me to go down there with bloody soap suds on my head? Did you not hear me? MEGA-LODON. I'll be Jaws' toothpick within ten minutes like this. Can you not portal us right into his castle or something?"

"I've never known you to be such a . . . bitch."

I paused. "Says the woman who's been messing about with the son of Poseidon."

Her jaw dropped and she narrowed her eyes at me.

"Right, don't think I don't know what you're on about." Inside the bubble, I could hear the sound of my own voice, like yelling inside of a tunnel.

"Do you want the thing or not?" She put her hands on her hips and tapped her foot at me.

I sighed. "Yeah, anything for Piper."

"Then this is how we do it." She stepped up to the edge. "I forgot to bring you a wet suit."

"Never mind that." I stripped off my jacket, scarf, and shoes. I stood there in just my sweater and dress pants. "This is good enough. The water is hardly as cold here as it is in England."

"After you, vamp." She motioned to the cliff.

I stepped up the edge and looked at the waves smashing against the rocks. The faster I got this over with, the faster I could get back to the Witch Queens and help them break my curse and the faster I could get back to Piper. I stepped off the edge and let myself plummet toward the surface. I tucked my arms into my body and straightened my legs. I plunged below the surface and held my breath out of habit. When I tried to kick to the surface, Tabi was there, pulling me farther down with her power over the currents.

"Don't fight me. I got you."

My body twisted and turned with the streams and propelled me forward. I shot straight down toward the underwater castle. When I struggled to find my bearings, my mouth burst open and I sucked in a deep breath. I expected the burning salt water to ache in my throat and force my lungs to seize up. When the pain and choking feeling didn't come, I tried to relax and let Tabi steer me with the tides. I floated along taking it all in. Before me stood a large piece of coral. Rainbow colors danced over it, and schools of brightly colored fish zoomed in and out of all the tiny crevices. It was like being on a close-up tour in an aquarium.

Tabi slowed us to a stop just outside an opening in the base of the reef, which was no bigger than one of those tubes kids climbed through on a playground. She pointed toward it. "Don't touch the side. Otherwise, *pop* goes the vampire."

"You know you've really got a comforting way about you. Quite calming, really."

"Funny . . . very funny."

Though our voices were muffled by the bubbles over our heads, I still heard the words clearly. I moved in front of her. "Give us a push, love."

I sucked in a deep breath and held it, even though I didn't need to. I let Tabi shove me forward with her power over the water. I threw my arms up by my ears, pulled my legs in close together, and let my momentum carry me through to the other side. My body twisted and turned like one of those bloody waterslides. I shot out of the coral tube like a missile from a submarine. The feeling of being weightless and floating in the warm sea made me forget, for a moment, the sense of dread I had hanging in the pit of my stomach since the day I met Piper.

Sharks, whales, and fish of all different sizes flowed to and from an opulent castle built entirely out of coral and shells. Rays from the sun beamed down through the water to spotlight the half-moon entrance. Glowing fish with tiny neon stripes down their sides swam in straight lines over every hard corner of the castle. Five smaller turrets rose up from the ground. Each one was connected by a wall of coral. Within that wall stood a building that could only be described as the Taj Mahal of the sea. A golden raindrop-shaped roof glinted in the sunlight.

Tabi propelled ahead of me. "We're almost there."

I kicked my legs and used my arms to propel me forward. I swam toward the castle, wanting to get this done, needing to be out of the water. Two hulking mermen saw up from the front door and raced toward us. Each one had tails like a shark and upper bodies the size of a rhino shifter. They looked like bodybuilders on steroid times ten. Each of them held a golden trident and pointed it at us as they charged full speed.

"You there! Stop!" Before they could reach me, they hesitated and then their eyes widened and they turned to swim away.

"What the hell?"

"GRAYSON, MOVE!" Tabi's panicked words hit me just as I turned around.

I kicked back, cursing at how slow my body moved in the water. I twisted until I about-faced and all I could see was an inky black cloud moving toward me. I swung my arms back, trying to propel myself toward the castle and away from whatever that bloody thing was. Two huge tentacles rose from the black cloud. They were bright-red and almost seemed to glow from within. It shot out and wrapped around my ankle. I dug into it with my fingers, ripping and tearing at the flesh holding me. Blood mixed with the ink, turning the water so dark I could barely see. Another tentacle snaked around my body and up my neck. The bubble over my head popped, and water rushed into my face. It burned my eyes and went up my nose. I tried to hold my breath, but I'd inhaled, and it burned down my throat and into my lungs. The thing yanked me down farther and the water grew colder and darker. Black dots swarmed my vision as I struggled to break free from a watery death . . .

CHAPTER TWENTY-FIVE

PIPER

"Why isn't this part of the city open? It looks about done." I gazed out over everything that Grayson had dreamed up, and I could see the whimsical aspects he used with touches of Old World England in the structures and Rome in the way things were carved out of stone. There was a touch of modern amenities in the lighting and how things worked. I could tell it was a labor of love. Grayson cared about this place, this project, and these people.

Prisha turned her head away from the city. "You'll see in about three ... two ... one."

Sunlight burst through a few cracks in the roof, sending rays of light dancing over the city. It glittered in an array of rainbow colors. My eyes widened, and my jaw dropped. It was spectacular how it gleamed in the sunlight.

"Piper, turn away. You'll burn your eyes," Sanchita

called up from her place just below me on the neck of the crane.

But my eyes didn't burn. They didn't even hurt. In fact, I could see hues of color I never even knew existed as a human. Before when the city had been dark, I only saw the night-blooming flowers, but now I was dazzled by the colorful arrangements all over. There was nothing dark or depressing about this vampire world Grayson had created. If he wasn't so damn wonderful, I'd hate him.

"You're not going to believe how beautiful it is."

"We believe you." Prisha climbed behind one of the poles, hiding away from how bright it was.

"Why can't they patch the holes?"

"The ground above keeps shifting and creating new crevasses. They're still trying to figure out the engineering behind it to keep everyone safe. Even now, those gaps come from hundreds of feet up." Theon squinted his eyes as he tried to look toward the roof.

"I figured, since The Night Spawn Headquarters start on street level and we just keep getting deeper and deeper, but the city feels so open, not closed-in at all." It really was a marvel.

Something in the shadowy distance drew my attention. It was a younger vampire. She had sickly pale skin and long, dark hair down to her hips. Her eyes were so bloodshot they looked nearly completely crimson. Her clothing was in tatters, hanging off her shoulder and down to her keeps. Dirt covered her legs, arms, and face.

"Hey, what's going on over there?"

The girl had hunched over and wrapped her arms around her midsection. Tiny pebbles rose off the ground and all shot toward her. A million pinpricks covered her body, and a pained wail escaped her lips. Dots of blood colored her tattered white shirt.

Martin shielded his eyes from the rays of sunlight in the distance and squinted in the direction I was looking. "I can't see, but it looks like . . . oh shit. It looks like she's going to meet the sun."

My heart leapt in my chest. *No. This can't be.* "Meet the sun?"

"She doesn't want to be in this world anymore." Prisha hissed. "It must be the sickness."

I tightened my grip on the metal pole, and it dented under my strength. They all looked at me as the metal groaned. A wide range of shock filled their faces. Sanchita motioned to my hand. "Damn, girl, you're strong."

But I wouldn't be distracted. "We have to stop her."

Prisha shook her head. "We won't get there fast enough."

"We have to stop her." I leaned over the side of the crane, nearly hanging off.

Martin pulled his tablet from behind his back. "I'll try to get someone here."

"There's no time." I had to help her. I didn't know how, but I was going to. I leapt off the top of the crane and plummeted to the ground.

"Piper!" Theon bellowed after me.

My stomach went up into my throat. When I landed, the ground dented under my feet. The impact vibrated up my legs, but I felt no pain. I heard the others start to climb down behind me. I couldn't wait for them though. The girl was only feet away from the sun. I pumped my arms, sprinting as fast as I could. The world blurred around me, and the wind blew my hair back from my face. She was just ahead of me. The others had finally hit the ground. Their footsteps echoed behind me.

"Piper, don't!"

But I wouldn't listen to any of them. The girl was only a foot away from the stream of light. I dove for her, hooking my arm around her waist. I twisted in midair and tossed her backwards as hard as I could to where I knew the others were. I only prayed they were fast enough to catch her. She soared through the air and right at Theon. He opened his arms, catching her as she slammed into his chest. They flew back with the momentum, and Theon landed hard on his back and skidded across the ground. I sucked in a deep breath as I fell to the ground.

Bright light shined down on me, warming my skin. I scrambled to my feet and stood there in the beam of sun. My pale skin glowed in the dazzling rays of sunlight, and I held my hands out. The others stood about thirty feet away, staring at me while trying to shield their eyes at the same time. A swarm of vampires in black army fatigues sprinted into the room in a blur of movement. Each of them had on thick black helmets and goggles, making their faces barely recognizable.

"Let me pass!" Marius bellowed from behind them.

They parted just for him, and he walked to stand as close as he dared. He held his hand up, shielding his eyes but still trying to see me as the army guys restrained the young, sick vampire. But Marius paid them no mind. He only had eyes for me. A wide wicked grin spread across his face, and it sent a chill down my spine.

"Well, aren't you interesting?"

I held my arms out and pulled my sleeves up, letting the sun touch my skin. I didn't realize how much I missed it until now. It was so warm and smelled of fresh dew and earth. The colorful rays danced over my skin, and for the first time, I could see how they caressed my skin tone, and everything looked like a rainbow of beauty. "I don't know what's happening."

Marius lifted his hand toward me like he wanted to grab me but didn't dare touch. Even this close, his skin started to smoke, and he took a step back. "Oh, I'd like to find out."

CHAPTER TWENTY-SIX

GRAYSON

*B*lackness swarmed my vision and my ears popped with the pressure of being dragged down. Blood and salt water flooded into my face, burning my eyes and making it impossible to see what the hell was going on. I curled my fingers into claws and dug at the tentacles holding me. Gooey, meaty flesh ripped in my hands and coated them in slime. My lungs burned for air as I kicked out, trying to find a glimmer of the surface. The water cooled around me and swirled with black ink.

Bubbles appeared all around me like a jacuzzi. The giant squid tightened its grip on my leg and around my waist. Pain exploded in my side and in my leg as the damn thing held me even tighter. Tentacles rose up around me and began to coil. My body twisted in the water as two dark eyes drifted up from the depths to watch as the breath left my body. There were more bubbles, and one formed around my head just as I was about to lose consciousness. I sucked in a gasping breath and then another. The burning in my lungs eased with each breath I took. Tabi floated up in front of me.

"My bad."

"Your bloody bad?" The squid twisted me upside down, and I felt the water pressure tighten along with its grip. The air I'd just gotten whooshed from my lungs and my temper flared. I felt the blood in the water from the monster and the impending predators being drawn to it.

Right, all I need now are sharks!

Enough was enough. My blood magic seeped from my skin with every infuriating passing second. "STOP!"

Everything around me halted. The tentacles stopped their constricting squeeze on my body, and those large black eyes narrowed in my direction. I would not be lunch today.

"Let go, you big slimy sod."

Inch by inch, its slimy tentacles uncoiled from my body and let me loose. I let my arms and legs float out to my sides as I righted myself. When the ink started to clear, all manner of sea life floated frozen around me. Tabi drifted by and I waved my hand, letting my hold drop on her.

"Apologies."

The moment my power dropped, she drifted to my side. "Apologies? No one said you had that kind of power. And what the hell? Why'd you use it on me?"

"In your immortal words . . . my bad." I felt ridiculous

floating there with a bubble wrapped around my head, having just been attacked by the creature from the deep.

"Yeah, my bad." She gave me the side-eye like she was seeing me for the first time in a new light. She waved to the sharks that hadn't moved. "But this is something else."

"Vampire blood magic is not to be taken lightly or used lightly, Tabi." I looked toward the squid and met his giant black glistening eyes. "Piss off back down the hole you came from."

I waved my hand, and my red mist filled the water and smacked into its face. The moment it did, the giant squid opened its tentacles and pushed away from me. It twisted back in that boneless way they rolled themselves over and disappeared in a cloud of ink. Bubbles flew from it and then, just as quickly as it showed up, it was gone. Other sea life lingered there, watching and waiting, and suddenly I knew what it felt like to be a fish in an aquarium.

"Right, off you pop." With one wave they were also gone, along with my patience. "I can't be doing with much more of this."

I was here to help Piper as best as I could, but wasting my time playing little merman wasn't on the agenda for today. No singing crabs or friendly fish. I twisted myself to face Tabi.

"Get us there ... now."

"Touchy touchy, vamp." Tabi flicked her hand and the current moved toward the castle.

It wrapped around my body, and I felt the cool water move through my clothing. The ache in my side and down my leg hadn't yet subsided, but I let the water carry me through. It sped past my body, and my legs drifted out behind me. If I hadn't had the bubble over my face, I would've had to close my eyes. The current carried us straight through the front gates and into the castle. For a split-second, I saw a large foyer before the current caught me and twisted us up a winding ramp. Round and round I went, higher and higher into the castle, like riding a waterslide backwards. I shot out on the top floor and a group of sea turtles whipped around me before disappearing back down the winding staircase.

I floated there, waiting for my head to stop spinning. Tabi floated to my side like she'd done this a million times before and it was no big deal. "Soft stomach, vamp. I would've thought you'd have an iron stomach from, you know all the blood drinking."

"Funny that, I drink blood, love. I'm not a monster."

"Others might disagree."

"Then I'm the monster who's going to get shit done." I started to swim forward.

Two mermen with tridents turned to face me. Bubbles floated around them from their quick movements. They darted toward us and I lifted my hand to use my magic on them, but yellow streams of magic rolled out in front of me, and seaweed shot up all around them, wrapping around their arms and tails. They swung to the sides and smacked into the rough coral walls.

I glanced over my shoulder at Tabi, who stood there with magic pouring out of her. "Nicely done."

"A pleasure."

I kicked my way down the hall and to the double door of Poseidon's room. "You're sure he's in there?"

She nodded. "I'm sure."

I shoved the doors wide open. I didn't get the satisfying slamming sound they would've made on land. Instead, they kind of just *drifted* open. There in the dead center of those walls was a towering man wearing nothing but tight wet suit pants that looked like black and blue fish scales.

His long hair drifted around him and looked almost trained to stay out of his face—unlike mine, which felt plastered to my head in this stupid bubble. In one hand he held a trident. The gleaming silver metal spiraled up to three separate points. Within the trident, bright blue flecks of shimmering sea glass sparkled with aqua-colored magic. His face was all angles, with a straight nose, sharp jawline, and high cheekbones. When I gazed into his eyes, they wavered like rough seas and changed colors from the deepest green to the most vivid aqua all in the beat of a moment. The muscle in his jaw ticked as he looked at the two of us.

"Do either one of you want to explain why you feel the need to shove your way into my home? My castle?"

Fury covered his features, and for a moment I was reminded of Titus when he grew angry at me. "We come for a favor."

He motioned to the two of us. "I'm not inclined to grant favors to intruders."

"Intruders? Hardly," Tabi snapped as she drifted up beside me to face him. "We've come because we know you can help us, and we know you could be quick about it."

He raised his eyebrows. "Just because you've gathered favor from a Prince of the Sea does not mean it carries over to me."

"A Prince of the Sea?" I gave her a sideways glance. "Oh really?"

"You, shut up." She turned back to Poseidon. "We know you have the blood pearl, and we know you haven't needed it in centuries. Why not give it to a young vampire who does need it?"

His brow furrowed and he looked at her like she'd lost her damn mind. "Because this isn't a charity, and nothing is given for nothing. What have you come to offer me? Your absence?"

"My absence?" Tabi crossed her arms over her chest. "Meaning?"

"Meaning you stay away from the sea and any who reside in it." He drifted back and a chair made entirely of bubbles rose up behind him. He rested his arms on it and let his trident float just beside him.

Her jaw dropped. "For how long?"

"Indefinitely." The word was a growl on his lips.

"Hold on." This seemed more personal than business, and I couldn't be doing with that. It was one thing for me to be messing up my love life, but it was an entirely other thing for me to be messing with anyone else's. "This sounds more like it has to do with your son than the business at hand."

Poseidon shrugged. "Business and pleasure can mix when I say so."

"Well, this is my deal, and I say not." The world was a mess, people were a mess, and even I was a mess. But I would not be dragging Tabi down with me.

"What could you possibly have to offer me that I can't fetch for myself? I rule the ocean the way The House of Shade rules vampires."

Our world worked like a hierarchy, where The Fallen sat at the top of the food chain. We all answered to them and their wishes. The Greeks came afterwards to help The Fallen in their mission for redemption. So, were they powerful? Hell yes. Did they have everything? Hell no. The rest of the supernatural world, like the witches, warlocks, and vampires, came after them. But on *that* food chain, I was at the top, and I could be top here.

"Everyone has a price, and a favor from The House of Shade could go a long way." He knew the sway we had wasn't just over vampires. Our alliances ran deep with the witches and warlocks, not to mention Titus' tie to The Fallen. He might've wanted to look like the biggest fish in the sea, but the truth was I could swim among the sharks just as easily as he could.

Poseidon sat forward. "An open favor from The House of Shade?"

This is where things get tricky.

Poseidon was known to have a temper just as unpredictable as the ocean. An open promise to him could mean anything . . . which was a lot, even if I was willing to give anything to help Piper. "Within reason."

He waved me away. "That's vague at best, which doesn't help me."

"Then let's not make it vague." When making deals, I hated showing my hand first.

"You get one veto."

"Five."

Poseidon rolled his eyes. "Right to refuse five times hardly seems worth it. Two."

"Four. You're not known for your calm demeanor. I prefer not to change a deal with The House of Shade as often as the tides change."

He chuckled. "Three."

When he extended his hand, I knew I wasn't going to get another counteroffer.

I swam forward to it. "Deal."

"Well worth a blood debt from The House of Shade." I hated putting myself in this position, but desperate times called for desperate measures.

"And now for your end of the bargain." He went to stand next to his bed and tugged on a long length of seaweed hanging there. The floor opened up before my feet, and a small pedestal rose in front of me. There on top of it was a big shell that seemed to glow from within.

"And you're sure it's in there?"

He gave me a withering look. "I'm sure."

I took the clam and shoved it in my pocket. "Pleasure doing business with you."

"The pleasure is all mine."

As I'm sure it will be, mate. I'm sure it will be . . .

CHAPTER TWENTY-SEVEN

ATLAS

"*A*tlassssss, don't you dare stop."
I threw her leg around my hip and drove into her hard with quick thrusts that I knew would get her there quicker. "Wouldn't dream of stopping."

This was yet another meaningless encounter, one among a stretch of many that wouldn't even register in my memory. To the upper crest of vampire society, I was the ultimate danger experience—the wild one night stand they'd whisper about with their girlfriends when they were married off to a very stable, very safe Barney-type who could barely dampen their knickers long enough to get a leg over. Their nights would be filled with dreams about me, their days filled with the monotony and safety that came with marrying a high-born vampire.

I ran my nail down the side of her throat and let the smallest trickle of blood well there. Her scent tingled my nose, and not in a good way. Still, I had to taste to know what I would do with her. If she was delicious, I might keep her for a time. If not, I would continue searching for something I couldn't find or define. The only thing I knew was that emptiness was a dark hole where my soul used to be. I ran my tongue over the drop of blood, praying it'd be the most delicious thing I'd ever tasted. But the second it touched the tip of my tongue, I fought not to recoil from the foul flavor.

The brunette below me screamed her pleasure at the touch of my tongue to her flesh. I felt her spasm beneath me, reaching her end in a matter of moments, whereas I'd barely gotten anywhere. I threw her leg over my shoulder, searching for pleasure where there was none to be had. The bed hammered into the wall over and over again, yet there was no ecstasy to be found. Frustration ate at me, and a piece of the headboard crushed under my tightened grip.

She reached up and cupped my face. "It's good for me too, darling."

If I were less of a gentleman, I'd have rolled my eyes. Three quick raps came on my door, and I halted. "It better be worth you knocking on my door!"

She ground into me. "More."

I looked down and met her eye. "Be still."

There were no words. Just three more quick knocks. *Saved.* I withdrew myself and wrapped the sheet around my hips. I marched over to the door and placed my hand on the knob. I didn't care who stood in the hall or saw who I was bedding. The brunette squeaked and pulled the blankets up over her head to hide from whomever was at my door, so clearly grand romantic gestures weren't her thing.

I growled and yanked the door open. "What?"

The soldier on the other side of the door flinched back for a split-second before he stood straight. He was dressed in black army fatigues, black boots, and a black beret. His shoulders were wide and muscular, and yet his eyes were round with surprise at the sight of me. He stood there frozen for a moment before his arm flew out toward me in a snappy mechanical way. "From Jester."

The paper was folded and crisp with not a single wrinkle in it. I looked down at it. "He trusted you with this?"

"Yes."

"Why?"

"Sir?" His brow furrowed.

"Why'd he trust you with this? It's obviously important." I let him stand there with his hand still extended. "Why not bring it himself?"

He swallowed and glanced down at the note. "Because I'm the one who discovered it."

"Where?"

"Night Spawn Headquarters." He lowered his voice. "You need to see this, sir."

I snatched it from his hand and ripped it open. My heart dared to speed up, but I forced it to a calm and steady pace, pushing myself not to react. "Have you reported this to anyone else?"

"Only Jester, sir." He looked me dead in the face.

"You saw this with your own eyes?" I held the paper out in front of him with two of my fingers.

He pressed his lips into a thin line, only letting the tips of his fangs show. "I did."

I stepped in closer and lowered my voice to a whisper. "If you're lying, I'll know . . . and nothing will stop me from hunting you down once I start."

He swallowed. "Understood."

Fuck. But even I knew it was too late. If he'd seen this with his own eyes, then so had enough vampires to start the rumor mill spreading. I crumpled the paper in my hand and turned back to the woman hiding under my blankets.

"Out. Now."

She peeked out from under the blankets. "B-but someone will see."

I rolled my eyes. "They've already heard . . . trust me."

A snicker escaped the soldier's lips, and I turned back to him. "Am I wrong?"

"Nope."

"Dismissed."

Without another word, he disappeared from my door. I turned and raced into my room, pulled on a sweater and trousers, shoved my feet into my boots, and headed for the door. I didn't bother turning around.

"Be gone before I return."

I ran through the castle, speeding toward the throne room. When I got to the double doors, I only slowed my pace long enough for the guards to scramble to open them for me. When I entered, Titus sat on the throne, but the room was filled with courtiers lingering about. Moira stood beside him as she always did, distant but present. I stopped in front of the throne, gave a quick bow, and turned toward the courtiers in the room.

"Leave." They all turned to stare at me. "Now."

I didn't need to bellow my words or use my power. Within seconds the room was empty except for Titus, Moira, and me. Titus chuckled. "And here I thought my power was impressive. Turns out your reputation is more so."

"I have no response to that."

Moira sighed. "You have a reputation for many things, Atlas."

Right, like I wanted the spotlight on me right now. "I have news of Piper."

"And?" Titus sat forward. "Did she hurt someone?"

I shook my head. "No, she saved someone . . . by walking into the sunlight."

Moira threw her hand over her mouth and squeezed her eyes shut. She pressed her other hand to her stomach. "Is she . . . is she . . ."

"She survived."

Titus rose to his feet. "How is that possible?"

"You know how." I didn't want to say the words out loud, but we all knew it was a big sign when a newly made vampire walked into the sunlight and didn't turn to ash.

"And I sent her away?" Titus fell back into his chair. "To be swayed by Marius."

"Piper is a smart girl. She'll see right through him." Moira placed her hand on his arm almost unconsciously but quickly pulled it away before he could place his hand over hers. "I just don't know how we got so distracted that we didn't see it. She was right under our noses."

"We know how, and we know why. The curse lingered. But looking at it now, we all refused to see it because we were protecting him. Fate is a fickle mistress ..."

I thought of the curse.
Born in blood of the human vein,
Bound in death she'll rise to reign.
By the crown, an heir will mark,
For in the sun, she'll bring the dark.
Lost in thirst, she'll kill for sport,
Seek the Prince who guards the court.
Mind the curse, yet hear her call,
For in her hands, we rise or fall.

This situation was getting more complicated by the second.

Titus shook his head. "Do we summon her back?"

"You can't, not without risking Grayson." Moira's voice was low and sad. "We can't lose him, Titus."

I didn't want to say it. "We can't leave her there with

Marius and Theon. If she is indeed the prophesied one, we need to bring her here."

When Moira looked at me with sadness in her eyes, I instantly regretted my words. But in my life, I'd always been for the crown and Piper was necessary for the crown. The House of Shade needed her. All vampires did.

Titus ground his teeth together. "In her hands, we rise or fall. And so it begins. Perhaps the only solution is to send Grayson away. He has many pursuits in other areas. I hear the witches are having a hell of time with some unexplained happenings. Yes, I think we should send him away, just for a while."

The sound of soaking, watery footsteps caught my attention a moment before Grayson appeared beside me. His clothing was drenched through, his hair slicked back to his face, and his skin held a blue tinge that made Moira look uncomfortable. He held a large pearl in his hand and looked Titus right in the eye as if he wasn't already a spectacle. "I most certainly will not be sent away. Now, what's this about?"

When he was greeted with nothing but silence, he glanced around at us. "Someone will speak, or I'll find out on my own. You know I have the means to do so."

Titus and Moira both looked to me. *Always doing the dirty work.* I sucked in a deep breath. "The prophecy is in motion."

Grayson chuckled and waved my words away. "Come off it."

"I do not jest."

He threw his hands up and let them fall against his soaking pants. "Great. Like we need another thing on our bloody plates. Have we found the vampire?"

"My dear, perhaps you want to clean yourself up? You seem to have created a puddle." Moira motioned to the water gathering in a small pool around his shoes.

"I will not. Not until you've answered me." He looked to Titus. "Come now, Uncle, we've never pulled punches in difficult times. Who is it?"

I ran my hand through my hair. "Piper."

Grayson scoffed. "Piss off. It's not."

"Intel says she walked into the sunlight."

"SHE DID WHAT?!" Grayson paled. His hands began to shake. "This is my fault. If I had just—"

"—And survived."

Grayson shoved the pearl into his pocket and shook his arms out. Drops of water fanned over the three of us. None of that seemed to bother him in the least. "I'm going to get her right now."

"No, let her stay." Titus' words brought him up short.

"You do realize that if she is the prophesied one, you have just laid her right in the hands of our enemy?" Fury colored Grayson's features.

"And have kept you alive and well in the process."

Grayson shifted from one foot to the other like he couldn't contain himself. "I don't bloody well care about me! She is there, and she is alone. That kind of power . . . Titus, you can't be seriously considering leaving her there."

"Marius is not an enemy. I have faith Piper will do well. She's brilliant. She will see through him."

"Oh, now she's brilliant? Go on and pull the other leg why don't you. You've shoved her out the door and into a world she doesn't know, and if she is THE ONE, she needs guidance for those powers. Are you really ready to let HIM of all people—that slimy, greedy, power-hungry leech of a person—be the one to teach her?"

"I didn't say that. I just said she'd be sorted for the time being. I have no intention of leaving her there."

"So, you intend to be rid of me?" Grayson's eyes widened and little red veins forked over the whites. "That's the solution to your problems?"

"Have you got a better one?" Titus said simply, like he was fighting with a madman . . . and maybe he was. But Grayson had a point. It was the point I'd made. She shouldn't be left to Marius. He knew it, I knew it, and Titus knew it.

"First thing is we bring her right back here. How's that for sorting things out?"

"And what of you?" Titus snapped back. "You're in a right state! Sopping wet and with no explanation of where you've been or where you're going."

"None of that matters because I am goinggg to retrieve my progeny. NOW." Grayson motioned to the door.

"No, you're not." Titus slammed his fist down on the arm of his chair. He jabbed his finger in Grayson's direction. "You are to clean yourself up and act like the *Prince* you are. And in one day's time, we will go to The Night Spawn City as we have done for years and engage in the Christmas activities *you* so painstakingly planned prior to your plunge into whatever you call your current state of being."

Grayson's face turned dark-red. He blew out a long breath. "Very well."

Without another word, he darted from the throne room, leaving a messy puddle in his wake. I narrowed my eyes at it. "Well, that was . . ."

Titus pointed in my direction. "Consider it your job to keep him in this castle for the next twenty-four hours."

Childminder . . . lovely.

CHAPTER TWENTY-EIGHT

PIPER

"What is this place?" My voice echoed off the rough, dark walls. It felt more like a cave than a room off a long, dim hallway.

"It's a room we usually hold those infected with the sickness in. But for you, we're just going to see what you can really do." Marius' voice came through an intercom in the room. It wasn't the best quality. His voice crackled, and the echo hurt my ears.

"And you have me in here because why?" I turned to what looked like a two-way mirror. My reflection shined back at me, and even to myself I looked dangerous, deadly even with my eyes so green they practically glowed and hair so dark it looked like a wild midnight curtain around my face.

The microphone clicked on. "Just to see what you can do."

"I got tested with Grayson. I have the standard skills: strength, speed, keen sense of sight, smell, and hearing. You know . . . your standard vampire stuff." I ran my fingers over the walls.

"And the sun wasn't part of that?"

I scoffed. "Would *you* just toss made vampires into the sun to see if they survive?"

"Fair point, but if you don't mind . . . I'd like to give it a try now?" The excitement in his voice was almost palpable.

"Go for it."

I'd barely gotten the words out before a buzzer sounded and the mechanical sound of gears turning filled the room. By now it was well into the afternoon and the sun would be at its highest and brightest. Dust rained down from above, along with tiny pebbles. The ceiling above parted and a beam of light showed through. It hit the table in the middle of the room. Light reflected in all different directions, but it didn't burn. In fact, it felt good, like sunning myself on a warm, breezy day. I reached out and put my hand in the direct path of the sunlight. As a human, I used to love the feel of it on my skin, but as a vampire, I appreciated the warmth and smell of it even more.

"Fascinating," Marius whispered over the loudspeaker.

"Yeah, you said that before." I stepped into the sun, and this time all I felt was a wave of calm come over me.

Before, I was terrified I'd light on fire, but now standing here, I felt strong and like I could do almost anything.

The doors overhead slammed shut and I was cast into darkness once again. "Are we going to play this game all day? Lights on, lights off?"

The door next to the mirror opened and Marius walked in. His face was lit up like a kid on Christmas Day who'd gotten the ultimate gift. "Do you know how rare you are?"

"No, tell me. Am I that rare?" I crossed my arms over my chest. I didn't know what Marius had in mind for me, but the way he smiled gave me the creeps.

He strolled farther into the room and pressed his fingers to his lips for a moment, seeming like he was choosing his words wisely. "You are the rarest among us. I believe even one of the most powerful."

"Powerful? What? Like the Blood Borns and their abilities?" My brow furrowed. I hadn't been in the world for a long time, but I knew Titus could control others through their blood, Moira could heal others, Atlas was just terrifying, and Grayson shared his uncle's power but refused to use it.

"Why can't we have power like them? What makes them that much better?" Marius' mouth twisted into a sneer. "They think they're so much more than us because of their lineage, because of their blood magic, but you could be the one to show them all."

"Show them all what?"

His eyes went cold and flat. "That we're just as good, if not better. Magic can be had. There are ways."

I didn't like the manic look in his eyes, like he had it out for The House of Shade. From what I could tell, they were trying to better this world, not bring it down. "I don't know much about this world, but I feel like magic is one of those things that either exists within someone or doesn't."

"I wish to test more things on you. Are you game?"

I glanced around at the room and through the open door behind Marius where Theon stood staring at me. He had his arms crossed over his chest and his eyes bore into mine. I couldn't tell what he was thinking, but whatever it was made me want to look away.

"Yeah, we can try. But I'm getting tired, so not much longer. Okay?"

"Of course, of course, you just got here. I must remember myself." He gave me a weird little nod, then backed out of the room and closed the door.

I heard the room seal like an air lock, and when my head snapped up to the mirror, his voice came over the speaker once more. No panic. I just want to make sure the water doesn't slip out.

"Water?" I did not like the sound of that.

Two huge pipes that I hadn't seen before shot water into the room like a cannon. I backed against the wall as the room began to fill. I pressed my hand to the glass. "I'm not sure how this is a test of power. I can assure you I can swim."

In seconds, the water was up to my ribs and still rising. Panic flooded my body. "Enough of this, Marius!"

My feet rose off the ground as the water reached my chest. My sweater felt like a sopping mess around my body, and I couldn't help but wonder . . . could I die again? The panic running through my body sure as shit made me feel like it was possible. When the water didn't stop, I knew what was happening. Arguing came from the other side of the two-way mirror and I knew Theon and Marius were in disagreement about what was going on. I just couldn't help but wonder who was on my side and who wasn't. I kicked my legs, holding myself just above the surface. The water rose so fast it would only be a matter of time before this room would entirely fill up.

If I hadn't known my own strength, I would've let the panic run wild with my body. Instead I felt my body buzz with life, and I sucked in a deep breath and let myself sink to the bottom. I turned to face the window and with both hands flipped them off. I knew my own strength, my own capabilities, and how well I did when angry. My anger was a superpower, and right now I was burning with fury.

I swam back from the two-way mirror and pressed my back to the opposite wall. I planted my feet against it and let my blood boil at being stuck in this situation. With all the strength I had, I pulled back and the water sloshed with me, moving to one side of the room. Bellowing came from the other side of the wall, but I didn't care. I kicked off the wall with all my strength and shot forward toward the mirror. The water rushed along with me, and with all the strength I could muster, I shoved my fists through the mirror. I expected the glass to shatter around my skin. I expected pain and cuts to explode over my hand and arms.

Instead, the mirror exploded outward and shattered into a million tiny pieces that mixed with the water. I tumbled out of the opening and into the room where Marius and Theon stood. The flood of water was too much. It knocked them both off their feet and forced the door behind them to open. We flooded out into the hallway, and I smacked into the opposing wall. When the water spread across the floor, I shot to my feet and shoved my hair out of my face. I marched over to where Marius lay sputtering and coughing in a puddle.

I jabbed my finger in his face. "What the hell is the matter with you!? I said you could test me, not drown me."

Theon staggered to his feet and wrapped his arm around my waist. "He just got carried away, Piper. Marius likes to push boundaries."

I shoved him back, and he flew across the hall and smacked into the wall. "Then you're as fucking crazy as he is."

Marius held his hand up as he coughed up more water. "I'm sorry . . . but you are . . . amazing."

"Seriously?" I was going to hit him or throw him through a wall—both of which would inflict some damage.

I took a step toward him when Theon launched himself between the two of us. He pressed his body in front of mine. Though he was bigger, taller, and more muscular than me, I got the feeling I could take him here and now. But when he wrapped his arms around me again, I suddenly felt exhaustion overwhelming my body and let him drag me back. Marius rolled to his side and pushed himself up. Strands of hair fell across his face, and as Theon dragged me farther down the hall, Marius stared after me.

"I'm going. I'm going." I pushed Theon off and let him fall into step with me. "Your boss is a fucking creeper."

"He's not my boss."

I narrowed my eyes at him. "Two words come to mind."

He shook his hands out, sending drops of water everywhere. "What's that?"

"Lap dog." Just then there was a clicking sound echoing down the hall and I spun on my heels. A ball of fire blasted from the room I'd just been in and out into the hallway. I felt the heat from the blast and the bright, flaring color stung my eyes. Marius fell back to the floor as it flew over his head.

"Fire!? Are you kidding me!?" I turned around and started moving down the hallway faster.

Theon followed close behind me. Why did he have to be so damn close? I whirled around on him. "What?"

"Are you going to your room?"

"Yeah, so?" I crossed my arms.

"So, you're going the wrong way." He mirrored my pose, and suddenly I decided that every man I had ever known wanted to drive me to insanity just to see if they could, or was that just vampire dudes?

I motioned down the hall. "Fine. Then lead the way."

He didn't move.

I rolled my eyes. "What?"

"You could say please." His lips curled up in a smile that was almost charming.

"Please," I said through thinned lips.

He clapped his hands behind his back and nodded down another corridor. "This way."

Jackass. I turned and walked silently behind him. The hallways were a maze that spread out all over the underground. Some of them looked like they belonged in a subway, but these passages looked like they'd been dug out by hand. They were rough and appeared more like caves than hallways. I glanced around, trying to remember my way. Doors lined both sides and I couldn't help but wonder where they all led. Each time I passed one, I peeked inside only to see more long, dark corridors. People lingered around the halls, shuffling about in a daze. The farther we walked, the creepier it got.

"Where are we?"

"Heading to your rooms." He said it so simply, yet there was an undertone to his words that I didn't like.

"You know you suck at lying." I stopped walking and looked around. Vampires of all shapes, sizes, and backgrounds lingered about. They looked like they'd been drugged out of their minds.

"Who says I'm lying?" Theon turned on his heels to face me.

"I don't know . . . maybe the icky feeling I get in the pit of my stomach every time you speak."

Another door opened, and when I looked in, my eyes widened. Madness unleashed. Vampires riddled with various stages of the sickness were trapped in that one hallway. It was like something out of a movie with an insane asylum where all the inmates went wild. Screams echoed down the hall. Vampires darted in all different directions while soldiers dressed in army gear tried to corral them into cells.

They were in hospital gowns, and madness colored their features. "What the hell, Theon?"

His face fell. "I know. The sickness spreads. We're doing everything we can to contain it."

"You need help here . . . *They* need help." I wasn't about to run to Grayson over this, but it was spreading and vampires were falling victim to whatever it was that was making them sick. "You need to find out what's causing this."

"You think we don't know that? Marius assures me he's doing all he can to help them."

The door slammed shut as I glanced back at it. "Does it look like that to you?"

"You've been here for all of one day. Don't you think

you should know your boundaries?" Theon glared at me like I'd insulted his family. In a way, I guess I had.

"You're right. I apologize. But it doesn't make me a bad person to want to help them." I motioned down the hall. "I'm tired now. Mind showing me back?"

"No, it doesn't make you a bad person, but it wouldn't kill you to give others the benefit of the doubt. Perhaps your words would not savor so strongly of the bitterness you feel right now if you did."

My eyebrows shot up. "Bitter? Really? Bit rude considering you barely know me or my experiences. And just because your defenses are up doesn't mean you get to take out your insecurities on me."

He chuckled. "You think I'm insecure?"

"I think you have doubts about things too." I took a step closer to him. "I know you're smart, Theon. I can see it in your eyes. You have sway here, and you care. Don't forget who you are."

His eyes softened. "How do you know who I am?"

I stepped back and sighed. "Just a hunch. When you grew up the way I did you being to learn about people."

"You don't know me well enough to lump me in with *people*. But you could…"

"Could what?"

He shrugged. "Get to know me. See for yourself exactly who and what I am."

"Tempting offer, but for tonight, I think it's been a long day."

He turned away from me and started walking back down the hall. "Then we better get you home."

There wasn't much I trusted about Theon and Marius, but there wasn't much I trusted about anyone besides Dice. Grayson had broken me, and while Titus had been fair and just, I got the feeling he wanted me to go as much as I wanted to. In the end, all I felt was completely and totally alone.

CHAPTER TWENTY-NINE

THEON

"Can you believe this?" Marius paced back and forth in front of me. His thick fur coat hung off his shoulders and pooled around his elbows.

"I can believe it."

He turned toward me and slammed his hands down on the table between us. His dark eyes were wide with excitement. "I heard whispers of the prophesied one. But I mean, come on, there's always such rumors in this world! I never thought it possible."

I leaned back in the chair. "Perhaps a calmer approach."

"How can I stay calm when she sleeps this night under our roof?" He turned from me and began pacing again. "Did you see her standing in the sun? I haven't seen the sun in centuries."

"Yes, and my retinas are still burnt from watching her."

"You don't share in my excitement." He ran his hand through his hair, shoving the strands out of his face.

"I rather err on the side of caution. It's not going to help your cause that you nearly drowned her tonight."

He waved my words away. "Did you see the way the water moved around her? I hardly think she noted it. Such power I've never seen."

"Power is nothing without influence."

"You think I have no influence?" He paused and pulled a chair around the table to sit across from me. As he sat, he chuckled and motioned to the ultra-modern office with dark marble floors and walls, his oversized desk, and the matching conference table that sat just across from it, which was where I now sat. "Have we not *all* the things?"

"Things do not garner favor or influence with someone like Piper."

He leaned back in the chair and held his breath. His cheeks puffed out a moment. "And what do you know of her? Are you an expert on a woman you just met?"

"Doesn't take a bloody genius to realize she's not after money or power." Piper was different than the others. She was observant and caring. Neither money nor status seemed to appeal to her.

"Then what is she after and how do we give it to her? Because I will have that one on my side no matter the cost . . . So tell me, what is the cost?"

I shrugged. "She's had privilege unbound within that castle with the Shade family."

"The House of Shade resides on shaky ground at best." He spat the words and rolled his eyes. "They do not hold true to their word, and it will cost others much . . . like they cost me . . ."

Ah, here we are: the crux of the problem. "And what did they cost you?"

"My life!" He balled his hands into fists and rocked back and forth in his chair. His dark eyes bounced around the room. "Lies roll so easily off their tongues. They take and do not give in return. I could've been great . . . I could've been MORE."

"So vague."

He pressed his lips into a tight line. "I dare not speak more of it, not until our position is stronger within the vampire world."

"And you think Piper will get you that?" I arched my eyebrows at him. "It'll take more than a single person."

"Not if that person is the prophesied one, and I know that she is!"

"She is Grayson's progeny, and if my instincts are correct, he was much, much more than that to her." As much as I didn't want to believe it, I knew they were lovers. I also knew she wouldn't have left him without good reason. "Her loyalties could still lie with The House of Shade."

"Then it's up to us to sway her this way." He looked me up and down. "There is a line of conquests out your door. What's one more?"

I chuckled and shook my head. "She's different."

"She's necessary." He glared at me for a long moment before he shot to his feet and began packing again. "And you will do what is necessary for me."

"If she is who you think she is, she won't be easily won over. She's not a slag who's happy with a bit of slap and tickle."

He paused his pacing to face me once more. Annoyance riddled his features. "Stating the obvious isn't going to get us any further with our goals."

I wanted to stand up and ask him what *exactly* our goals were. Were his goals still mine? Did I truly believe in what he did? Or did his pitch for how life *should* be just sound the best? I'd like to think I was a man of individual thought, but Piper had a way about her that made me question who I was and where I was going. Was I helping myself, or was I doing this for the benefit of all vampire society?

"And what are your goals?"

A wide smile spread across his face and his fangs extended down past his lip. "No less than the world."

CHAPTER THIRTY

PIPER

*P*ounding . . . so much pounding. I curled to my side and pressed my hand to my head. *Stop the pounding.* I didn't think vampires got headaches like this. But then again, I also thought vampires slept in coffins and rose from sleep to awake in the blink of an eye. This felt like waking up with a hangover, and I hadn't even had tequila in years—not since the night I got drunk on it, lost my shoe, and woke up with Dice on a rooftop in the Bronx when we lived in Salem. Neither of us remembered how we got there, but we swore of tequila since then. *This* splitting headache felt worse than that.

I groaned. "Why is there still pounding?"

"Because I'm still knocking." Theon's voice came through the other side of the door.

I shot up in bed and glanced around my new apartment. My bed was a rumpled mess. It looked like I'd been a tornado in my sleep. One pillow hung off the side of the bed while the other had landed somewhere across the room. The sheet had popped off the corner of my bed and was balled into the middle. I scrubbed my hand down my face. The bags of blood I'd gotten from Grayson yesterday lay empty and spread around the room. Knots riddled my hair, which was wrapped in angry snarls from my neck down.

"Um, Theon?"

"Come now, Piper. You know it's me." He gave three lighter knocks. "Don't you want to let me in after what happened between us last night?"

I lifted the covers and sighed with relief when I realized I was still fully clothed. I hopped from the bed and hurried to the closet. I yanked my sweater and jeans off from the previous night and tried to think of what happened once I got back to my room. I remembered walking back to the room in awkward silence and falling on my blood supplies like a lunatic. I was so starved I blew through the bags.

I grabbed a shirt from the shelf and yanked it over my head. It was a bright-red, oversized cable-knit sweater that fell to my knees. "Oh, and what happened between us?"

"The world appears in a whole new light because of you." His British accent rolled over the words like a poem.

I made a loud gagging noise. "Does that work on other women?"

"I wouldn't know, I've never said that to anyone before." He chuckled. "But it would be nice to say it to someone's face and not through a door."

I yanked on a pair of black leggings and darted to the bathroom. When I flicked on the light, I cringed at my own reflection. My hair was indeed in tangles, dark circles hung under my eyes, and I looked like I hadn't slept a wink. My stomach cringed with hunger, and I wrapped my arms around myself. I closed my eyes and sucked in a deep breath, then blew it out.

"Ah, but it's early and you didn't tell me you were coming, sooooo you can wait, my guy, while I wash my face."

Again, he let go of that smooth chuckle. "As you wish, love."

He sounded like Grayson, and for a moment I felt his absence like a hole in my chest. I shook that empty feeling away before attacking my hair with all the frustration that I felt. I pulled the comb through my wild waves. But anyone with even remotely curly hair knew it was a bad idea to brush them unless they were to be tied up or braided right away.

"Not your love," I called back as I shoved my hair up into a messy bun. I walked out of the bathroom and grabbed my phone.

I pulled up Martin's text thread before I opened the door. My fingers flew over the screen. *'Send help.'*

I hit send, then slid the phone into the side pocket of my leggings. I pulled the door open and there stood

Theon. He was freshly showered and freshly dressed in a white button-down, black V-neck sweater, and black trousers. And he smelled like heaven. He was sleek and classy in that 007 kind of way. He held a small potted flower in his hand. When he glanced down at me, he held it out toward me.

"What's this?" I reached out and took the little plant from him.

It was unlike anything I'd ever seen. The single flower stood in the middle of the pot with a thorny stem that reminded me of a rose. But the flower itself was more like peonies, with petal upon petal that looked like puffy ruffles. A warm glow emanated from the center of it and tiny glittery particles danced in the air around it. It reminded me of the ones that were planted around the new city.

He leaned against the door frame and shrugged. "Peace offering."

"I didn't realize we were at war." I stepped back from the door and motioned for him to come in.

"I've never met anyone like you."

I gave a light chuckle-snort at that as I turned from him to put my new plant on the center of my tiny table. "Somehow that doesn't sound like a compliment to me."

"You should take it as such." He dropped down into one of the chairs at my little table.

I raised my eyebrows at him. "And what have I done to deserve such praise?"

"You see the world in a different light . . . I like the

way you see things." His eyes lit up as he looked me over. I didn't totally hate the idea of Theon. He was young, clearly ambitious, and had helped me at every possible turn.

I sighed. "You'd be the first."

"It's all about being fair and balanced, logical even."

"You sound impressed?" I dropped down into the seat across from him and I felt my whole body ache from head to toe. It was difficult to know how much longer I had until I lost control, or if I *would* lose control. As a human, I could function even while starving. I could at least hold off for a while until I could eat. As a vampire, starvation brought hangry to a whole new level.

"You're an impressive type of woman." He leaned forward in his chair and smirked at me.

"If we're going to be friends, then you gotta stop with the cheesy pickup lines." I sighed. "Tell me something real about yourself that isn't meant to impress."

He crossed his arms over his chest. "Like what?"

I thought for a moment, trying to focus on anything else besides the ache in my stomach. "What was your life like when you were human?"

His brow furrowed. "What relevance does that have?"

"Because if you remember who you were beyond who you have become, that to me is something real. Starting off as friends should be honest." I waved him on. "So what ya got for me?"

"Alright, let me think on it a moment." He leaned back and his face smoothed. His green eyes darted around the room as though he were thinking. His lips pulled up in a small wistful smile, then it fell. "I've got one."

"I'm waiting."

"On the night of my death, my parents sent me down the road to collect milk from the local dairy. It was barely past sunset, hardly dangerous hours in those days. And yet . . ." his frown deepened, ". . . yet I was in the wrong place at the wrong time. It happened quickly enough. I remember the sharp pain in my neck and feeling the world fade around me . . . Kind of like fainting, you know?"

I shook my head. "I don't know, but please go on."

"After that, I grew angry for a time, I didn't want to leave my parents or my little brother. I was twenty-five when I died. I was of marrying age. I stayed in the forest around my home for a while, but I think . . . well, I think, deep down, my mother still felt me. They searched for a month. Finally, I let my hat and coat float down the river. I wanted to give them the closure they deserved. It was better they thought I drowned than believe I would return someday."

"Oh, Theon." His life had been whole, complete, and he'd been snatched from it. I found myself starting to like this side of him.

He gave me a sideways glance before continuing on. "Anyways, my mother would visit often and leave flowers on the headstone they'd made for me. My father would hold her as she wept while fighting back his own tears. It took everything I had in me to not go to them as I was.

But how could I? Their son who never changed, never aged as they grew older and gray. And when they passed, my younger brother laid them beside my headstone. He visited all three of us for many years, taking care to clear the brush away and lay new flowers. But no human can withstand the test of time."

I reached out and placed my hand over his. "I am so sorry."

Sadness riddled his features. "It wasn't all bad. I was able to help them from afar. Their land was always tended to, and magically, somehow, wealth fell right into their laps."

"So, you took care of them?"

He sighed. "As best I could."

I gave his hand a squeeze. "Thank you for telling me that."

He twisted his hand so his fingers could wrap around mine. He caught my eye and his gaze bore into me. "Real enough for you?"

I swallowed around the ball in my throat. The unshed tears I felt for him and his family prickled my eyes. "Yeah, thank you for telling me."

"I understand that it appears we're on the opposite sides of things, but that is not the case. These vampires . . . They're my new family, and I intend to treat them just as well as I did the ones I lost." His skin was warm against mine, and for a moment, I found myself believing him. "I'd like for you to give me the chance to prove that to you. Can you do that for me?"

I didn't want to believe him or fall into another trap with a charming Brit, but there was something about Theon that rang sincere with me. I wanted to give other people the benefit of the doubt and see if they would give me a pleasant surprise. Because for every letdown, there was someone willing to stand up. Dice was proof of that, and now maybe Theon was too.

"Yeah, I think I could do that."

"Then our bargain is struck."

"Am I interrupting something?" I hadn't even heard Martin walk into my room, but he stood there with Prisha and Sanchita on his sides. The three of them all had their eyes locked on where Theon and I had joined hands across the table.

I slipped free of his grip. "No, not at all."

"Speak for yourself." Theon turned toward Martin. "Do you always walk in without knocking?"

"I don't have to knock." He sauntered across the room to stand next to me. "I'm Martin."

When his eyes roamed over me, I knew he was seeing all the things that were easy to hide from Theon: the bags, the messy hair, the fatigue I'd been fighting since last night . . . He held his iPad as always and started hitting buttons faster than I could register. There was comfort in knowing he was on top of things and knew my hunger was getting the better of me. I just didn't know how long I had until it took over.

Sanchita walked into the room and sat on the foot of my bed. She'd since changed her clothing into a long deep-red skirt and dark-emerald shirt that made her eyes look even more green than yesterday. Her hair was loose and curling down her back. The little bell earrings she wore made a light tinkling sound. She looked at the empty blood bags on the floor. "Someone had a party last night."

"Someone looks like she's starving this morning." Prisha hopped on the bed next to her sister and looked equally as festive in a pair of black pants and a white and red striped shirt. Strands of tinsel were threaded through her long, straight hair.

"And you both look very festive. Where are you off to?" I didn't need all these new people to know I was starving and could only live off the blood of Grayson. It'd make me a freak among them to know I was trying to play the bity-bite game with Grayson.

Prisha beamed. "The Night Spawn are having their underground Christmas party. It's one of the best parties you'll ever go to. We thought you might want to go with us?"

"I have no doubt it'll be an awesome party, and I'd love to go with you all." I tried to show the same enthusiasm she had now, but the longer I went without feeding, the more rundown I felt.

They all fell silent for a moment and stared at me. I glanced around. "What?"

"Umm, people are talking about you." Prisha wrung her hands. "Gossip travels fast in the underground."

Greatttt, I came here to get rid of being talked about, and here I am not even a full day later and boom . . . gossip. "What are they saying?"

Sanchita glanced at Prisha. They shared a look before Sanchita answered. "They're saying you're some kind of super-vampire that the history books talk about."

I rolled my eyes. "What, like Wonder Woman?"

"No, more like some kind of King Arthur shit."

I turned to Martin and Theon. "I just walked into the sun. It's not a big deal. Right? Other people have done it?"

Theon cleared his throat. "Um, Piper, only born vampires can walk in the sun. As far as we all know, you're the first made one to be able to do it."

Before I could think of anything else to say, my stomach let out a growl loud enough that everyone looked like they wanted to step back from me. Prisha popped to her feet. "I've got some blood in my room."

Panic filled my body. I didn't want to tell them I needed Grayson or what would happen to me if I didn't have him. I turned to Martin. "Oh, don't worry, Martin's got me covered."

He held his iPad up and hit a few buttons. "How can you ever doubt me? Your delivery is arriving as we speak."

"See? He's got it all set."

The blare of trumpets sounded through the whole underground. It was impossible to ignore or even talk over. "What the hell was that?"

Prisha and Sanchita bounced up and down with a

high-pitched squeal like they were fangirling over a movie star. Theon sighed and rose to his feet. "They've arrived."

"Who?"

"The Crown Prince Grayson and King Titus." Martin beamed and rocked back and forth from his heels to his toes. I was about to pale, thinking they'd come for me, but he continued on. "They're here for the festivities."

Martin grabbed my hand and tugged me to my feet. "We must be off now."

"What? I thought you were going with us?" Theon offered me his arm. "Or are you going to go get your delivery? I'm sure Martin can handle it and get it to you."

If I was going to keep the way I fed to survive a secret, then I would have to play this game and pray my control didn't slip. I took Theon's arm. "Let's go."

He tugged me toward the door. "Lovely."

I glanced over my shoulder. "Martin?"

His eyes were wide as he looked me over. "Everything is under control."

Everything . . . except me.

CHAPTER THIRTY-ONE

PIPER

*I*f New York style Christmas were on crack, then sprinkled with Whoville and a touch of Hallmark, that would be Christmas with The House of Shade in the Night Spawn underground. Martin had gotten me back to the main area that reminded me so much of a mall, with multiple floors that overlooked a wide-open main level. Witches walked down the main floor like it was a parade. Their magic flew in all different directions, covering the floor and winding around the pillars and rails of each floor. It was like a light show with all the different colors. Wildly colorful Christmas decorations exploded in all directions.

Colorful specks of light flew up in the air and landed all over the place. They flickered and glowed like lightning bugs, except these were red, green, silver, and gold. Bright-colored tinsel and streamers flew through the air like confetti. Christmas trees popped up from nowhere and ornaments magically appeared in the hands of the vampires surrounding them. I smiled to myself. I loved decorating trees. The smell of warm cookies and pine filled the air. Everyone smiled and laughed as perfectly wrapped presents fell from the sky and into their hands. Christmas music blared through the whole place, and a feeling of lightness came with it.

I expected Grayson and Titus to be riding in some kind of carriage, but the only carriage I saw was one pulled by reindeer with a Santa throwing out candy canes. Grayson and Titus were just walking through the crowd, stopping and chatting with people. From here I could see their smiles and the way these vampires embraced them. I knew all of us were full-grown vampires, but the sense of fun and joy was in the air with all of this. Everyone was dressed like the Gupta sisters in their festive best. It wasn't about anything more than hanging out together and just celebrating the season.

Theon smiled down at me. "Not too bad, is it?"

Martin scoffed. "It's the coordination of perfect planning. The House of Shade would settle for no less than wonder for its people."

"Indeed, and your devotion knows no bounds, but I was asking Piper."

"I believe we all have opinions that are free to be shared." Martin looked down his nose at Theon. "You share yours readily enough, even if they are wrong."

"Boys, maybe we could just enjoy the day without all

this . . . testosterone," Prisha chided them both. "Besides, I'm hoping to get a glimpse of the Royals. It'd be very cool. Last year, I swear I saw the back of Grayson's head."

Sanchita bumped her with her shoulder. "Did not. That was Fred with the good hair from the blood-coffee shop."

"And I keep telling you it wasn't."

"And yet we all know it was."

"I didn't realize the Prince was such a spectacle to see." Theon rolled his eyes. "You lot are a bit much. Anyways, PIPER, back to my original question. It's not too bad, is it?"

"No, there are some things about this world that are way cool. Humans would lose their shit if they knew magic was real." Just as I said that, magic exploded over my head and rained down on me in silver glitter. I held my hand out and chuckled at how it gathered there like fake snowflakes. For a moment, I almost forgot the ache in my stomach and the burning in my throat.

Prisha and Sanchita bounced at my side. Sanchita practically vibrated with energy. "We've been waiting for this."

Prisha spun in a circle catching magical, fake snowflakes in her hands and letting it fall into her inky hair. Presents dropped right into their hands, and Prisha tore into one, tossing the paper aside. It was a long, flat white box, and she held it to her chest.

"What is it?" I tilted my head to the side, trying to get

a glimpse at the cover.

"I'm not telling." She wagged her eyebrows. "All I can say is it's absolutely perfect."

I chuckled. "How random that you get the perfect magical gift."

"It's not random. The House of Shade makes it so." She leaned in closer to me. "It's part of the reason why I said they care."

I arched my eyebrows. "That's really . . . amazing. This whole thing is."

"Isn't it just?" Marius seemed to melt from the crowd to stand on the other side of me. He plastered a smile on his face that felt about as genuine as the knock-off purses Dice and I used to buy in the back alleys of Boston.

"I think it's pretty wonderful." Marius gave me the full on *icks*. Not to mention, I think my extreme thirst was partially his fault. It took a lot of energy to walk in the sun, and then he nearly drowned me.

"You're still too human." He glared at the decorations. "This is trivial. Vampires are easily bought with minor trinkets."

Theon sighed. "Not everything is political. Sometimes life is worth enjoying."

Marius narrowed his eyes at him, and his lip curled back in disgust. He sucked in a breath like he was about to spew some venom toward Theon, and I felt myself tighten my grip on Theon's arm, ready to lay a verbal smackdown on Marius if need be.

"—Yes, I've always thought there was a time for politics and a time for enjoyment. Well said, Theon."

We all turned at once to find King Titus standing in our little group. Everyone around us immediately dropped into a bow. Marius even ducked his head lower. "Your majesty."

"Marius, glad to see you're enjoying things." Titus' face fell into a stern harsh scowl when he looked down on Marius. "Is it not a wonderful thing to give back to the community?"

"It is indeed, sir." Marius straightened and looked almost pained when he gazed upon Titus. "I was just saying that very thing to this group."

Liar liar, greedy pants on fire.

"Were you? Because from where I stood, I could almost sense the smell of bitterness." When Marius tried to speak, Titus clapped him on the shoulder. "Come now, old friend. Don't get yourself in a strop. After all, even the Grinch learned to enjoy Christmas. Save the sour sow routine for another time."

"Yes, your majesty." His eyes blazed with annoyance, but he gave Titus a single bow and then slithered back into the crowd where he'd come from. I found myself even more relaxed the moment he left. There was no longer any doubt in my mind that Marius was a slimy bastard, and I couldn't help but wonder why The House of Shade let him continue in his role as the Ambassador to The Night Spawn.

"He needed a moment to gather himself." Titus

chuckled and turned toward me. "Piper, my dear, you're looking well."

When I bowed to Titus, he tucked his finger under my chin and gently urged me up. When I met his eye, he grinned. "I think we're past formalities, don't you?"

"I'd like to think so, your majesty." To say I was surprised was an understatement. To say the others nearly keeled over would be accurate.

"Glad to see my family making nice with others." Grayson casually strolled up beside Titus. His eyes lingered for a moment on my hand wrapped around Theon's arm.

Prisha grabbed Sanchita's wrist and yanked her to her side. They vibrated with excitement as they faced Grayson. They turned red-faced as they fought to keep their lips pressed into demure smiles. He glanced their way, and they both gave him a low bow. He turned that breathtaking, cocky grin on them that I knew would send them into a tizzy. Because even now, even after everything he'd done, when he smiled like that it sent my heart fluttering against my own will.

"Ladies." He nodded to them. "I take it you're Prisha and Sanchita Gupta? Piper's new friends."

"We are!" Prisha bounced as she spoke.

"We've been taking good care of her!" Sanchita cut her off.

"I have no doubt," he said so smoothly. "I've heard such lovely things about you."

"Are you spying on me, Prince Grayson?" I tried to keep my tone casual, but deep down it'd only been one day without him and it had me already missing him. I still hated that we weren't what we could've been, and that was on him. But as long as I only admitted my feelings to myself, then no one else had to know. Desire and anger were starting to go hand in hand for me when it came to the sexy bastard.

His eyes darkened, and with all the confidence in the world, he reached out and plucked my hand from Theon's arm. He held it up to his lips and pressed a light kiss to the back of it. His mouth was warm and soft on my skin. Memories of his body tangled with mine flooded my memory, and I sucked in a quick breath to steady myself. His heady red wine scent flooded my senses, and my mouth watered for a taste of him. He flipped my hand over and placed a little white box in the center of my palm.

"What's this?" I fought the urge to rip it open. Curiosity mingled with my indignation. I wanted to know exactly what he'd gotten me, but my pride refused to let it be so.

"The perfect gift." His voice was so calm, so smooth, like he didn't get tied up in knots at seeing me the way I so clearly did when seeing him.

Martin scrolled through his tablet, furiously switching from screen to screen. "I'm sorry, sir, that's not on my list."

Titus chuckled. "Martin makes his lists and checks them twice."

"Only after Grayson approves every single thing for the gifts and festivities . . ." He stepped closer to Grayson. "Sir, I apologize if I've missed—"

"— Martin, you are perfection as always." Grayson held his hand up to stop Martin. "But this was my own doing."

I held the box out toward him. "You don't have to buy me things."

Prisha and Sanchita both gasped and whimpered at the same time when I declined his gift. I could see them shaking next to me.

Grayson plucked the box from my hand. "I didn't buy it."

I rolled my eyes. "Then you didn't have to *make* me something."

"I didn't make it." He chuckled, and when his eyes met mine, it felt like the whole world drifted away and it was just the two of us once more. Fire burned between us, and I felt myself wanting to be closer to him—like he was the sun and I was a planet caught in his pull.

"*Steal* it then . . ."

"Would I do such a thing? Oh, such little faith you have in me, Little Creature. But I can assure you *this* you *will* want. Practical with a touch of beauty, which is no match for your own, but one does endeavor to try."

Theon cleared his throat, trying to break the tension

between us. "Will you be attending the after-party, your majesty?"

Titus chuckled and shook his head. "No, a party like that is for the young, which I am not, but I'm sure the Prince will be happy to attend in my place."

Grayson still hadn't looked away from me. "Only if Piper is okay with it."

I tried to shrug but it came out like a half-shrug, half-twitch. "I don't care what you do."

I'm a horrible liar. I cared so much.

Sanchita and Prisha groaned at my lack of eagerness to have Grayson near me. Grayson shook his head and chuckled. "Such sweet lies roll from your lips."

"I really don't care," I said, trying to sound more convincing.

"Lovely, then I will be attending . . . so long as you don't care."

Theon groaned. "Then of course we're happy to have you."

Gray still hadn't looked away from me, and now he held the box up once more. He pulled the lid back, and my breath caught in my throat. There in the center of the box was a perfect pearl the size of a quarter. It was creamy-white with an iridescent sheen to it. It sat wrapped in a platinum setting ordained with tiny diamonds that wound around it like a snake. The chain was thin but twisted into a sturdy cord. I sucked in a deep breath.

I loved it instantly. "I-I can't accept this."

"Of course you can." He pulled it out of the box. "Won't you?"

"Yes, won't you?" Prisha practically growled at me.

"She absolutely should," Sanchita insisted.

I didn't want to make it awkward or cause a scene in front of all these people. I could always take it off later in the privacy of my rooms. Perhaps I could even pawn it somewhere to help pay to get Dice to me. Even as I had the thought, I knew I'd never let it go. I cleared my throat. I wanted to say yes. It was beautiful, and deep down I loved gifts.

"Yes, of course . . . Thank you." I held my hand out for it.

"Allow me." With his vampire speed, he lifted my hair and latched the necklace in less than a second, but it took long enough that I could feel his heat and I drowned in his scent. My stomach tightened and my fangs throbbed to sink into his skin.

The moment the pearl hit my skin, it warmed. I felt its power lingering deep behind that glossy exterior. I held it in my hand and watched as it turned from creamy-satin to a deep blood-red color.

Prisha sighed. "Oh, how lovely."

Grayson's eyes widened, and he held his hand out to me. "Come with me."

I hesitated.

"Piper, come with me. Now."

Damn he was sexy as fuck when he laced his voice

with that commanding tone. I could've said no. Told him to go fuck himself. And I was tempted to.

"Now, Piper."

Shit . . . New kink unlocked. I placed my hand in his and let him take me . . .

CHAPTER THIRTY-TWO

PIPER

The moment my fingers wrapped with Grayson's, electricity shot down my arm. Fire sizzled between us, and I felt my need for him in more ways than one. Our relationship was a mess of desire, lust, pain, and need. I wanted him more than anything I'd ever wanted before. His touch was a balm to the weariness I felt deep in my soul. Everything was a connection for us, and right now I reveled in it. He tugged me through the crowd at a pace only I could keep up with, but even still, the other vampires clearly saw us. There were shocked gasps and wide-eyed gazes as we passed.

I didn't know where we were going, but Grayson did. This place was so huge I still got turned around, but Grayson knew his way, and when he pulled me into a dark room with no windows and only one door, I froze in the middle of it. "What are we doing?"

He ripped his shirt over his head and threw it to the

floor, revealing the taut muscles and skin of his upper body. My fingers curled to touch him, to feel his skin against mine. His eyes bore into me. "Feed."

I took a step back. "No, we can go to the lab or something."

It wasn't that he wasn't tempting. The desire to have his delicious taste in my mouth nearly had me leaping on top of him. That close, the intensity was difficult to resist. It was like my body and emotions just took over and my mind was gone. He took a step toward me and laid his hand over the pearl around my neck. Heat spread from his touch, yet I could discern the cool feel of the pearl under his palm against my skin. He backed me up against the wall, and we were only a few inches apart. Our breath mingled together and warmth spread low in my belly.

Fuck. I wanted him. He knew it. I knew it.

"This gift is not only beautiful, it serves a purpose to help you." He hadn't removed his hand, and I didn't want him to.

I hated that this close he made me feel whole and complete, like without him I was only halfway alive. But when he was with me, the world lit up. I resented him for it. Why did he have to be my light but also bring so much darkness?

"Help me?" My words came out less harsh than I wanted. "How?"

"The deeper red it gets, the more in need you are of me."

There is a pearl that can tell I want to bang the hell out of him!? My eyes widened. "Kind of private don't you think? Take it off."

His deep chuckle vibrated in my chest. "It'll help teach you to control your thirst. The darker it gets, the closer you are to losing control."

He lifted his hand from the pearl to show me the color. "So dark it's nearly purple. Not good, Little creature, not good. *You. Need. Me.*"

I hated the way he said it like I needed all of him to survive. I could survive without anyone if I was forced to. "I think that you like that I need to *feed* from you."

"Are you saying you don't have need of me for anything else?" His mahogany eyes melted for me and a smile played on his lips.

"Only your blood . . . for now . . . until we figure out another way to make me better." I didn't want to need him. I didn't want to have this desire between us. It was a thin line of pleasure and pain that I walked each time I was near him.

"If you say so." His tongue darted over his lips, wetting them, and even in the dimness of this closet-like room I could see them glistening with temptation.

"Why do you want me to want you when you so clearly have cast me aside?"

"It's a twisted web we weave, and sometimes our lives aren't our own to do with what we like." He tilted his head to the side, exposing his neck even more to me. "Come, Stubborn Creature, take what you need."

I didn't know what he meant, and I was tired of asking more questions about why he seemed to want me with every fiber of his being but in the end left me so easily. The pulse in his neck called to me, and suddenly I couldn't resist any longer. My fangs lengthened and throbbed with the need to pierce his skin and feel his goodness fill my mouth.

I wrapped my hand around the back of his neck and jerked him toward me. I struck hard and fast. My teeth sank into his skin, and his taste flooded my mouth. My eyes rolled into the back of my head, and all I could feel was him all around me. Connection sizzled between us, and when the muscles in his body tightened, he pressed his whole body against mine. I could feel his excitement through my leggings, which were too thin and too tight. When his hand wrapped around my back and traveled to my hip and caressed the curve of my ass, I moaned at the touch.

Everything was him and I wanted it. I hopped up and wrapped my legs around his hips, and he pressed me back into the wall harder, lining up his hard excitement with my own. His hips flexed and the perfect friction between us had my eyes rolling in the back of my head. I didn't know what we were doing, but this close I couldn't say no. I didn't want to. I rocked my hips forward, grinding against him.

"Your little body is my addiction." He groaned and threw his head back as his hips moved with mine. We'd found that perfect friction, like two kids making out in the back of a car. Except we weren't kids, and I couldn't stop this moment if I tried. *Why does it have to be like this? Why does the fire only spark for him? Why does he hold the key to my passion?*

Anger and need warred within me, and I found myself grinding against him harder and faster, needing some kind of release. His blood sang through my body and the pleasure of his flavor, his touch, his groaning voice in my ear was too much. Ecstasy exploded over me, and for a moment, I saw stars in the darkness of the room. I flew so high I never wanted to come down. I pulled my teeth from his neck and let my head fall back on a moan. Grayson was right there with me, and he pressed his forehead to my neck. I felt his panting breath fan over my skin. My whole body tingled with awareness for him. He was everywhere—too close, too much.

I unhooked my legs from around his hips and slid down his body. When he leaned into me, I ducked under his arm and away from him. I threw my hair out of my face and straightened my twisted clothing. *I can't believe I just did that.* I swiped the back of my hand over my lips, and when my tongue darted from my mouth, I tasted him lingering there. He turned around with a self-satisfied grin on his face that made me want to hit him. He pulled his shirt off the floor and yanked it back over his head. My little fang marks peeked out from the collar like I'd branded him.

"Well, thank you for that." His blood surged through my body, and my energy returned to full force. There was no fatigue, no hunger, and no pain. He'd taken it all away. "Piper, look—"

"—We can't keep doing things like this."

"I won't let you starve." His eyes burned into mine.

I headed to the door. "I, um . . . I don't want to be mad at you anymore, but this can't be. I need to just get over you in my own way. So, if you don't want to let me starve, then we'll make an arrangement through Martin."

He tugged his sleeves up to his forearms "We live in the same world. We can't avoid each other."

Watch me try. "Public gatherings then, and Martin will arrange for my supplies."

"Piper." He stepped toward me, reaching for my hand.

I took a step back. I felt a hot ball of emotions well up in my throat. I was tired of hating him, tired of loving him, tired of never being everything to him that he so clearly was to me. I wanted to stop, to find peace here. Grayson wasn't a bad guy, he just wasn't the right guy. I heard the message from the universe loud and clear . . . Time to be the adult.

"No, I can't." My words were so calm, not filled with the anger I felt before. "We can't."

I pulled the door open and walked away, leaving him there like he'd left me so many times before.

CHAPTER THIRTY-THREE

DICE

"*H*ave a holly jolly Christmas. It's the best time for the tears! I don't know if they'll be snow but have a cup of beer!" Ophelia bellowed at the top of her lungs while sitting in the middle of the room surrounded by boxes, glitter, decorations, ornaments, messes of lights, and so much more. It was like her craft room threw up on the floor and she decided to sit in the middle of it with her favorite knife and stab things until they vaguely resembled some form of a Christmas decoration.

"It's *cup of cheer*." I hung another ornament on yet another tree.

According to Ophelia, options were always necessary, so she lined her throne room with Christmas trees and insisted on decorating each one with a different theme. It was like Christmas threw up in here. We had a gold tree, a silver tree, and a tree decorated in needle-sized daggers that from afar looked like dark tinsel but up close looked like a thousand papercuts waiting to happen. There was a Disney-themed one, a hot-pink one, and now a hodgepodge one where she insisted on cutting out all the decorations using construction paper, duct tape, and a knife. Needless to say, I was getting my fill of Christmas.

But it made me miss how Piper and I spent Christmas Eve. We'd get all our presents out and place them under our little tree and light a fire. We'd hang out with soft music, a shit ton of snacks, and whatever books we were currently sucked into. It wasn't much, but it was what we did. This was the first Christmas Eve in years that we weren't doing our little tradition.

"Oh oh, the missile ho. Hung where you can seeeeeeee. Somebody waits for you. Sounds like an ambush to meeee." She hummed to herself as she pulled things from the potion pouch hanging on her hip. One minute she had a paper mess, the next she smashed a little vial on it and *BOOM*—some kind of origami-looking decoration that would've taken any human hours to fold. At first their magic freaked me out, but I'd been there long enough that I was kind of used to it . . . kind of. I thought it was the coolest thing ever, and I always knew there was more out there, so I just had to let myself live with it and keep being full of wonder about it.

I groaned and sighed. "That's not how it goes. It's—"

"—don't bother. She marches to her own tune." Cross moved to the other side of the tree and hung a long string of hot-pink paper that was cut into one long curl. He shoved it in between the branches.

I sucked in a breath and sighed. "I can't just stay here trapped on this island."

"I know." He turned and walked away from me.

I didn't feel safe per se, but I didn't think I was in immediate danger of being killed either. It was clear Ophelia and Cross were dangerous. They didn't even bother putting their weapons away around me. Like if I grabbed one and tried to hurt them, they'd be just fine, which is why I hadn't even tried to yet. There was only one way to get out of this and it was when they were good and ready to let me go. Piper had to have had a plan in mind when she sent me here, but this shit just wasn't making sense.

I stuck my hand in my pocket and felt my dice warm under my hands. I wanted to pull them out and let them roll across the floor to tell me something comforting, but how could I do that here? With them?

"You should use them." Ophelia appeared just beside me, only a foot away from my face.

I startled and jumped back. "Don't sneak up on me like that."

"If I was sneaking up on you . . . you'd never know it." Her eyes were wide and round. "Come on. Show me."

I curled my hands around my dice. "Swear you won't take them."

"I'll take what I want, but in this case, I like you, so I won't take *them* until you give them to me . . . In which case, the law of presents applies, and I can't be held responsible for what happens after that."

I wrinkled my brows. "What?"

"Whatever you got in your pocket is fine." Cross rolled his eyes as he kept putting more decorations on the tree.

I pulled my hand from my pocket and held my dice between us. I felt their warmth in my hand as they moved around. Each of their sides was a symbol that had no words, but I still somehow understood perfectly. She grabbed my hand and pulled them closer to her face. She poked one with the tip of her finger, and it rolled in my palm. A light-blue color glowed from within it.

She placed her finger on one, then snapped it back just as quickly, shaking it out. "Fascinating."

"What does that mean?" I shoved them back in my pocket. "Do you know what they are?"

"Yep." She sat back in the middle of her construction pile.

"Well, are you going to tell me?" I put my hands on my hips.

She paused what she was doing and pressed her lips into a line as though she was thinking. "Nah."

"Nah? Just like that? Nah?" I threw my hands up and let them slap down on my thighs. "Ok, I can't stay here anymore. I want to leave and go find Piper."

She shrugged. "Okay."

"Really? You'll take me to go see her?" I didn't want to let hope bloom in my chest, but there it was anyways. It'd been weeks since I last saw her, weeks of missing my bestie and wondering what the hell actually happened to her.

"Sure." She dusted her hands off and popped to her feet. "I've always wanted to throw a human-ish thing in there and see what happens. I'm wondering if it's like Shark Week or more like Jaws."

Sometimes she confused the shit out of me with her cryptic words. "What?"

"Let's go. I'm bored, and I want to see Christmas in other countries."

"Piper is in another country?" This was the first information I'd gotten about her from any of these magical people.

"Um, yeaaaah."

Cross peeked his head around the side of the tree. "Niceeeee."

A bright blue light flooded the room, drawing all our attention to where the throne would be. It swirled with color and power. Neon-green smoke flooded from the magical doorway and into the room. It crept across the floor toward us, and I found myself stepping closer to Ophelia.

Cross walked up on my other side. He didn't seem bothered by this at all. "Maze."

The man I'd seen in my bar all those months ago, Maze, appeared in the opening. His magic whipped around him in a wild tornado. Tarot cards whirled above his head, and his eyes were milky-white with a hint of glowing green. Strands of his dark hair fell over his face, and he looked as though he was looking at nothing and everything all at the same time.

He didn't step through the doorway, yet I felt he was here for a purpose, and then his voice boomed across the room. "A blood on the streets. War colors the horizon for the House in peril. Death beckons one and all."

The portal snapped shut, and I felt the heaviness in the air around us. "That was eerie as fuck."

"I hate when he does that shit." Cross ran his hand through his hair. "But you get used to it."

I looked to the empty space like he was going to appear again. When he didn't, I glanced to Ophelia. "What does that mean?"

A sinister grin spread across her face, and she started pulling knives from all kinds of hiding places on her body, checking them, then putting them back. "It means I get to do what I do best."

I was afraid to ask. "And what do you do best?"

Cross shook his head and waved my question away. "You don't want to know."

"Tell me." I sucked in a breath and held it.

Ophelia paused in checking her personal arsenal. "Kill things that have it coming."

"And what about me?" I didn't want to be trapped here forever.

"Sorry. You'll have to stay a bit longer." She shrugged. "But at least there's plenty of food, you have a nice room, and hey, you're living in a castle on a tropical island. Be a little grateful."

I swallowed around the nervous lump in my throat. Maze said something about death and blood on the streets, and somehow I felt that was about my bestie. "And Piper? What about her?"

Ophelia rolled her shoulders and bounced on the balls of her feet like she was warming up for a workout. "I like that one . . . Let's hope she isn't one of the ones who has it coming."

CHAPTER THIRTY-FOUR

GRAYSON

The world seemed so monochromatic without her in it. Everything was black and grey with shades of drama. The pressure of not being close to her was almost too much. If one had a source of life, then how did one stay away from such a thing? When the curse was cast on the generations of The House of Shade, whoever had done it had known the pain it'd cause. That kind of bitterness and need for vengeance would drive us all mad, and deep down, I couldn't help but wonder what my family had done to deserve such misery. With the history of Evermore and how bloody violent it was, there was no telling. All I *did* know was that this was what misery felt like.

It was sorrow deep in my bones, seeing only her when I closed my eyes. Her scent lingered in my memories. Everything about her consumed me. She was my curse . . . and my obsession. Even now, watching her from across the room, I could barely tear my gaze away from her. Yet I had to fake my way through this, and for The Night Spawn, I would.

The party was in full swing. It wasn't a huge affair like the ones we did at the castle. It was more like an after-party or college dorm room party. One of the larger apartments served as the venue, and it was packed with vampires all drinking spiked blood, eating little snacks, and chatting in small groups. Christmas decorations were sparse in the apartment, but it almost looked purposeful, with a tiny tree and little Christmas magnets on the fridge.

Everyone was dressed in some kind of Christmas sweater or holiday outfits. There were Christmas hats and noisemakers. Music filled the room, and they all looked so happy to just be there with their friends. When I glanced at Piper once more, she stood in a small group with the Gupta sisters, Martin, and Theon. She'd found herself quite the little niche in the underground. And she looked so . . . comfortable.

"Your Highness!" A young male vampire ran up to me with a camera in hand. He was short and slight, with wide, dark eyes that matched his skin and short, tight curls.

I forced my gaze from Piper to turn to him. "Hello there."

He extended his hand toward me. "I just wanted to say thank you, Your Highness. You know, for the camera. I've always wanted to be a photographer, and this equipment . . . Well, it'll get me started. And I'm so . . . I'm so grateful."

My lips curled into a smile automatically, and I took his hand. This was what I wanted for the Night Spawn: the freedom for them to choose their own lives and pursue dreams, to be able to really live and not be relegated to hunting the night. "Of course. I'm just pleased we could be of use, Steven."

His jaw dropped, and his eyes widened. "You know my name."

I was about to confirm that I did indeed know his name, but he spun on his heels and ran across the room where a group of his friends watched our interaction with excited interest. His voice rose over the light hum of the crowd. "HE KNOWS MY NAME!"

I shook my head and chuckled as the rest of his group clapped him on the back. The truth was I was attempting to learn the names of the vampires in residence in Night Spawn City, or at least have some general knowledge. In this Titus was right: know thy people and know thy enemies.

"Your Highness! Over here!" Prisha waved me toward their group.

Piper's head snapped up, and when her eyes met mine, I could see the sadness and disappointment there. I didn't know what hurt worse—being a disappointment to her or not having her. I wanted to walk up and claim her as my own for all to see. But that wasn't how this worked. I kept the smile on my face as I walked over to their little group. Theon moved closer to Piper and pressed his hand to the small of her back. The moment his hand touched her, I was tempted to rip it off.

I could rip it off before he even knew it. Matter of fact, I could just command him to rip his own arm off. Tempting . . . Oh so tempting. I never wanted to use my powers before, but with Theon . . . I could make an exception.

"Your Highness—"

"—Please call me Grayson or Gray." I didn't need everyone fawning over me. I much preferred to be treated like everyone else.

She sucked in a sharp breath and visibly vibrated in front of me. "Okayyy, *Grayson*."

"What's it like in the palace? Is it cool to be royalty? Or is it like an insane amount of pressure and all you want to do is escape? How did you know what to get for everyone? Are you psychic or do you just have really good spies? When you were gone with the Witch Queens, what was that like?"

"Whooaaaa, Prisha. Take a breath." Theon chuckled. "I'm sure the Prince hasn't come here to get interrogated."

"I think I can decide for myself." I turned to Prisha. "And I'm happy to answer your questions. Being a royal has its perks and responsibilities, so I suppose it is kind of cool. The Witch Queens are something to behold, there are no words. No, I'm not psychic, and Martin knows all and sees all. I've enlisted his help on many projects, and not once has the man ever let me down."

Martin nearly cracked a smile. Instead, he ran his hand over his iPad and straightened his tie, then cleared his throat. "One endeavors to do as much as one can, sir."

"Modest as ever, mate." I patted him on the shoulder. "It's people like Martin who make the job easier and well worth doing."

His cheeks warmed to a deep-red. "Thank you."

Sanchita clapped her hands together. "It really is a pleasure."

"And for me as well." This was all part of the job, but in truth I wanted to know who Piper had chosen as her friends. She was picky when it came to people, and I wondered why they appealed to her. "In fact, you all should come to the Christmas Ball tomorrow at the palace so you can see it for yourselves. Piper will be in attendance."

"I will?" Her eyebrows shot up.

"As my progeny, of course she will. I'm sure she'd love your company."

She smirked at me. "In that case I'd love to."

Theon scoffed. "And how would the Blood Borns react to that? Having Night Spawn at their gala?"

"I suspect however I choose."

Silence fell over the little group. Theon moved closer to Piper, and I fought the hiss that wanted to burn up my throat and threaten him. She glanced between the two of us and sighed. "Guys . . . behave."

"Is that it then? You command and others fall into line

around you?" Theon chuckled and smiled, but there was an edge to his words. They were more accusing than playful.

I shrugged. "Indeed. Yes."

He held a cup to his lips and took a deep drink. "And what of forward progress? Change?"

"Change is subjective."

"So, you agree that you want to maintain our stations?" He scoffed. "Quite vexing, I must say."

"I think the message you'd like to convey is quite clear to your mates here, picking an argument to impress others. If you're after the affection of one such as Piper, it would be ideal to make yourself look like David versus Goliath. To that, I say *piss off*. You are no David, and I refuse to play the role of Goliath." I leaned against the counter next to us, making sure to look relaxed just to get the point across that he was no threat to me. "It's an interesting tactic."

"Come on, Theon, lay off," Prisha chided him. "You know Grayson has done so much for us already. We're getting a new city and new opportunities all the time."

"Right, like I'm to believe he's the one taking on that bill?" He shook his head and took another sip. "Ten quid says that's a publicity stunt."

"Actually," Piper said, "it is true. He is paying for it all."

Silence.

She held her hand out toward him. "I'll take that ten quid now."

Laughter bubbled up my throat. "Well done."

Theon didn't think it was funny. "And what of the rest of it?"

"Are we to discuss politics all night or is this a party?" *How many times did I find myself in this position at any number of these gatherings?*

"It's so rare that we have you here. Can't fault a guy for taking the opportunity to have a conversation." He handed me a cup full of blood.

Not wanting to be rude, I took it. "No, you can't."

"See? We're all friends here." Piper twirled from Theon's grip and met my eye. "Just friends. Now, if you'll excuse me."

She strolled away from the group and headed for the door.

Friends.

Just friends.

Heat and anger shot through my body. I'd said we were friends to her, but somehow when she said it the sting was acute. I couldn't take this much longer.

Just friends . . . To hell with that.

CHAPTER THIRTY-FIVE

PIPER

*S*exy cocky bastard. *Just friends? Who was I kidding?*

The world could light on fire and I'd only have eyes for Grayson Shade. Theon was nice enough. He was trying to learn and be more. I liked that about him. At least he was moving in a different direction than what Marius suggested. Could the same be said for Grayson who followed along with what the crown demanded? Or was that just an excuse? Either way, I didn't know what I was thinking saying it was okay to be around him publicly . . . that I could handle it. The audacity of me thinking I actually could and not feel one of the five hundred warring emotions I felt within my own body for him.

I needed a breath, a moment of reprieve from his smirk, his quick mind, his tempting scent. The way he consumed me was not easy to deal with, so I strolled away . . . just for a moment . . . just to breathe. But I felt him at my back, moving silently as I wove my way through the crowd and out the door. I stepped to the side and paused as more vampires wandered in and out of the party. It reminded me so much of the house parties people had around the colleges in Boston, except we were deep in the underground, and I wanted the outside air to breathe. Grayson sauntered out after me just as I leaned against the wall and sucked in a deep breath.

His eyes blazed, and he stepped in closer. "Just friends?"

"That's right," I lied. "Just like you said."

He placed his hand beside my head and leaned in so close I could feel his breath fan across my cheek and caress my ear. "We will never be *just friends*."

"Grayson, I—"

His hand snaked up my throat and he let his thumb draw small circles on my jawline. "You and I will never be *just friends*."

"You're right." My words came out as a whisper.

Other vampires stopped to peek at the two of us, and I felt their gazes on us. He must've too, because for a moment he looked like he was going to back away. Instead, his tongue darted out and he ran it over the vein in the side of my neck. *Holy fuck.* Sensations racked my body, and I wanted to feel it again, wanted to feel his teeth slide into my skin. My eyes rolled and I tilted my head back in a silent plea for him to do it here and now.

A low growl rumbled in his chest, and his grip tightened for just a second before he stopped, picked me up, and took off running at full speed. The world flew by in a blur. I barely had a second to think before he kicked open the door to a room I'd never seen and threw me across it. I sailed through the air and landed on a soft, cushy surface. Gray was there next to me as my head hit the pillow.

"*Friends.*" He hissed the word as he grabbed the hem of my shirt and fisted it. "Tell me to stop now or I won't until we're both screaming in pleasure, *then* we'll see how friendly I can be."

I hesitated.

He loosened his grip. "Patience is not on my agenda tonight, Indecisive Creature."

Who was I kidding? I was a goner for him. I groaned and lifted my arms up. "Don't stop."

"Good girl." He pulled my shirt up over my head.

His movements were fast and rough, like I was seeing the vampire in him for the first time. He hooked his finger into the front of my bra and ripped the material. The cups flew wide open and cold air drifted over my breasts. Grayson's hand covered one while he took the other in his mouth. I arched my back, urging him onward. This was too much. It was fate. His hand slid down to the waistband of my leggings, and in one quick jerk, they too were gone, and I was completely bare.

His hand dipped even lower, and when he felt how ready I was for him, his breath hissed out. "Just friends."

He flipped me over on my stomach and pulled my

hips back so I was on my knees with my face pushed into the pillow. I heard the sound of his pants unzipping, and a moment later I felt him pressing into me. My body gave around him, and I felt him moving inside me. Pleasure ripped through me, and I pushed back into him to find that perfect glide. His thighs slapped into mine and I felt the brush of his trousers on my skin. Something about being completely bare to him made this stolen moment that much more scintillating.

His fingers pressed into my hips, and he dragged me back along him. His breath hissed in and out, and I felt myself just wanting this, wanting him. He rolled onto his side, dragging me with him, and suddenly I was the little spoon. His hand curled around my body and reached down between my legs. His fingers danced over the most sensitive part of me as he drove into me from behind. My body was a mix of sensations: longing, need, pleasure, desire. Grayson was all-consuming, burning me from the inside out. But deep down I knew that I scorched him too.

He was everywhere at the same time. His kisses were on my skin, his hands all over my body. This wasn't just a hard fucking, this was him taking possession of me . . . of my body. And holy hell I wanted it. I wanted to give in to him and let him do what he willed. And I did. His hand moved in perfect rhythm to his pumps, and I found myself going to new heights, rolling in the pleasure he gave me.

He growled in my ear. "I can never be just friends

with you, Piper. You're my obsession."

I felt my body quicken around him, my muscles all tightening, ready for that explosion of pleasure I knew only he would bring me so perfectly. He moved faster and harder, his body slamming into mine. My little moans filled the air. I couldn't think. I could barely breathe. There was only him and only us in this moment.

"That's it, Sexy Creature. So close. Come on." His hips slapped into my backside, and he never let up that punishing pace.

One of his hands fondled my breast while the other rubbed between my legs. He ran his tongue over that pulse in my neck, and I couldn't take it anymore. It was too much. He was too much. My body exploded around him. I threw my head back, crying out at the pleasure running over me. My muscles that'd been so tight let go all at once and turned to Jell-O in his arms. Ecstasy had me flying high with him inside me. The room was dark but glittering lights danced in my vision. I never wanted to come back down, never wanted this moment to end.

He pumped me harder and faster. Sweat slicked my skin, and I felt him racing to his own end. His body jerked within mine and I felt his spasms of pleasure deep within. He shoved into me and held himself there while he found his end. His breaths tickled my shoulder as he sagged into the bed. His arms constricted around me, pulling my back to his chest. He curled around me, our bodies still linked. We laid there for long moments, just breathing and listening to the sound of our pounding hearts. He pressed a kiss to my shoulder, and when I tried to get up, he held me tighter.

"Stay."

It was one word but it had me lying there with my muscles feeling like goo. He brushed my hair away from my ear and whispered, "Just stay."

When I nodded, he said nothing else. He just held me tighter against his body, like at any moment I'd slip away and he couldn't bear the thought of it. I didn't know how long we lay there or how I could only listen to his breathing. I didn't want to think about the loss or pain anymore. We could never be just friends, but we could never be more. When he finally fell into a deep sleep, I turned in his arms and took in his devastating face. Everything about Grayson was gorgeous and heartbreaking. He was both love and pain, fulfillment and loss, pleasure and sin.

I didn't want to fall asleep in his arms and wake to another awkward conversation about what we were and could never be. There was only one thing I could do at this point . . . leave. I slipped from his grip and crawled out of the bed. As a human, he might've awakened with my movements. But I was no human, and this was a moment that I wanted to forget but was sure would forever be burned into my memory. I'd never known such a man, such a contraction. He could give me the world and take it away in less than a second.

And for all that . . . I slipped away into the night.

CHAPTER THIRTY-SIX

GRAYSON

"And then she just... left."

If there was any group of people who could help me with my plight, it was these guys. So, here I was back at Evermore Academy, standing in one of the empty classrooms with my best mates and a few others. The walls were the same dark-grey stone the exterior was made of. Desks were lined up in rows in the classroom, and at the head of the room stood a larger desk where the professor would sit, and behind that was a lone chalkboard. I sat with my legs dangling off the professor's desk and my hands folded in front of me.

Tuck, Beckett, Maze, Logan, Kylian, and Brax all sat around me with grave looks on their faces. Tuck sat there tossing a fireball up and down. He shook his head, sending that wild auburn hair flying in all different directions. The smell of burnt embers filled the room.

"I mean, you're screwed. You can't just mess around like that."

I ran my hands through my hair. "You think I don't know that?"

"It is my experience that if one acts like a big teddy bear, one will get treated as such," Brax rumbled in his deep Russian accent from his seat at the back of the room.

"Riigghhhtttt."

Kylian lifted his hand. "What exactly am I doing here?"

"We're here to help out our friend . . . Ya know, give advice?" Beckett, my other closest friend, sat beside Tuck. He was the model sort, with blond hair and ocean-blue eyes.

"I'm not qualified for this shit."

Maze's eyes swirled from milky-white to green and back again. "Yeah, and you won't be for a while."

Kylian's head snapped up. "Did you just check with your little psychic powers?"

Maze pulled a crumpled-up bag from the side pocket of his army pants. He reached in and pulled out a wad of white paper, then proceeded to unwrap it until he had a mushed-up BLT sitting on his desk. He reached into the other pocket and pulled out a handful of loose fries and dumped them on the desk. He did this several times before deciding his pocket was sufficiently empty.

"Yeah, I checked. You're gonna suck big time."

Kylian placed his hand on the floor and copper-colored light glowed from beneath his touch. A chunk of the stone contorted within his hand until he had a perfect ball of sand. Once he did, he fisted it and threw it right as Maze. Neon-green smoke poured from Maze's hand, and a single tarot card flew from his pocket and hovered right in front of him. The ball of sand crashed into it and exploded. Sand rained all over the side of Maze's head and jacket, but he didn't pay attention. Instead, he plucked up a fry, blew it off, and then ate it.

He scoffed. "Touchy."

"I don't suck at anything." Kylian flipped him off.

Logan, who usually remained silent, flicked his hand, and his smokey magic wrapped around Kylian. "Tell the truth."

His powers of charm could get anyone to do virtually anything. It was a dangerous magic meant only for those who could handle it. If he'd been the old Logan, I'd have complete faith in him. But there was a side to him now that we all needed to be wary of. I'd seen it before and hoped to never see it again. Sweat beaded Kylian's brow, and his body quaked. When Kylian pressed his lips together, trying to fight Logan's power, all Logan did was chuckle.

"I'm barely toying with you . . . Don't make me ask again."

"Enough." Beckett sighed. "Let him go, Logan."

Logan dropped his power and Kylian sucked in a deep breath. "Fine. You want my two cents, leech? You done fucked up with this girl."

"Speaking from experience, are we?" Tuck stared him dead in the eye.

"Can we focus?" Logan pointed toward me. "That thing with Angel has nothing to do with this. Focus on the vampire. We're not talking about me. We're talking about him and how bad he messed up."

"I bloody well know that. I'm here to figure out what to do from here . . . or how to sort it . . . or how to coexist for longer than twenty minutes without trying to kill each other or rip each other's clothes off."

"I fail to see the fault in the last one." Kylian leaned back in the chair and crossed his arms.

"Right, you should not be giving advice to anyone." I turned back to Beckett and Tuck. "You lot have gotten the relationship equation figured out. What do I do?"

They exchanged a look, then both of them kind of glanced away. Frustration grew and I couldn't take it anymore. "Oh, come off it. Right, I'm not a bad guy, I've just done some bad things . . . for her own good."

"Yeaaaaah, butttt from her perspective, you're just a bad guy at this point." Beckett ran his hand over the back of his neck. "Hard to come back from that. Trust me."

"And she doesn't know they were for her own good." Tuck still tossed the ball of fire up and down like it was some kind of game.

"I told her it was for her own good."

Beckett shook his head. "But it's like, you can't just *say* it's for their own good. You have to explain *why* it is for their own good."

Tuck nodded. "Took me a while to learn that one."

"Me too." Beckett sighed.

"Weird, right?"

"Right, like they claim to trust us, but they need to know the why behind everything."

Tuck threw his hands up and let them fall on the desk. "I know, right?"

Beckett sat up straighter in his desk. "Does a four-star general explain to the troops why things are done a certain way?"

"No!" Tuck slammed his fist on the desktop.

Beckett's voice rose. "Does the chef explain to the cooks why they need to prep food in the kitchen?"

"No!" Another slam of the first.

They'd gotten themselves wound up, and I didn't know how to stop it until Maze started laughing so hard he couldn't take another bite of his sandwich. He threw his food down on the table and dusted his hands off.

"Yeah, but you're both forgetting one very important thing."

Tuck turned toward him. "Oh yeah? What's that?"

"You're not the generals . . . they are." He popped another fry into his mouth and dug back into the sandwich.

We all fell silent for a moment while they took that in. Kylian chuckled and shook his head. "You all are weak with these women."

Maze chuckled. "And you think you won't be?"

"Not a chance."

"Care to make a wager on that?" He took a bite of the sandwich and a piece of tomato fell out and slapped on the white paper.

Kylian's eyes widened. "You know something."

"I know all things."

"Tell me."

"Not a chance." Maze scoffed.

"I don't care about your rules. You will tell me." Kylian sat forward in his seat as if about to pounce on Maze.

"Nope." He popped another fry in his mouth.

Beckett sighed. "Maze, stop fucking with him."

"Why?"

"Because . . ." Beckett paused. "Actually, nah, go ahead and fuck with him. I'm entertained."

Kylian flipped them both off, then crossed his arms over his chest. "Next time you want to go on a killing spree, you're gonna go by yourself, and I'm not gonna help any of you find your targets."

Maze shrugged. "There's always Ophelia . . . She knows how to find and kill things."

"Da." Brax shivered. "Tiny human is terrifying."

We all took a moment and nodded.

"Can we focus for a minute?" My world was crashing down around me, and this lot couldn't seem to scrap a shred of good advice. "So, what, I'm to pack it in? *Piss off* is what I say to that."

"Not pack it in, but maybe your only saving grace is to tell her the truth?" Tuck shrugged. "It always works for me."

"My sympathies, Grayson." Brax placed his hand over his heart. "I find it difficult to keep things from Elle as well. Humans are so fragile."

They all turned to look at him. Tuck chuckled. "And how is it going with her?"

"Surprisingly well." Brax turned to me. "Not telling is difficult."

"Damn right it is. And what of Titus' gag order? I can't very well walk up to her and tell her I'm cursed and that's why I have to stay away, particularly when it's quite obvious I cannot." This was a disaster. "And she just . . . left."

"Can you blame her?" Logan chimed in. "It's a kind of mental torture. I want you . . . I don't want you. Bit of a dick move if you ask me."

"That's right helpful." I knew this whole situation was a balls-up. "Perhaps we can think of something useful aside from me being a dick."

"You are a dick, leech," Kylian grumbled under his breath.

"Don't get yourself in a strop with me. Not my fault your future is a mess. You're a sour git, you are." None of this was helping. "I need solutions here, and I've come to you lot for them."

Beckett shrugged. "Break the hold your uncle has on you, tell her the truth, then stay the hell away from her until the Witch Queens figure out a way to help you. At least she'll understand and not think you're a total jerk off."

"That easy, is it?" I sagged. "That seems the only solution."

He held his arms out wide. "The truth will set you free, my friend. Besides, I've never come up against a curse the Witch Queens can't break."

The door flew open with a bang, and in strolled Zinnia along with Astrid, Serrina, Tilly, and Tabi. Astrid walked over to where Beckett sat on the desk and hopped up on the desktop in front of him. She turned and met my eye. "We can't break it."

"Fucking hell." I ran my hands through my hair and tugged at the strands. I wanted to rip them out. "Can not *one* bloody thing go right?"

"YET! We can't break it *yet*." Zinnia put her hands on her hips. "We're still working on it. Adrienne and Niche are buried in books and they refuse to come out until they find a solution for you."

Silvery power rolled off her. It was as if she had so much extra her body couldn't contain it. Astrid too was looking powerful as ever with golden magic rolling down her arms and legs. It was almost second nature to the two of them. While Tilly wasn't a queen, she had some kind of weird power connection with Maze that let her wield some of his power—mixed with whatever was left over of the short time she spent as a demon.

Tabi hopped up on the desk next to me and bumped me with her shoulder. "How did the gift work out?"

I tried not to think of what happened after I gave that pearl to Piper. "Better than expected."

"So good . . . and then she left him," Kylian blurted out.

"Right. You're not invited to our chats any longer. I can't be doing with you right now." I pointed toward the door. "Shut it or leave, wanker."

"I'll stay." He leaned back in his chair.

Tilly moved over toward Maze, and he silently offered her the last bite of his sandwich. It was just one gesture, but to me it said it all about their relationship. She smirked at him and shook her head, pushing the bite toward him. Instead, he grabbed the last fry and handed it to her. There was a silent battle of wills, and finally she took the fry and ate it. In that moment, he smirked to himself like he'd won by getting her to eat the last fry. It was such a loving motion coming from him—so small but so important—because Maze didn't share food.

"Oh, will you pack it in." They all turned to look at me. "What? You're all so happily soulmated and I'm drowning here. Now will someone offer some sort of plausible solution or *something* to help?"

Zinnia pulled a vial of glowing purple liquid from her pocket. She shook it up, then handed it to me. "We haven't figured out how to break the curse . . . yet . . . but this will give you a thirty second delay."

I took the vial and stared down at it. "Thirty second delay until what?"

"Until you fall to the curse."

Her words fell heavy in the room, and I wanted to laugh and play it off like nothing could touch me, like nothing could bother me, but we all knew better. "This is it then . . . You all think I'm going to fall, do you?"

When they didn't respond and all I could see was the sadness in their eyes like I was already gone, I slid the vial into my pocket. "Yeah, me too."

Damn that curse . . . damn this life . . . and damn my heart . . .

CHAPTER THIRTY-SEVEN

PIPER

"I don't really understand men." Prisha walked into my closet and pulled another dress out from the stack hanging in the corner. "I mean, you like them, you don't like them. Why can't they just be normal and good and make it easy to like them?"

This conversation was hitting a little close to home. It was normal to gossip about guys and stuff when chilling with my friends, but I was still reeling from the night before and didn't know how or what to do now. I hadn't heard from Grayson, but Martin had a brand new batch of blood delivered for me early that morning. So, he was thinking about me enough to feed me but not enough to even call. It didn't help that I now had a phone to keep on checking. *If Dice were here, she'd tell me to forget his ass.* But something in me just couldn't let go.

"No one understands them." I didn't want to tell them about my night spent with Grayson or the complications between the two of us. I'd just met them. It felt kind of wrong to unload on them the way I unloaded on Martin before. I also didn't want them to have a bad opinion about their Prince. It was sad I wanted to protect his reputation, but I still felt something for Grayson. Last night was evidence of that.

So here we were picking dresses for the Christmas Ball at the castle. I didn't want to go, but everyone expected me to be there, and I wouldn't let them down. At least this part felt more familiar, with my friends picking through my closet. Dice and I practically shared a closet when we lived together. Having the Gupta sisters here doing the same thing kind of made it feel like a new start to a new home.

"Oh, I don't know. The Prince seems to have eyes only for you, Piper." Sanchita spun around in a circle in a tight black dress that hugged her body from neck to knee. Three round cutouts revealed the dark skin from her ribs down to her hip. I had no idea who put that number in my closet, but she could totally have that one because it looked amazing on her.

I sat back on the bed and toyed with the edge of a dress that'd been thrown there. I forced a laugh. "Does not."

Prisha peeked out from the closet and looked to Sanchita. They both broke out into fits of laughter. She walked out holding an emerald floor-length gown. "He rushed out after you last night like his ass was on fire. What did he say anyways?"

"Oh, um." I didn't want to lie, but his words echoed in my mind. *We will never just be friends.* "He just wanted to make sure I'd be attending the Christmas Ball thing with you guys. You know, his *progeny* is expected to be there."

"Well, I wish *any* guy would show that kind of interest in me." Sanchita slid her feet into some matching heels. "I mean, is it too much to ask to find my soulmate and just be tied together forever and forever?"

I rolled my eyes. "I'm not even sure soulmates exist."

"Oh, they very much do exist." Prisha stopped in the middle of the room and put her hands on her hips. "I'm telling you."

"Yeah, but like, how do you even know? It's just a feeling." I used to think Grayson was my soulmate, but now I was sure we weren't. How could he be when he hurt me so easily but couldn't let me go. A soulmate wouldn't do that.

"Not for vampires." Prisha took the dress off the hanger and pulled it over her head. "It's like a whole thing for us. And you know right away."

"I find that really hard to believe." Soulmates always seemed like such a myth, like something for the fairytales, not real life.

Sanchita pulled the back dress off and grabbed a red one that was draped over the foot of my bed. She stepped into it and pulled it up, then turned to Prisha to zip the back up. "It's not the same as humans. They have to guess at their feelings. In Evermore, all the species have soulmates. For the witches and warlocks, it's at first touch, which is nice because it's right away. You know that the universe has picked this person just for you."

My thoughts turned to Grayson if only it had been that easy So simple as just a touch. Things might be different between us. When he'd first touched me, I thought we were soulmates. Maybe he needed something more to convince him of what I believed so long ago.

"And for vampires?"

"Oh, it's kind of hot." She lowered her voice. "It's all about the bite."

"What?"

She extended her fangs. "If you bite him and he bites you, and you're soulmates, the mark appears on your body. It's like a sign you belong to one another."

Prisha sighed. "It's more than that. Blood is our life force, so when you bite each other, it's like exchanging life forces. You become bonded and start to share everything and make each other stronger. I've even heard you can feel each other's emotions."

Just hearing about it made my heart hurt. It felt like too much to hope that Grayson belonged to me. He'd spent enough time running his lips over my skin to never have even attempted to bite me. Did that mean he knew I wasn't his soulmate? Or he just didn't want to find out? Was he avoiding it with me? Every single one of those options stung.

"It sounds kind of fairytale-ish to me."

"Doesn't it to us all?" Prisha sighed. "Even so, Grayson kind of looks at you in that way."

"No. He really doesn't." I rose to my feet and walked into my closet. I ran my hand over the last few dresses hanging there. But nothing felt right for the Christmas Ball. I wanted to be classy but pretty . . . with a touch of sexy.

Sanchita's voice rose so I could hear her. "Well, he seems like the right type to be a soulmate. Handsome, rich, powerful—"

"— Don't forget kind and generous," Prisha added.

Don't remind me. "Yep, I'm sure he'll make someone very happy someday." *Just not me.*

I grabbed a dark-plum dress from the rack and walked out of the closet. It was one of those mermaid dresses—short in the front and a long train in the back. It would be tight across my body and flowing at the bottom. I bit my bottom lip. "I don't think this one is right either. What do you think?"

They both stood there staring at me. When neither of them answered, I grew impatient. "What?"

"We both know something's going on with you and the Prince. If you don't want to tell us just yet, that's okay, but don't ignore the signs that there is something between the two of you. Give it a chance." Prisha moved to sit on the edge of my bed and the dress she had on puffed out around her.

"You're not wrong. There's something between us, but it's not what you think, and he is a great guy . . . just not with me."

Before I could clarify any further, there was a harsh,

brisk knock on the door. I dropped the dress and walked over to the door. My brow furrowed as I opened the door. Marius stood there in all his self-important glory. The fur collar of his leather coat was even fluffier than usual. He wore a dark-black button-down shirt under it with leather pants and thick boots. His hair was styled to fall all around his face, and I was sure he had on dark-black eyeliner.

"Ah, it looks like I'm just in time."

"For what? The party isn't for another few hours." My brow furrowed in confusion.

"For this." He swept his arm to the side and a tall, thin vampire pushed in one of those rolling racks full of all kinds of dresses. The rack overflowed with all kinds of material of different colors and shapes. "I thought you ladies might want some options to choose from."

Prisha and Sanchita fell on the rack like it was the sales rack at Louis Vuitton and everything was ninety percent off. They started pulling dresses off right away and tossing them to each other. At this point, my little studio apartment was going to be one big pile of clothing.

"That was very kind of you."

"A peace offering." He smirked. "For my bad behavior."

"You think dresses make up for almost drowning me?" I shook my head. "You've got a lot to learn about women."

"Yes, Theon said as much." He sighed. "But I thought this might be a baby step toward getting on."

"Theon was right. It takes more than a pretty dress to make up for that." I crossed my arms over my chest. I didn't want to wear a single thing he brought for me. I'd rather pick a dress I already had here.

"Perhaps you could attend the ball with us then? And we could start there?" He hung his head like he was trying to appear apologetic.

"Thank you, but I'm going with my friends."

He motioned to the sisters behind me. "Yes, of course, I meant your friends as well."

"We'd love to!" Sanchita called out with a hint of laughter in her voice.

I sighed. "Yes, I suppose so."

"Lovely. Then I shall return to collect you all in a few hours." He gave me a small bow and then backed out of the door and nearly collided with Martin who was on his way in with a big white box.

"Pardon." Marius eyed the box but didn't say anything.

Martin's brow furrowed and his lip curled in disgust. "What did he want?"

"To bribe me into trusting him." I groaned.

"Hope that didn't work." He adjusted the box in his hand.

"You know me better than that." I pointed to the box. "What's that?"

"I don't know if I want to show you now." He held it away from me.

I giggled and reached for it. "Come on, deep down we all know I like gifts, just not from Marius."

"Finneeeee." He held it out toward me. "It's from Grayson."

I lifted the lid and sucked in a deep breath. There among bright-red tissue paper was a white silk dress. It was simple but classic with spaghetti straps and shining material that matched the pearl hanging from my neck. I lifted it out of the box and held it to my body. It was elegant, beautiful, and sexy as hell with a slit in the side.

Prisha froze in her hunt through the dress rack. "Wow."

"Yeah."

Martin sighed. "It's perfect."

"It really is." I paused. "Did he have you pick this out for me?"

He chuckled and shook his head. "His majesty did this himself. I'm simply a messenger."

"What a vampire." Sanchita sighed.

"Like a real-life Prince Charming." Prisha's voice was laced with yearning.

"There's a note." Martin handed over a perfectly folded piece of paper, and my heart sped up as I took it.

Grayson had always known how to do things. This wasn't a bribery dress, this was a dress bought with care because he just thought I'd like it, and that melted my heart from the inside out. I really didn't want to love him, but it was like trying to fight a riptide in the ocean. Eventually, no matter how hard I fought, he would drag me under. I felt myself slipping into that world where I knew the pain would come but I couldn't see a way of stopping it. He was all-consuming in a way that made me putty for him. I opened the paper and smirked. There in his perfect scrolling handwriting was one sentence.

With my regards—just your friend . . . Gray.

CHAPTER THIRTY-EIGHT

PIPER

Mirror portals were an odd thing. It wasn't that I didn't trust myself after my last little exploding mishap. *Okay, maybe it was.* But we stood in the middle of the lobby at the front of the Night Spawn Headquarters. The last time I was here I made this very same mirror explode out all over everyone. Now I was even more pressured as there were a group of my friends now standing behind me to witness what could possibly be a mishap.

"You know you can do this, right?" Theon leaned in on my side to whisper.

"I love the confidence you have in me," I murmured back.

"Off you pop then." He nodded toward the mirror. "We can't keep everyone waiting."

I chuckled. "Has anyone told you you're a dick?"

"Plenty of times."

I stepped forward and studied my reflection in the full-length mirror. The dress hugged my body, not leaving much to the imagination. The bottom had a slit that went high up on my thigh, and I stood out from my friends in the light, cream-colored dress as opposed to the darker colors they'd all selected. Prisha had chosen the emerald-green ball gown, and Sanchita selected the black dress with the cutouts that went from her ribs down to her hips. Martin had chosen to arrive with me rather than stay at the castle. Even he wore a dark tuxedo and black bowtie. Theon had also opted for a traditional tuxedo, except he wore a black tie that ran down the center of his chest. His hair was combed back from his face, letting everyone see his bright-green eyes and the chiseled planes of his cheeks. Marius watched me like a hawk at the back of the pack. He was still dressed in the same fur-lined leather coat and pants—like he couldn't be bothered to dress up at all, like he himself was enough. Yet when he looked at me, it was nearly covetous. It felt like he would reach out and chain me to him at any moment.

It sent a shiver down my spine, and I focused my energy on getting us to the castle in one piece and not covered in mirror particles. I placed my hand against it and closed my eyes, thinking about exactly where I wanted it to go. I felt it turn cool and goopy under my touch. I took a small step back.

"Go ahead." I held my hand to the mirror as they passed through.

Theon was first through the mirror, with Martin right behind him. Prisha paused in front of it. "This is the first time I'm ever doing this... Does it hurt?"

I chuckled. "Not at all. It just feels kind of sticky for a minute, then you'll be totally fine. Promise."

She stepped through and Sanchita waited for the mirror to return to its moving, gooey state. "This so cool, Piper."

Marius waved his arms. "Right, off you go. No use hanging about."

"Someone has got himself into a strop." She rolled her eyes and walked through.

He stood before me and offered me his arm. "Piper, my dear, care to join me?"

Ew, no. "I have to concentrate to keep the portal open."

The muscle in his jaw ticked as he dropped his arm down to his side and curled his hands into fists. "One day you won't deny me. Don't think I didn't notice that's not one of the dresses I provided."

"Lady's choice." I arched my eyebrows at him.

He straightened his lapels by slapping them against his chest. He squared his shoulders and marched into the mirror. I was so tempted to let him get stuck there, but this was supposed to be a night of celebration, and no matter how much he deserved it, I wasn't going to start it off with pettiness. Once he was through, I stepped into the mirror, and the cool liquid melted around me. It clung to my skin and slowly peeled back with every step

I took. Part of me was ready to panic at the thought of sending all of them to the wrong place. The other part of me knew I'd done it. The closer I got to the castle, the more I felt it.

When I came through on the other side, they were all standing in a long hallway waiting for me. I dusted my hands off and held my shoulders back, trying to play off my excitement. "Everyone ready?"

I walked past Marius and the sister to the head of the group where Martin and Theon were waiting. Theon held his arm out, not knowing I just turned Marius down. "Shall we?"

I took it and didn't bother turning around to see Marius. I was too acutely aware of his barely audible hiss. No one else seemed to hear it, and I pretended not to. When we reached the end of the hall, I stepped through the mirror and shivered as the chilling liquid peeled over my body. We stepped through into the hall of the castle that was just outside the giant throne room. I'd grown so familiar with my surroundings while there that I almost felt a tiny bit of tension leave my body.

"Which way do we go?" Prisha craned her neck, looking at all the other vampires wandering up and down the halls. I'd never seen the castle so busy as it was now. Vampires from all over the world were in attendance here. I heard the accents, saw the different styles of dress. They came from all over. I smiled to myself. If humans only knew how many of them there were, they'd freak out. I motioned down the hall.

"This way."

Marius pushed past the twins and Martin to stand on the other side of me. "I know the way."

"I wasn't talking to you. I was answering Prisha," I snapped more forcefully than I intended, but his ego was bigger than I could put up with, and I didn't appreciate it.

"Your attitude leaves something to be desired," he hissed at me.

"Stop. Talking. For like ten seconds, would you?!" Annoyance filled my words, and I felt something shift within my body. A fine pink mist left my body and slammed into him, and he pressed his mouth into a tight line. *What the hell was that?* I'd never done anything like that before. I did a quick glance around, but no one else seemed to see it. Marius scowled at me but said nothing. I could feel the agitation rolling off him and running right into me. "What? You enjoy the sound of your own voice too much."

The Gupta sisters giggled, and Martin actually cracked a smile. Theon scowled at me. "Don't be too hard on him. This is a big event for us all. It was only a few centuries ago that the Night Spawn were first invited to something like this."

I tugged on his arm. "Then I guess we better get moving."

"Of course." He waved his arm down the hall. "Lead the way."

We began to weave our way through the mass of

vampires toward the entrance of the throne room. "It's very crowded."

Before I could say another word, the crowd started to part in front of us, and I smiled over my shoulder at the sisters. "Looks like we're in luck."

The throne room had always impressed me with its tall ceilings and stained glass, but tonight it was even more beautiful. Candles of all shapes and sizes floated above our heads, bathing the room in warm light. The ceiling had been spelled to look like giant glittering snowflakes were falling over us, but they disappeared before they could touch any of us. The walls were covered with garland that twinkled with little lights and bright ornaments. When a group of vampires walked up to one of the main trees and hung an ornament, my brow furrowed.

Martin stepped around us to explain. "Titus would prefer not to receive gifts. Instead, he asks that everyone donate to the rebuild of Night Spawn City and to put an ornament from their country or something that means something to them on one of the trees around the castle."

"Oh, how lovely."

"It's a political move, nothing more." Marius sneered.

I ignored him and kept looking at all the things. On either side of the throne room, big doors were open. They led to other rooms full of all kinds of food. Blood fountains stood in all four corners of the room and were being attended by the servers. It was all so extravagant but at the same time classy enough to bring a touch of awe.

Behind me, Prisha and Sanchita kept pointing things out to each other. Their voices rose with excitement. Martin joined in with them, murmuring at them to look at the ceiling, windows, or something else. But my eyes were drawn to the dance floor at the center of the room. A string quartet played a song I wasn't familiar with but every vampire dancing seemed to be. They whirled around each other in perfect rhythm. It was so beautiful, like a ballet.

When the vampires around us started to part even more and back away, I turned to find Titus and Moira heading our way. Theon straightened his stance, and the others all dropped into a low bow.

Moira beamed at me. "Piper, my dear, you look exquisite."

"Thank you. As do you. Lovely as always."

"Yes, we all aspire to be so refined." Marius bowed in front of her and took her hand in his. He placed a kiss on the back of it but continued to hold it there while he maintained his bow.

"Marius, always a pleasure." She withdrew her hand from his, choosing instead to fold them in front of her.

Moira was always the picture of perfection with her deep eyes and long, flowing chocolate hair that was so similar to Grayson's. Her dress was a bright-red corseted ball gown that flowed down to her feet. The sleeves were tight to her arms and covered in golden glitter. Titus looked over the King by her side. He'd changed his long burgundy-red jacket for a deep emerald-green one. Gold filigree was embroidered down the lapels and around his wrists. Underneath he wore a pressed white button-down shirt and matching white pants.

"Piper, I wonder if you won't come by tomorrow? There is something of great importance I'd like to discuss with you."

His rumbling words took me by surprise. "Oh, yes of course. I'd love to."

"How ominous." Marius pressed his hand to his chest. "Should we all be concerned?"

Titus shot him a glare. "None of *your* concern."

"Oh, I would think the prophesied one is all of our concern, don't you?"

The vampires around us all grew silent. Even the sisters behind me stopped whispering to each other. All eyes swung toward me, and I swallowed. "What's he talking about?"

Marius arched his eyebrows in a fake surprised look. "Oh, they didn't tell you? How interesting."

"What's this? Is it true? The prophesied one has come?" Clive Cristian, the Ambassador to the Blood Born Vampires, melted from the crowd to join our little group. He was as oily as I remembered, with his slicked-back hair and tiny mustache. He looked like something out of a period picture with his old-style English attire complete with waistcoat.

"Nice of you to join us, Clive." Marius spat his name like a curse.

Clive barely spared him a glance. "Hmm, Marius."

"There is no such evidence." Titus held his hand between the two of them. "Perhaps if you both would give us time, we can sort this out."

Once again, all eyes swung toward me, and I felt Theon's arm tightening beneath my fingers. "This is, after all, a party."

"Why do I feel like you all are talking about me?"

Marius turned to face me. "Because we are. You. You are the prophesied one all vampires know about and refer to in our world. For in her hands, we rise or fall."

Clive's voice rose as he turned an accusing eye on Titus. "How could you have known this and not told us?"

"Indeed." Marius crossed his arms and smirked, looking so satisfied with himself.

"As I said . . . gentlemen. Nothing is known yet." Titus' voice was laced with finality. "We will look into all possibilities."

I didn't know if they were talking about me or what, but I didn't like it one bit. I held my hand up to get their attention. "Someone speak now, and tell me what's going on."

"They think you're the vampire from an ancient vampire prophecy," Grayson said, sliding into the group. He was completely devastating in his navy-blue suit. It was tailored to him perfectly and cut in slim to his body.

One of his hands was casually in his pocket while the other motioned between the factions. His eyes drifted down to where my hand rested on Theon's arm.

He turned to Marius. "Accusations do not become us."

Then he faced Clive. "Neither do overreactions."

"She walks in the sunlight." Marius pointed an accusing finger in my direction.

Grayson chuckled and shook his head. "As do I. As do most of the born vampires. The truth is, we haven't had a progeny made with royal blood until now, so you might just be jumping to conclusions. We don't know, but all will come to light soon, gentlemen."

Marius chuckled and narrowed his eyes at Grayson. He sucked in a breath and his whole demeanor shifted to a fake pleasant that I did not trust. "The young Prince is right. We shall all drink and be merry on this holiday."

A waiter walked by with a tray of glasses, and Marius stopped him. He grabbed glasses and handed them to Titus, Moira, and Clive. He tried to give one to Gray, but he shook his head. "Perhaps later."

"More for the rest of us." He held his glass up. "To the future."

The others murmured something to that effect and clinked their glasses together, then all took a sip. Once it was over, they all seemed to take a step back and breathe a collective breath. When Grayson looked at all of them, they disappeared, leaving me with my friends and him.

I pointed toward Grayson. "I don't know what's happening, but you will explain it to me."

"But of course." He motioned to the room around us. "But first this is a party, so everyone, please do enjoy."

They all took the hint and started to disperse amongst each other. But now even more eyes lingered on me, and I shifted a bit closer to Theon. He seemed the most calm of all. He placed his hand over mine. "It'll all be okay, Piper. Shall we dance?"

"Yes, I'd love to. But I just need a moment." This was all too much. Did I really have something more to do with this world? Had my fate been written centuries ago? Was my death meant to be all along? Was I always made for the vampire world?

Grayson waved for a server. "Perhaps a drink first."

When the waiter hurried over, he stopped in front of me with a goblet full of the most delicious smelling blood. I took it and glanced at Grayson. He gave me a small nod. "From my own personal storage."

His words were subtle, but I knew it was his.

Theon turned toward the server. "Brandon, I didn't realize you were going to be working here."

"We have most of the Night Spawn here either as guests or volunteers to help with the festivities, like Brandon." Grayson shrugged. "We enjoy having *all* here."

Atlas moved to stand next to Grayson. His eyes slid down to my hand, and he scoffed and shook his head, then turned back to Grayson. "All seems well."

Prisha and Sanchita vibrated with excitement. Prisha tapped me on the shoulder and jutted her chin toward Atlas. I took the hint and introduced them. "Prisha,

Sanchita, this is Atlas Savage. Atlas, have you met my new friends, Prisha and Sanchita?"

"I haven't had the pleasure." He looked Theon up and down. "I'm familiar with you."

"Atlas, always good to see you." Theon chuckled.

"I do not share your sentiments," he said bluntly.

Theon rocked on his heels. "Oh, come now. I'm not so bad as all that."

"If I had a bucket of water and you were on fire, I would still bathe in it. That's how much I loathe you."

"So, what you're saying is, we can't be friends?" Theon nodded to himself. "Noted."

Grayson held his hand out toward me. "Shall we, Piper."

I finished the contents of my glass and glanced at the others. I slipped my hand from Theon's arm and placed it in Grayson's. "Alright."

He pulled me toward him and led me toward the dance floor. Other vampires cleared the way for the two of us, and I found myself being more self-conscious than ever before. I was slowly becoming a showpiece to these people, and I didn't like it. Grayson gave my hand a squeeze. "Eyes on me, Little Creature."

"They're all staring."

"Look at me, Piper." When my eyes snapped to his, all I saw there was a calm I did not feel. I took a deep breath and felt myself forgetting all the people around us. It was just us in the middle of the dance floor.

He wrapped his hand around my waist and dragged

my body close to his. I rested my hand on his shoulder, and when the music started, I felt my body easily glide and move with his. We spun in a perfect waltz, like we'd taken lessons. In reality, he probably had and was making me look good.

"The dress suits you," he whispered in my ear. "Quite ravishing."

"We're going to talk about my outfit?"

"Do tell me what you'd like to talk about, Little Creature." He lifted his arm and spun me around.

"Prophesied one?"

He dipped me low, and I felt my back arch into him and my breasts nearly spill from the top of my dress, yet they stayed in place and he pulled me back up. "Yes."

"Do you think I am?"

He pulled me in hard, and I felt his body against mine. "Nothing isn't possible in this world, Piper."

"How very vague of you."

He chuckled. "It's all I've got right now."

He spun me again, and my head swam. "Why do you hide so many things from me? I can tell, you know? We'd do much better if you just told me the truth."

His chest rose on a heavy sigh. "Yes, that is the advice I've been given."

"Whoever said that is a brilliant man."

"I quite agree."

We twirled around faster, and the world blurred around me. I couldn't tell if we were moving too fast or if

I felt too overwhelmed. "You should try the truth and see what you get."

"I will endeavor to do so in the future."

The music slowed to a stop, and he held me away from him. When he gave me a bow and the other ladies began to curtsy, I followed suit. "In the future . . . meaning not now." I sighed and grew suddenly so tired.

I took a step away from him when he reached out and grabbed my hand. "Piper, I—"

There was a loud bang from the other side of the room, and his head snapped in that direction. He dropped my hand. "Just let me go check on that."

Never the right time and never the right place. That is how it would always be with Grayson. "Of course."

I turned away from him and hurried to where Prisha, Sanchita, and Theon stood. Sanchita fanned herself. "That was some dance."

"I could feel the fire from here." Prisha too made the fake fanning motion. "You two really have something."

"Ah, well, that's inconvenient since I've decided to try to hate him for eternity." Even I knew how silly that sounded and couldn't stop myself from laughing.

They broke out into fits of laughter, but I didn't have the energy to join them. I swayed on my feet and Theon caught my arm. "Are you well, Piper?"

"Actually, I don't think so." I didn't know if this was all too much or if there was something else wrong.

Marius hurried over to us. "What's happened?"

"Piper isn't feeling well." Theon answered for me.

I pressed my hand to my mouth to fight the neausea rolling in my stomach. Grayson had given me the blood, but this felt like something different. I glanced down at my necklace and the pearl hadn't darkened to red. It was still a creamy white. "I think I might be sick."

"Quickly take her home to rest," Marius commanded. Another sound came from the other side of the room, and his head snapped up before turning to us. "She must lie down."

For once his words made sense. The room spun and I grabbed onto Theon to steady myself. "I think he's right."

"Take her to your place, Theon, and keep an eye on her," he commanded.

"Alright." Theon took my arm and guided me toward the door. I didn't have the willpower to argue with him. The only thing I wanted was out of here. I'd had enough of love, politics, and prophecies for one night. Clearly my stomach agreed with my desire to leave. "It's okay, Piper. I've got you."

I tilted my head up to meet his eyes. "Can I trust you, Theon?"

"I'll see you well, Piper. I promise. You can trust me."

... *but could I?*

CHAPTER THIRTY-NINE

GRAYSON

I hurried across the ballroom to see about the ruckus, weaving my way through the crowd. I arrived near one of the blood fountains at the corner of the room where a server was trying to pour a carafe of blood into the fountain to refill it. Clive held the young vampire's wrist.

"What is this swill you are serving us?" He shook the man, rattling his bones. Clive's vampire power was his strength. He wasn't just strong, he was abnormally strong. But he never used it in public. He preferred to let his wealth do his dirty work.

"Clive! What are you doing?" I snapped. "Unhand him."

Clive stumbled back as though he was drunk and dropped the vampire to the ground. "It tastes awful. I would think The House of Shade could afford good blood."

He staggered back and tripped over his own feet. My brow furrowed. "What is the matter with you?"

"I. Don't. Know." He dropped to the ground and lay there for a moment.

I motioned to some in his entourage. "Come pick him up. Let him sleep it off."

When they rushed to his side, they too looked slow in their movements. Something wasn't right. My pulse quickened. All around me vampires were acting out of sorts. They dropped their glasses, staggered in different directions, and clung to the walls for balance. I glanced toward Atlas, and he was at my side in a moment. "What's happening?"

"I don't know but the Blood Borns seem to be the ones most affected," he answered quickly.

I spun in a circle, taking note of the same thing. Something was wrong. I felt it in my gut. The air smelled both sweet and sour at the same time, not the normal rusty scent of blood. Adrenaline flooded my body as I searched for Piper in the crowd. Yet I didn't see her anywhere. "Find her."

He gave me a single nod and pressed his finger to his chest. Red mist covered his body and Poe erupted from his skin, taking flight over the crowd. I ran to my mother's side and took her elbow. "What is happening?"

She held her hands out and her healing poured from her. It hit a few people, and she stumbled back into my arms. A sheen of sweat broke out over her skin. "I don't know, darling. But they are not well."

Titus ran to the two of us and took my mother from my arms, allowing her to lean into his side. "This is madness!"

Atlas darted to stand in front of Titus and my mother. He pressed his finger to his forearm and his red blood magic swirled up and down his body, then his swords peeled from his skin. He took up a fighting stance. "She's not here?"

"What?" *Piper is missing amidst this chaos!?* "She has to be."

"You doubt me?"

Atlas was never wrong and never untruthful. But I had to find her before something worse happened. "Uncle, can you look after Mother?"

My mother reached out and grabbed my shirt and wound it in her fist. "No, Gray. You mustn't go. She will be the end of you."

"She already is." I gently unwound her hand from my shirt. "I must find her."

"You will not." Titus' power wrapped around me, and for a moment I felt myself compelled to stay and do what he told me to do. But the desire to find her was too great. The yearning to see her safe was all that mattered to me now.

My own blood magic rose to the forefront, and I shoved his away. "You will not command me."

In that instant, I felt myself break free of any kind of hold he ever had on me. My power rose and swirled within my chest. I didn't want to fight with my family, but Piper was my family too now. I had to protect her. I had found something more important than myself . . . I'd found *her*. I had to get to her now.

The ballroom descended into chaos. The Blood Born vampires were falling down, staggering around as though they'd been drugged. They were completely disoriented, like they'd been poisoned or something. Two of the servers dragged a table into the middle of the room, and Marius hopped up onto it. He held a goblet of blood in his hand. "Ladies and gentlemen, may I have your attention please."

A hush fell over the crowd. Marius kicked a glass that'd been left on the table. It sailed across the room and exploded into tiny shards the moment it hit the wall. "For years the Night Spawn have crawled beneath your feet like worms in the darkness. No more! You think because you were born with blood magic in your veins that you are better than us, but what if that magic was no more? What if it was all gone?"

When the room gave a collective gasp, he threw his head back and chuckled. "Now you will see who the power belongs to and know what it feels like to eat under the table instead of claiming a seat at it. Too long we have served. Too long we have remained compliant. Too long has our kind been relegated to the basement of your world. It is our time now. Let us see how you debutants fair without your blood magic to protect you."

He held his glass up high and dumped the blood on the table at his feet. "Cheers!"

CHAPTER FORTY

GRAYSON

"That son of a bitch!" I took a step forward, then froze. When I glanced over my shoulder, Titus and my mother were barely able to stand.

"Mother!" I raced to her side. "Are you okay?"

Her eyes fluttered in her head. "I think so."

I turned to Atlas. "You have to get them out of here."

"I'm not leaving you in this madness." A vampire ran at him with his own set of knives in his hand. Atlas chuckled, leapt over the vampire's head, then shoved his swords straight through his chest and spread his arms wide, cutting the man in half.

"You can and you will. Secure the crown and then come back to help me." When he hesitated, I flicked my hand at him, letting my power smack him in the chest. The moment the command hit him, he had no other choice but to comply.

"You're a daft prick." He turned and shoved Titus and

my mother toward a hidden door at the back of the room.

A blast of fire shot over my head, and I ducked down and rolled behind another table. When I peeked around the side, I spotted a made vampire throwing flames from his hands. I pulled my throwing stars from the small pouch around my ankle.

"How in the hell does he have fire power?" Made vampires weren't supposed to have any kind of magic.

This wasn't possible. Their bodies weren't made for it. Yet there he was dressed in a server's uniform with his hands on fire. When he turned the force of his power on the table I'd ducked under, heat licked at my face and the tablecloth burst into flames. It burned and sizzled around me. Sweat ran down the sides of my face and rolled down my back. *Where is the freaking phoenix when you need him?*

"Oh, fuck all." I sprang from my hiding spot and threw two of my stars in his direction. The first ran across his neck in a smooth line. The second followed and soared in a perfect line cutting a line on the back of his neck. His eyes widened for a second, and then his head slid from his shoulders and fell to the ground. The stars circled back around to me like trained boomerangs. They weren't the typical sort that only had one throw in them, but that was the benefit of being friends with witches.

I caught them and turned toward another made vampire who cackled while he created a small tornado that spun around a group of high-class Blood Borns. Screams rang out through the room. Vampires stampeded to get to the exits and away from the attacks. Everywhere I looked a new power arose that shouldn't have been possible. Not like this. And not within The Night Spawn. This was all wrong. Titus and I had worked to keep the peace and make sure there was growth. There would never be peace now.

The room shook, And as the wind whipped around, I sprinted through the chaos and wrapped my hand around the wind-vampire's neck. I lifted her off the ground and held her there. "How did you come to be like this?"

All she did was smile and kick her legs. Her eyes shot to the side and suddenly I was slammed in the side of my head by a huge boulder. I dropped her and my body went soaring through the air. I twisted and felt myself spinning in all different directions, caught in a tornado. She threw me to one side, and I slammed high against the wall. The tornado twisted around the room, collecting tables and chairs along with other vampires. I had no way of stopping it. I was caught within her grasp and slammed into another wall. My body collided with all the debris. Dizziness overwhelmed me and my stomach turned.

Poe soared through the air, and when I snapped my head around, there was Sav running across the room toward the wind turbine. His body was cloaked in black, his face and head were hooded, and he had those swords pressed back along his forearms. From the corner of her eye, she spotted him, but it was too late. He dropped to his knees and slid around the floor. His blade ran across the back of her knees, and she fell to the ground.

All at once I came crashing down to the ground with the debris all around me. I smacked into a large table, which cracked under the pressure. The room continued to spin, and I forced myself to rise to my feet. I staggered out as Sav was standing over the female vampire. I placed my hand on my head and felt the blood trickle down from a bump there.

He held his swords up. "For that . . . death."

"Sav." He froze, holding the executioner's swords over her waiting for my command. Terror and pain contorted her features. "Take the hands. I have questions for her later."

"No, no, no!" She tried to scramble back, but her injuries were too great to heal so quickly . . . But hands . . . A made vampire may never grow them back.

"With pleasure." His swords came down, and in one shot both her hands were gone.

Her screams echoed around the room, but I needed to find the one who was responsible for all of this. "Marius!"

I gazed around the room and found him holding Clive up against a wall. His head snapped around and a wide smile spread over his face. I pointed my knife at him. "You're dead."

He threw Clive over his shoulder and ran for the

door. He called out to his band of trouble makers, "Stop them at all costs!"

Clive fell on the floor in a heap and didn't move. I didn't know if he was dead or not. I didn't care. I was here to stop this from happening. Bodies of both made and born vampires littered the Great Hall. Tables and chairs were smashed to pieces and scorch marks fanned over the stone walls and floor. It was a complete disaster. Blood ran down the side of my head, and I felt the splitting pain that went along with it. I swiped my hand over my face and watched the other vampires facing us slowly start to fan out. Had the Born Vampires still had their powers, the fight would've been even. But this was a slaughter, and I loathed it when the powerful prayed on the weak, especially when they poisoned them to do so.

They spread out to face just me and Sav. The male vampire on the end was hulking with biceps the size of his head. Tiny pebbles spun around him like gnats, and I recognized this power over stone. The male next to him was smaller with frizzy red hair, freckled skin, and clothes that were three sizes too big. His hair stood on edge with tiny sparks flowing through it. The girl next to him had water droplets hanging in midair. Her hair was soaked, and it looked like she was sweating bullets. Her skin was ashen, and every so often she let out a wheezing cough that sounded like she was drowning on dry land.

What had been done to them to make them like this? Even looking closer, they didn't look right. They were different, unhinged, manic even. Another girl stepped out and her fingers dripped lava. The floor around her melted, and I wondered if she could actually turn it off or if she was forever bound to not touch anyone ever. Her clothing had holes burnt into it, and her hair looked like it'd been set on fire more times than I could count. Next to her was a vampire who glowed like he was radioactive.

I couldn't help but wonder. "What the hell happened to all of you?"

"You're dead," the girl in the middle proclaimed as water bubbled up from her mouth.

"Right then . . . piss off. You had your chance."

I glanced at Sav and he let his mask drop from his face. A deadly smile spread on his face, and he chuckled deep in his throat. It was a dark rumble, like he was enjoying this moment. Where he went, death followed. There were no doubts about it. I smirked to myself, feeling my own blood magic swarm through my body. "I'll give you one warning and one warning only. This is Atlas Savage." The line of them paused. I chuckled. "Your reputation is getting right awful, mate."

"You're bloody welcome." He hauled his arm back and hurled his sword at the bodybuilder. It moved so quickly I couldn't track it with my eyes. The bodybuilder went flying back, with the sword plunged through his eye socket and stuck into the wall behind his head.

The others all screamed and ran toward us as fast as they could. Water flew at me, and I dove to the side. Sav rolled in the opposite direction, and I'd had enough of this bullshit. These baby vampires with witch powers they didn't understand were too dangerous. They weren't built to contain magic like this. Fury flowed through my body, and my power exploded out of me.

"STOP!" Red mist filled the room, and no one moved. They froze like statues, their stolen magic hovering in the air around them. Even Atlas was trapped in my mist. I waved him over. "Atlas, you're free."

I dropped my power around him. He rolled his shoulders and sauntered over to my side. "This is a step up in your blood magic. I've never seen you do this to a group before."

"Nor I." My fury still burned hot and heavy. There were too many things on my mind, too many things I had to take care of and this wankers were out of control. "Titus? My mother?"

"Safe," was all he said. Atlas knew better than to leave them vulnerable or disclose their location with so many treacherous ears listening.

I turned to the water girl. "Where is Piper?"

When she didn't move, I pulled my magic back ever so slightly. "Speak."

The rest of her body remained frozen while her face contorted in pain. "I'll never tell."

"Then I'll hang you upside down and you'll drown in the power you stole."

I turned to walk away when she called out, "Wait! Theon took her."

I was going to fucking murder Theon. "Where?"

"His quarters."

I headed for the door. They came into my house, attacked my guests, and took my Piper . . . and they thought *Atlas* was death . . . They had no idea.

"What do I do with them?" Atlas called after me.

"I'm sure you can think of something interesting." My mind was focused on one person and one person only . . . Piper.

The thought of her in danger or hurt made my blood boil. Red mist floated around my body as I ran toward the mirrors we'd set up for our guests. I barely registered the destructive remains that were the castle. It was all in ruins from this little attack Marius had arranged. We'd survived it, but not without our losses. He would pay. They all would. As I approached the mirrors, I didn't stop. I just let my mist roll out before me. All at once they vibrated and exploded inwards. I didn't care. I had a visit to make, and it would be Theon's last.

CHAPTER FORTY-ONE

GRAYSON

Visions of her broken, beaten body filled my head. If they had mutated those other vampires, then what would they do to her? To my progeny? To my everything? To even try to picture a life without her was impossible. There was nothing without her. She was the air I breathed. Letting her go was stupid, pushing her away even more so. I needed her. If they hurt one hair on that wild, stubborn head of hers, I would burn the world down around them, and there would be no factions left once I was through.

With my speed, I was through Night Spawn City in moments and at Theon's door. I paused, listening for a struggle. Theon's voice carried through the door. "There now. Just rest. Tuck in."

"Tuck the fuck in." I grabbed the handle and ripped the door off the hinges and threw it behind me.

Theon's eyes widened, and he took a step back from

the bed where Piper lay all tucked in and comfy, with her hair spread on *his* fucking pillow and her scent in between *his* sheets. She sat up in the bed. "Grayson, what are you doing?" She looked me up and down. "What's happened?"

I couldn't speak, couldn't breathe. She was in his fucking BED. I leapt forward and wrapped my hand in Theon's shirt. "She is MINE."

I threw him across the room and into the wall. Before he could fall to the ground, I was there to grab him again. I dragged him around the apartment, breaking his furniture while using his body like a sledgehammer. Piper screamed my name, but I couldn't look at her in that bed. I threw him toward the ceiling, slamming him there repeatedly until it dented to my satisfaction. Blood poured from his mouth, nose, and ears, yet I couldn't stop. He did this. He was part of this. "You traitor!"

"Grayson! Stop!" Her words wrapped around me like a blanket, and I threw Theon out the door and turned back to her.

I couldn't be without her, not for one second longer. This was everything the world had to offer, and she was it. She grabbed my arm and shook me. "What the hell have you done? What is wrong with you?"

"YOU!" I grabbed her shoulders and jerked her toward me. "You are what's wrong with me."

"What?" Confusion riddled her features.

I couldn't resist her any longer. Her blood had called to me the moment she turned into a vampire. I needed her . . . needed us. My fangs dripped for a taste of her. I couldn't stop now that the tight control I had over my emotions was gone. I struck out hard and fast. My fangs pierced her skin and her warmth flooded my mouth. My eyes rolled into the back of my head as she cried out from my bite. Her little fingers dug into my back, pulling me closer. It was heaven, it was hell, it was . . . everything.

CHAPTER FORTY-TWO

PIPER

*P*leasure wracked my body from head to toe. Connection burned between the two of us. It was so hot and heavy I could feel his frantic madness in my own chest. I pulled him in closer, wanting him near me. He pulled his fangs from my neck and backed away from me, pressing himself up against the wall. He reached into his pocket and pulled out a vial of purple liquid and popped the top, chugging it down like a shot.

"Gray, I—"

"I loved you the moment I met you." He fired the words out so fast. "I knew you would be it for me. And you always have been."

Bright red light flooded from under the sleeves of his coat and shirt at the same time as my own forearm started to glow. When I looked down, there was a makr there that'd I'd never seen before. Black lines that looked like vines ran from the back of my hand, around my wrist, and up my forearm. Sharp barbs poked out from each of the lines like barbed wire. I turned my arm and there on my forearm were two roses. Their petals were a deep crimson. Each was tucked into intertwined vines covered in spikes. Blood drops dripped from the single spike touching the center of each rose. My jaw dropped at its gothic beauty. My heart soared at its simple beautiful perfection.

"Grayson?"

He ripped his sleeves open. We matched perfectly. "You're my soulmate, Piper. I've always known you would be."

His body shuddered from head to toe and red veins forked out over the whites of his eyes. Dark circles surrounded them, and his skin paled till it was nearly blue. His fangs descended down past his lips, and when he looked at me, I felt like an animal about to be hunted. I didn't know what was happening to him, but he grew bigger, his muscles more well-defined. His suit coat tore to shreds and fell in pieces around him.

"Piper, listen to me." He caught my eye.

My heart hammered in my chest. "What's wrong with you?"

"Piper, I love you." His entire body shuddered as though the words themselves hurt to say.

"I love you too." I took a step toward him, but he held his hand up waving me back.

"Good. Now do something for me." He froze. His eyes met mine, and a cold chill ran down my spine.

"An-anything." I wanted to go to him but every instinct in my body told me not to move, that this wasn't the Grayson I knew and loved. This . . . this was something else.

A growl ripped from his throat as he tensed his whole body to spring at me. "RUN!"

Want to find out what happened to Grayson and The House of Shade?

Click the link and pre-order Wicked Thirst now!

https://mybook.to/wickedthirst

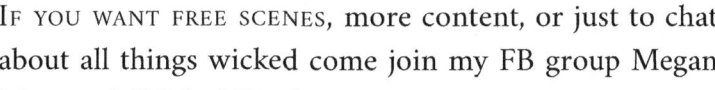

If you want free scenes, more content, or just to chat about all things wicked come join my FB group Megan Montero's Wicked Readers.

Click here to join the Wicked Readers

DON'T MISS OUT ON THIS FREE BOOK!

THIS POWER CHOSE *ME*...

Within the supernatural world of Evermore everyone prays their child will be born with the Mark of the Guardian for they have unparalleled strength, intelligence, and *power*...but they have no idea what it's actually like. I didn't wish for this *gift* and I definitely don't want it. I was born a prince, I already had it all. This Mark on my neck stole all of it from me and forced me into a dangerous life I'd gladly trade away if I could…

But now the Witch Queens have ascended and it's time to try and defeat the evil King once and for all. For over a thousand years his cruelty has spared no one as his torturous power grows stronger. He must be stopped now, before his reign destroys everything and anything in his way. So I must push aside my dreams of returning home to the family that cast me out. I must step up and claim the power that chose me. I *must* enter the Trials and become a Knight in the Witch's Court.

There's only one way to prevent the tyrannical king from destroying everything I love…I must become the one thing he can't beat.

Click here to get your FREE book now!

INCASE YOU MISSED the first season of The Royals: Witch Court check it out now!

CLICK HERE TO GET YOUR WITCH COURT BOXSET

It's time to claim my power...

ALL MY LIFE I've lived under lock and key, always following the strict rules my mother set for me. A week before my sixteenth birthday I sneak out of my house and discover why. Turns out I am not just a normal teenager. I'm a witch blessed with a gift someone wants to steal from me.

And not just anyone…the evil King Alataris.

For a thousand years the people of Evermore have suffered under his tyranny. The Mark on my shoulder says I am the Siphon Witch, one of five Witch Queens fated to come together and finally destroy him. The only thing keeping Evermore safe is the Stone that shields the witch kingdoms from Alataris's magic…and now he's found a way to steal it. Suddenly, I'm sent on a quest to find the ancient spell to protect the Stone. My only hope for surviving is through my strikingly beautiful and immensely powerful Guardian, Tucker. The laws of Evermore state that love between us is strictly forbidden, and it appears I'm the only one willing to give in to the attraction…

When the quest turns more dangerous than expected I realize I have absolutely no idea what I'm doing. I was raised human. But I have to learn my magic fast because If King Alataris gets his hands on me he'll steal my magic and my life…but if he gets his hands on that Stone we all die.

THE MAGIC CONTINUES in the second season of The Royals: Warlock Court Now in this completely set!
CLICK HERE TO GET WARLOCK COURT

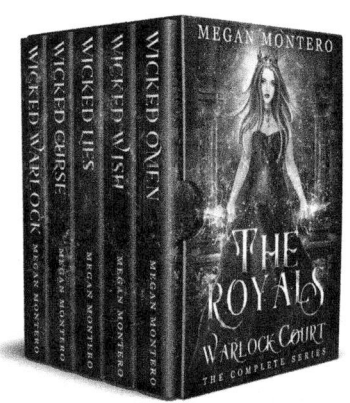

THERE'S **no such thing as magical powers…**
All my life the only kind of magic I'd ever seen was the sparkling jewels on fifth avenue. On the night of my sixteenth birthday all hell breaks loose, and by hell I

mean me! I never felt power like this, so dark, so tempting, so out of my control! No one is safe around me. And now I'm being thrown into Warwick Academy.

An academy for the darker side of magic. . .the warlock side.

My captor, my savior, and the bane of my existence, Beckett Dust insists on keeping me here even though we can't stand each other. I don't care how drop dead gorgeous he is or that he rules the school like he owns it, I need to stay as far away from him as I can. His deepest desire is to turn me into a weapon in the great war to come. My deepest desire is . . . him. There's a thin line between love and hate and right now I'm walking it.

IF YOU'RE all caught up on The Royals don't worry there's more to come. In the mean time check out The Night Realm: Magic Marked my awesome co-written series with Chandelle LaVaun.

CLICK HERE TO GET MAGIC MARKED

He put a spell on me...

Or at least he *must* have, because none of this makes any sense. None of this can be *real*. I'm not a mage with magical powers...I'm just *me*. Ellie Sutton. Your average, everyday seventeen-year-old high school *human* student. My biggest concerns are bullies, failed exams, and missing the express subway twice in one day.

Magic is something I read about in comic books, it's not real. People don't move things with their minds or summon lightning with their hands. I don't care what Stellan Wentworth says. It doesn't matter that he's breathtakingly beautiful or that his eyes sparkled when I challenge him. He's the kind of hero found in romance novels, not my real life. I'm dreaming, I have to be.

Because if I'm not, then what he's telling me is true. This gorgeous, terrifying world is in turmoil...and if I don't learn how to use my magic overnight...they'll all die.

Published by Leo Press

Copyright © 2022 by Megan Montero

Cover Design by Lori Grundy @ Cover Reveal Designs

Artwork by Samaiya Beaumont @ Samaiya Beaumont Art

This book is a work of fiction. Though some actual towns, cities, and locations may be mentioned, they are used in a fictitious manner and the events and occurrences were invented I the mind and imagination of the author. Any similarities of characters or names used within to any person past, present, or future is coincidental.

All rights reserved.

No part of this book may be reproduced in any form or by any electronic or mechanical means, including information storage and retrieval systems, without written permission from the author, except for the use of brief quotations in a book review.

❦ Created with Vellum

*To Topsail Island my little slice of heaven.
The one place I always find peace and myself.*

ABOUT THE AUTHOR

Megan Montero was born and raised as sassy Jersey girl. After devouring series like the Immortals After Dark, the Arcana Chronicles, Harry Potter and Mortal Instruments she decided then and there that she would write her own series. When she's not putting pen to paper you can find her cuddled up under a thick blanket (even in the summer) with a book in her hands. When she'd not reading or writing you can find her playing with her dogs, watching movies, listening to music or moving the furniture around her house…again. She loves finding magic in all aspects of her life and that's why she writes Urban Fantasy and Paranormal.

Learn about Megan and her books by visiting her website at:
   Www.meganmontero.com

ALSO BY MEGAN MONTERO

The Royals: Witch Court

Wicked Witch

Wicked Magic

Wicked Hex

Wicked Potion

Wicked Queen

The Royals: Witch Court Boxset

The Royals: Warlock Court

Wicked Omen

Wicked Wish

Wicked Hunt (A Warlock Court Novella: Ophelia)

Wicked Lies

Wicked Curse

Wicked Warlock

Wicked Ties

The Royals: Vampire Court

Wicked Bite

Wicked Vampire

Wicked Thirst (Coming Soon)

The Night Realm (Co-Write With Chandelle LaVaun)

Magic Marked

Midnight Mage

Marvel Mage

Master Mage

Court Marked

Fatal Fae

Fiery Fae

Final Fae (Coming Soon)

Christmas Marked

Bite Me, Santa

Jingle My Bells

Trim My Tree

Ride My Sleigh

Stuff My Stocking

Printed in Great Britain
by Amazon

40214765R00233